Blood Fruit

Karen Kennedy Samoranos

...

ᔕ

Gallatin Peak Productions

Warning

This book contains adult language and scenes. This story is meant only for adults as defined by the laws of the country where you made your purchase. Store your books carefully where they cannot be accessed by younger readers.

For Felicidad

The Jungle

My paternal grandfather was born an American citizen in 1926, the son of Ilocano Filipinos recruited to work the sugarcane fields and pineapple plantations in Kauai, part of the U.S. Territory of the Hawaiian Islands.

In Grandpa's family room in Sunnyvale, California, is a fire-resistant safe in dual use as a side table. Here is the stash of irreplaceable documents, birth records and baptismal certificates, and the original U.S. passport used to bring his children to the mainland United States when they were still too young to form reliable memories of their journey by ship.

Grandpa once showed me his own birth certificate, the black-and-white copy mimicking a photo negative, with his father's elegant signature in graceful white curves against a sea of black. The document clearly states our family name as *Benitéz*, with a *Z*, but the subsequent generation somehow morphed the *Z* to an *S*, the phonetic Spanish pronunciation, and so we are consequently known as *Benités*. In America, the Spanish configuration is often discarded, corrupting the elocution to *Buh-NIGHTS*.

The work in Hawaii ended when the Stock Market crashed. Within a year, my great-grandfather, Ferdinand Benitéz, moved his wife and four children back to the Philippines, to Narvacan in Ilocos Sur, where they lived in pastoral calm, until the Japanese invaded the Islands during the darkness of World War II.

The war served as an interruption, a threat to the recall of our family's historic continuity, and a traumatic rite of adulthood for my Grandpa Feliz, who relates his past haltingly in phrases colored by the beloved familiarity of his regional accent.

He still can remember running through strips of jungle that stood between cultivated fields, hiding in deep shadow formed beneath the full moon, breathing so hard that his father bade them all to cover their mouths to drown their gasps, lest the Japanese soldiers detect their laboring breaths and shoot at them blindly through the trees. They ran until their bare feet bled, and still, kept onward. Under this same cycle of the moon, Grandpa witnessed the murder of his eldest brother at the point of a Japanese soldier's bayonet. He recalls it painfully in black-and-white, colorless beneath a bitter moon.

I was a young girl, barely twelve, when Grandpa shared the compelling horror of these childhood memories. If I am haunted by the anguish of his recount, I imagine my grandfather never rests. The past and its relevant bloodshed have merged into Grandpa's legacy.

He is now eighty-two, rather hard of hearing, and obstinate, fixed in his habits much in the way the moon cannot possibly deviate from its preordained course. We always know the cycle of the moon, we expect it to fulfill its destiny, and we map its route. Grandpa knows his path, start to present, and can presume the coda. His vision and memories are linear, unfaltering, affixed by the light of the moon.

* * * *

I have my own memories illuminated by moonlight. The strongest lessons I have absorbed were transacted in Grandpa Feliz's post-war habit, coerced by lunar cycle.

The night of this particular reminiscence is alive with subtle sounds, small animals moving restlessly through the grass, and night birds calling with tones to mute the distance between their roosts and prey. Soft clicks and rustlings penetrate the foliage, insects on constant march through the leaf litter. The wind kicks up, moaning along tree limbs, fitful across the vast range of hills, from cove to summit, until it breaks free of the land. Once its breath is past, the creatures with their frugal motion can be heard again, hidden in the undergrowth and meadow verge.

Pretty soon, as the night air draws, comes the smell of the feral pigs. They are not as rank as their barnyard brethren, with an unforgettable, earthy reek. After the scent, rises their speech, the chomp of jaws, and soft grunts of communication that tie each pig together while they forage. I can conjure the smell to this day, blended with grass and wind, the tendrils of morning glory caught on my heel, and the rustling of deer mice in the blades. The mice feel the pigs rooting the soil, and glance away from the steady rhythm, for surely some will become a quick meal between tusk and tongue.

My father has taught how feral pigs are the wickedest form of prey for man or beast. They are light on their feet, ill tempered, and deadly in the heat of self-preservation. His younger brother, my Uncle Mark, once leapt for a tree in less than optimal conditions, and had his calf laid open by the tush of a boar. Because of negligence, Uncle Mark walks with a slight limp, and took to hunting feral pigs with a pack of well-aimed pit bulls.

I witnessed that once, and never again, because of the brutality. I am no fan of overkill, and even less enthusiastic in being reminded of what need humans fill to stay on top of the food chain.

When Uncle Mark brought the dogs, there was no call for stealth, he just took them into the hills and set them on scent. Dogs are tireless athletes, dedicated to the chase until their target is exhausted, like wolves on a moose. They'll maneuver a boar with its back against a tree, and commence bloodletting. There are elements of savagery in the carnage wrought by a pit bull's jaws as they clamp onto a pig's face or shoulder. I have admiration of the pig's courage, and yet, I also appreciate the focus of the dogs. Don't ask me to reconcile the reason for the hunt. That one experience I survived because I could accept the toll up in the windswept hills, but once I returned to mundane suburban existence, the moonlit hunt acquired the cadence of a nightmare.

The peaceful childhood forays with our father into the hills near Tres Piños, in San Benito County, was for purposeful listening, not to hunt. Hunting was a facet of my father's past, before marrying and having children. But he did want us to appreciate nature, as we were so insulated in our day-to-day life in the suburbs. Although we were girls, he developed our connectivity to the outdoors absent of gender stereotype while we were naive and malleable.

Dad would guide us to climb to oak woods and wait, ghosting around nervous deer, avoiding thickets of poison oak; and he would ask us to describe what we heard. We held our breath when the pigs worked past. I think they know the smell of a hunter, the odor of aggression. Since we were only listening, if they scented us, they'd slip away rather than chase us up a tree. There's no posturing from a wild animal. They often have better sense than humans do, and waste no energy without justification.

* * * *

We are a family rooted deeply in tradition and social custom. Though I am only half my father's blood, I'm attuned to the eloquent pull of his cultural undercurrent. But if my grandfather's generational contribution to the tenuous archive of family memory is plagued by the horrors of World War II, I don't suppose much has changed. And, as I've learned, when my eldest sister killed a man, we all eventually drift into some kind of war zone, either by rote or by design.

3

1. Blood

The telephone call came through after two a.m., accompanied by pouring rain. Along the roofline, the storm washed away dust and fire smoke of a drought-wreaked summer, a net of fine ashes mixed with pigeon droppings that cement-like, would probably endure the deluge.

On the other end of the line was the voice of my eldest sister, Mallory, who spoke softly, drowned by the crash of rain. We have always been close, and I suppose that's why she called me first. In my sleep-addled speech, I must have angered her somehow with a smart-aleck response, because I found myself holding the receiver a foot or so from my ear.

"Do you *hear* me, Madeline!"

I imagined Mallory's smooth face livid and bulging with veins in her aggravation. Usually in control of her emotions, she was prone to brief spikes of bad temper. I reasoned had I heard her, I would probably not be half deaf at that moment, with the phone sizzling in my hand.

"Yup," I confirmed with a sigh.

"I did it, Madeline," she claimed, a tinge of hyper-excitement in her voice, while exhaustion strained her words.

My drunken stupor of the previous hours blurred my immediate grasp of the situation. I teetered as I crow-hopped in the darkness of the bedroom, locating pants and t-shirt, and nearly tripping over my boots. With the phone against my ear, I could get dressed and still hold a conversation.

"Mallory. Where are you?"

"I'm in custody," she offered, as though carefree and heading off to vacation, or in Mallory's case, a dance club. But maybe her bravado was her way of fending off disaster.

"Custody?" I was now fully alert. The sludge of alcohol fumes wisped into nothingness through the power of dread. "Where?"

"What do you mean, where?" She seemed to be fading away slowly in the murky dim.

"Are you in town?" rephrasing the question. "Can I drive for less than one hour and find you?"

4

She cleared her throat. "I'm at the San Mateo County Sheriff's department. Just a twenty-minute drive." She could have been asking me to dinner or a movie, with that casual tone.

Come on up, Madeline, she'd often urge. *We'll find a restaurant, and hit a movie, and then, if we're still awake, I know this club...*

I'm not a party girl, so I seldom stay awake long enough to make it past dinner.

"What do they think you did, Mallory?"

I fished around for my keys, lost patience with my inability to find them, and switched on the bedside lamp. The light anchored all particulars, including Mallory's voice. The wad of keys sat huddled on my bureau, bypassed with every stab of my hand. I vowed to at least drive within the lane markers, as I caught up a sweatshirt from the foot of my bed, and pulled it on.

"I think I killed somebody, Maddie," she told me earnestly.

I sucked in a breath. "Careful. This phone call's probably recorded."

"But I did, I think I might've killed him." She was adamant I believe her.

"Give me the address," I demanded, to shut her up.

She rattled off numbers and a street name, but I was familiar with the area, and it was only a means to refocus her conduct.

"I can't believe it," she whispered, reverting immediately to the previous subject matter, and that's when I lost it.

"Christ, Mallory, shut the hell up. I'll be there soon."

I threw the telephone across the room, where it hit the edge of the fireplace mantel. I could hear it clatter to the floor, defusing my irritation, and I turned away, making haste for my truck.

* * * *

The rain was dying to a light shower, pushed by a burly south wind. The curb across the street from my house fronted a flat of bare earth, reinforced by gravel, and the raised bed of a single-track rail line. In the ambient suburban glow, the parallel of the steel rails shone brighter than the sad wash of my headlights. Wind tossed the trees wildly, ornamental pears at least thirty years old, eking an impoverished living off the hardpan. Leaves stuck to the windshield of my truck were the first to sweep away as I headed toward the freeway.

In the allotted twenty minutes, I had plenty of time to think about my own problems, which had begun last night. I willingly built trouble for myself, but none seemed as dire as this fix Mallory had created. While the rain strafed the windshield intermittently, the thin traffic on the highway at this hour swept past my work truck with rooster-tails of standing water from the grooved roadway. In the cab, my red-eyed gaze in the rear-view mirror complemented the sharp smell of my sweat which, hours ago, had drenched my pullover sweatshirt. Not until I turned off the freeway, and waiting for the signal light to turn green, I noted the dark splash marks across the front, a spray of my victim's blood, matched by bruises and cuts across the stiff knuckles of my right hand.

At the Sheriff's facility, Mallory was watching for me inside the foyer, an attendant male Sheriff's deputy close to her left hip. The white-haired deputy could fog the glass with the heat he was exuding, amazed how Mallory attracts men, young and old. I could discern through the rain-streaked side window of my filthy truck she was dressed in street clothes. I'd been expecting to find her in an orange jumpsuit, cuffed hands chained to her waist, but then she would have called me to county jail.

As soon as she recognized my rig, she raced out the doors, leaving the deputy embraced in his testosterone disappointment. He raised one hand unconsciously, trailing his fingers in her wake.

"Maddie!" Mallory leaped inside the cab, and I could immediately smell her perfume. Even one brief session in police custody hadn't destroyed her femininity, evidenced by the sea of body spray blinding my vision.

"Ugh, what *is* that smell?" But I hugged her close anyway.

While she struggled with the seat belt, I noted a familiar pattern on the lapel of her suede jacket caused by blood marks and falling rain.

"Thanks for picking me up." She ignored my crankiness. "They just wanted me to make a formal statement." Her hands shook as she secured the belt.

"So…am I taking you home?" I asked, as I put the truck in first gear, and headed away from the lighted bulk of glass and concrete.

She lived up in the hills above Woodside, in a 1930s cottage she shared with one roommate or another to make the mortgage payments. In my condition, the thought of negotiating all those winding roads made me faintly ill.

"No." Her hands waved in front of her, poised to repel my suggestion. "Anywhere but home, please." She forced a smile, though I read trauma in her eyes.

"Okay, not home, but then where?"

"Let's find an all-night diner or something."

Exhaling, she leaned back against the seat, and fell asleep, head lolled to one side, facing passing traffic.

* * * *

When I drive, I often reflect on the task at hand, but there are times my mind forgets where my calling lies. I think it's a practice I use to stay awake, one eye on the road, and the other on the internal film looping in my head. The reality of the present fades, the wipers, traffic, and soft static voice of talk radio, reduced to insignificance. Time shrinks, manifesting a similar effect as sleeping off the miles.

When I reached home, self-proclaimed meditation trailed away to the hum of the engine and the roll of Mallory in sync with the truck's motion. I reflected on the dark nature of human behavior, marked by my sister's mysterious ordeal. Turning off the freeway, I drove the fresh, empty streets with an indefinable dread, and parked beside the rail line.

"Mallory." I nudged her shoulder, and she awoke, eyes nearly as bloodshot as mine. "Come on, stay with me tonight."

"What?"

Her head rose off the seat, and she studied the gnarled pear trees, leaves being stripped by the wind. A couple of the trees hadn't figured out winter yet, in full bloom, pale flowers whirling away with leaves. Though most were either naked or shedding patchy autumn colors, others were brightly green, a cycle gone haywire from pitiful, starving lives between the row of old houses on Bassett Street, and heavily traveled rail line. A freight train lurched along southbound; cars stacked with lumber from northwestern mills, announcing its presence before the Agnew crossing in a long, brassy blast of the horn.

"Come inside, I'll get you something to eat," I offered.

She shook her head, pressing against her stomach with both hands. The blinking lights of the rail crossing reflected faintly across the whites of her eyes.

"I...couldn't possibly eat anything."

"A drink, then. Come on."

She obediently followed me into the green-painted bungalow, my home for three years. Inside, the wood stove was warm enough to keep the damp chill at bay, but too hot for Mallory, who embraces the cold.

Mallory threw herself into one of my side chairs, and kicked off her shoes. There is a teak bar in my living room, and I dug around for a couple of tumblers and a bottle of Scotch, and poured two drinks. Though Mallory is a fitness trainer, she would never turn her nose up at a single malt.

"Tell me about it," as I sank into the closest side of the sofa, and set my drink between my knees. "What happened to you?"

Now the light was better, and I noticed an abrasion on her right cheekbone and small cut across her top lip.

"Well, Maddie. I've been doing some serious damage."

"I doubt it. I mean, they let you leave, right?" referencing her exit from the Sheriff's facility.

"Maybe you've been up to no good yourself," she said in disgust. "What happened to *you*?" pointing at the blood across my sweatshirt. "And you stink," she added. "If I hadn't been asleep, I would've said something."

I recalled my brief experience of laying in the proverbial gutter the previous evening, but decided not to say anything about it until Mallory had given up her story.

"Yeah, huh." I shrugged. "Mine's no big deal, you go first."

She swigged at the Scotch. "It's just like I told you on the phone. I might have killed somebody."

"How are you so sure?"

Her face was ashen, but she drained the glass, and stood just long enough to set the tumbler on the bar.

"Do you remember me telling you about a guy who was stalking me?" she asked.

I frowned. "Was it Roger, the one you got a restraining order against?"

"That was a year and a half ago, and he moved out of state. No, this was a man from the fitness center. I'd met him a couple of times when I taught a step-aerobics class. He was creepy, and getting creepier. I just had a restraining order served on him."

"What was he doing?"

"Hanging around the gym after class, watching me. Leaving notes on my windshield."

"Maybe you're paranoid." But I recalled the deputy, the dire expression of pain on his face as Mallory ran out the door. She oozes vitality, often the target of unwanted male attention. "Maybe you have, I don't know, super pheromones, or something," I theorized aloud.

"Whatever, this guy was really scary. You know the eucalyptus grove above my house?"

There's a slope rising at about a ten-degree grade behind the house where my sister lives, a staggered woodland of live oak and bay trees fronted by a grove of enormous eucalyptus, overgrown with English ivy in the process of choking the trunks. Mallory had often remarked she intended to have the trees removed, but there are seven of them. At a thousand dollars each to hack out of a sheer slope riddled with poison oak and thorny blackberry vines, she had never gotten around to hiring an outfit for the formidable job.

"Sure, I know the place."

"My roommate caught him looking in our windows with a pair of binoculars. I wasn't there—well, my car was, but I was out jogging on the county road. Kelly, she freaked out and called the cops, and they caught the guy trying to run. I guess he tripped in the bushes or something. He was arrested for being a peeping Tom. And I don't know how the hell he got himself up there in the first place without anyone seeing him."

"Is that when you decided you needed a restraining order?"

"That's when it started. I kept finding notes on my car, and photos of me stuffed into the mailbox. I actually caught the guy following me in his car one time while I was running."

"Have you been given a status, whether he's just injured or—?"

"I don't know, Maddie. He might be past tense. Last time I looked, he was in my carport lying in a pool of blood, with paramedics doing CPR."

I sat forward, nearly spilling my drink. "What did you do to him?"

She raised her brows. "I hit him with a piece of concrete." She shook her head slightly, almost a tremor, and her hands were clearly shaking. "I only meant to stop him, but then his face...and there was so much blood." She seemed pale and about to vomit.

"Stop him from doing what?"

Mallory removed her suede jacket with care, and peeled off her long-sleeved t-shirt, revealing a mass of bruises on her upper arms.

"What the hell is that, Mallory?" I clutched my drink with both hands. "Since when do you bruise?"

"Since he tried to rape me," she whispered, sitting motionless in a navy-blue bra.

I made the mistake of laughing, a serious personality deficit, often used as recourse to anxiety, or when I'm about to cry.

"And that's *funny?*" Mallory seemed as horrified as I.

"It's *not* humor." I pressed both hands to my eyes, to stop the burning tears. "You teach self-defense, so it's more of an irony."

Mallory stared at me in shock.

"Please, go on," I urged in an apologetic tone. "What happened next?"

"He grabbed me, hit me a few times around the face. There was a struggle, and I kicked him in the groin. Then, I picked up a piece of concrete." She motioned at an invisible prop on my living room floor. "The parking stop in my carport's been broken since I bought the house. There's rebar sticking out, you know? I picked up the part of the block that separated, and I hit him across the face." She moved her hands gripping the supposed weapon from right to left mimicking the swing of a bat. "I swear, I never knew you could literally take off someone's forehead with one try." She leaned back in the chair; face buried in a hand.

"And the Sheriff department's not charging you?"

"Not yet." She removed her face from her hand. "Not unless he dies, I guess."

"You'd better hope he doesn't."

"I don't know, Maddie. How could someone survive after being assaulted that way?"

I set aside the drink, and went to comfort her. Maybe it was the shock of the experience, but she seemed so unyielding beneath my encircling arm.

"If I didn't have the R.O., I'd be in a hell of a lot of trouble," she added, as though impervious to being consoled.

"Did the county take pictures of those bruises?" Sitting up, I fished around for my digital camera, finding it in the drawer of a side table.

"A detective snapped some photos."

I began to shoot with the flash, walking around her to make certain I had a thorough record. Later, I'd look closely at the photographs, and wonder if my sister were shrewder than she'd let on, as there was a subtle rancor in her gaze that defied her supposed anguish.

"What are you doing, Maddie?"

"Never trust the cops," I advised, as though an expert. "Don't assume they'll take care of you. You have to cover your own ass."

She melted into the sofa with a heavy sigh, exhausted.

"Why don't you get some sleep?" That final swig of Scotch was surprisingly sharp as I forced it down my throat. "You can have my bed."

"As long as your sheets are clean." She could still mock me with one eye closed.

"You know me. I never bring men here."

"You never bring men anywhere."

While my sister dozed on the couch, I stripped sheets from my bed, and put on a set of fresh sheets and pillowcases. When that was done, she staggered in and, removing her athletic shoes and jeans, fell onto the mattress like a slowly toppling tree. I think she was asleep before her head hit the pillow.

When I knew she was safe, I made up a place for myself on the sofa bed in the living room. The wood stove was radiating heat, and I lay with the covers off, one leg hitched over the other, waiting in vain for sleep. I guess that's because I kept the film of last night's event playing over and over in my mind, and guilt is never a sleep aid.

2. The Poison Tree

If you don't understand the definition of "Paradigm Shift," I'll educate you on its merits and the potential of a crippling aftermath. Once in motion, the Shift can spell either positive change or catastrophe. On one side, you're uplifted and redeemed, but its descent is equal to being a crushed insect beneath the sharp heel of a heavy boot.

Oddly enough, when I am convinced my back is to the wall, I reflect on the late Agapito Cassin, Grandpa Feliz's maternal uncle. I never met Agapito, but he has exerted influence upon me without his consent. If I know anything about ol' Agapito, it's that he was a font of wisdom.

There is a memorable and half-skewed platitude dished out by my stately forebear, who was alive for at least a part of my father's childhood, long enough to impart some tantalizing dogma.

"Collect and select," Agapito enjoyed telling those members of the family swimming in youthful male hormones. He never spoke this phrase to the girls, as it might suggest that Agapito condoned all sorts of sexual possibility. But to the young men, it implied the need to date heavily until you found just the right virgin to hold close as your wife, sans promiscuity. *Collect*, meant putting together a list, based upon pedestaled feminine attributes, disqualifying those with libidinous histories; and *select* was what you did when you verified her as unsullied treasure.

What you can't perform are resections upon your own family. You're stuck with whoever was dealt into your family hand. Therefore, you acquire patience and charity to survive one another's eccentricities.

But apparently this premise of *Collect and Select* can be extended to the unsanctioned few who belong to your lineage without your consent. And my father, Mitchell Benités, is to blame for unwittingly bringing his personal curse to life.

* * * *

My father is a professional musician, a guitar player by trade, making a decent living from his field of choice, subsidized by teaching. That's one of my mother's jokes, Dad financing stage performances from income earned in the home studio.

At age twenty-five, with my chosen career as a general contractor, my preferred haunt for alcohol consumption has evolved from my father's least-favorite place to park his axe. It doesn't take a rocket scientist to figure out I don't want my historically confrontational father to be privy to my personal method of entertainment.

It's neither the decor nor the consistently intoxicated patrons that magnify Dad's reluctance to haul into JJ's Blues Lounge in San José, as many of the in-house musicians have been his musical acquaintances for thirty years. It's the fact that when Dad hits the stage on an open-mic night, his musical acrobatics generally chase off the playlist of guitarists waiting a turn. This strangely reinforces the Benités family's cultural aversion of calling attention to oneself.

Due to its pulse of lament and acrid cigarette smoke, JJ's is such an unsuitable place to embrace ghosts, even those belonging to another man's past. Entering the bar is slipping into an era of down-and-out Memphis wannabees on the West Coast. There is honesty to the players, the embodiment of raw suffering, especially when a man is forced to sell his guitar to pay rent or feed the kids.

I go on the nights when the local players are pounding the stage, wandering in after work. You can drive past the frontage on any given night, and get a whiff of pungent smoke and an earful of guitar-driven riffs from the genre most rooted in heartache.

As Mitchell Benités' daughter, the old-timers are familiar with my paternal connection. In the trait of culture, it's my liability to buy my elders their drinks. For that, I bless my financial prosperity. Besides, most look out for me, conscious of my father's temperament coiled like a basking snake, and they're ever watchful on his behalf. No man in that joint wants to own up to having lost track of Mitchell's girl as she's victimized by some drunken jerk.

I often meet one of my best friends from high school days at JJ's. Kevin Gerard played football at USC, and then lost his college scholarship during freshman year by virtue of a blown knee. Kevin hobbled back to Santa Clara after that tragedy, and pieced his life back together, belying critics' predictions. Even with the limp, he can easily secure construction contracts under license. He's reliable and meticulous, stature he acquired to compensate for the college maiming.

On the winter evening, in time parallel to Mallory's horrific event, I

13

parked my work truck. Though it was nippy out, the orange flush of a sunset peering beneath rain clouds along the hills, in JJ's the Blues were already in motion, and sweat sheened on the musicians.

Kevin was seated at the bar, hunched over a Seven & Seven, talking to the bartender; and at the same time, being coaxed by a middle-aged biker chick to join her out on the unobstructed dance floor. If I know Kev, he wouldn't budge, as his living arrangements include a thirty-seven-year-old female roommate who lawyers in the District Attorney's office. She doles out a weekly *per diem* to Kevin of three hundred dollars, Kev's compensation for being horny and hard. Knowing him the way I do, I seriously doubt he'd screw up the home situation for sidebar ass.

"There, see? I told you." Kevin pointed to me, slapped the edge of the bar, and nearly upset his drink. "I told you she'd show."

I yanked out a barstool, doing my best to ignore his comment.

"Anything, Maddie?" Doris, the bartender asked. She can hold a conversation with a customer, and keep an eye on the door, especially on this relatively unpopulated Tuesday evening.

"Just a shot of *reposado* with a Corona."

"With pleasure," Doris smiled, serving a shot of tequila, and a beer with a lime wedged into the mouth of the bottle.

"Mmm, thanks." I slid her a couple of bills exceeding the tab. I shoved the wedge down with one thumb, until it joined the golden beer, sending up a rush of bubbles. Tossing back the tequila, I took a swig of the beer.

"Dude, Maddie," and Kevin pointed to the heavy-set fortyish woman at his far side. "This is Linda, she rides a Harley." And he had the audacity to wink openly at me.

"Hi," I said, nodding cautiously. Linda seemed to take an interest in me, and my instincts braced against the inevitable.

"I told her you drive a Kawasaki." Kevin referred to my Nomad 1600 cc, a fully dressed cruiser.

"Yeah?" I set down the beer. "That's just...great. Aren't we all hot stuff, now."

"It's nice to know another young person who rides the streets. Mine's a Softail," she elaborated, as though I gave a damn. "Y' always gotta be careful, right?" Linda spoke the slur of intoxication. I was hoping she didn't intend to drive off in her present state.

"Right," I kept up the head-wag, and an exaggerated expression of intense concentration.

Eventually my lack of any interest beyond nodding my head, Linda picked up the cue to move on. After a couple of minutes, she found her mark, and proceeded to work an older male barfly with her spiel.

"You're not real friendly tonight, Maddie," Kevin feigned scolding me.

"Hey, last thing I need is a woman coming on to me."

Though the way Linda was dancing with her new fixation, she seemed anything but a door that swung both ways. All that drunken tottering to *Mustang Sally* meant it wouldn't be long before the two departed the bar for a cheap motel, or perhaps the bench seat of a car.

Doris set another beer and shot onto the bar before me.

"From Cale," she motioned to a middle-aged guitar player, Caleb Benchley, a decade shy of being elderly enough to have fathered me. My age of consent aside, he knew my dad, so it was indecent to buy me a drink when Mitchell Benités was nowhere in sight.

I nodded my thanks to Cale, and then turned my back on him.

"That old dude has balls," Kev grinned, nudging me.

I rolled my eyes. "Funny. I was thinking he was a coward to try to liquor me up when Dad's not here."

Doris returned to our quadrant of the bar. "You know, Maddie." Her brows were puckered. "There's been a guy in here asking about your Pop."

"Well?" I shrugged. "Maybe he wants guitar lessons."

"I don't think so." Doris seemed conflicted. "He said he'd heard Mitch hung out in here sometimes."

I flinched at *Mitch,* since my father preferred *Mitchell,* and would shorten another's name in line with their chummy come-on. This would often result in a witty turnaround, when the speaker might be lucky enough to comprehend the gist of Mitchell Benités' irritation. There was a priest at a Diocese event I recalled, Father Horace, who had the misfortune to call my father *Mitch,* after he'd been introduced as *Mitchell.* I would guess the priest was genuinely baffled as to why Dad referred to him continually as *Father Whore.*

"Dad comes in here maybe three times a year."

"That's true," Kevin agreed, as though he'd counted.

"And he always comes in with Mom," I added.

I pulled out my wallet from a back pocket, stereotypical men's style, and fished out one of my father's business cards. Under the yellowed glare of JJ's lighting, the slick business card with its color photo of a Gibson L5 CES, one of the jazz archtop guitars in Dad's impressive collection, seemed to reflect an oily sheen.

"I love this card," said Doris dreamily. "So, what? Do I have to give it up? Can't I keep it?"

"You can give it to the guy who's been asking about my dad. Though you know, Dad is listed in the phone book."

"Yeah, that's right." Doris frowned.

"What gives, Doris?" I asked bluntly.

"He really wanted to talk to your Pop in person," she repeated.

I was hoping she'd elaborate, when Cale Benchley pulled a stool up beside mine, and leaned close.

"Hello, Madeline," he spoke in a sultry voice, flavored by cigarette smoke. He smelled of the gin he was swilling, and the Marlboros he furtively smoked outside the bar.

"I dare you to try a pickup line when my dad's here," I bristled. Sliding off my stool, I very obviously moved my seat away from him, while Kevin, no help at all, cackled loudly.

"I ain't going to try it when Mitchell's here," Cale admitted, which was the gin speaking. Cale Benchley was a smooth talker once prepped by liquor, but only to lonely bar females who visited JJ's for the reason of fornication. My justification for dropping in was more of a personal buzz.

"What's wrong with you?"

"Come on, baby. You gotta know I've been wanting you, ever since I knew you were legal." He was leaning toward me again. "I mean it has a mind of its own." The barstool was rearing up on two legs.

Deliberately, I yanked one floor-bound leg of the stool with the top of a steel-toed boot, and the seat shot out from under him. Good thing Cale Benchley was drunk enough to follow the flow of his descent, because he might have been injured had he tensed for even a second. He seemed to find the tip-over hilarious, and just lay there on the floor, giggling, until he began to hiccup.

"Come on." Kevin helped Cale to his feet, while I righted the stool.

"Damn, Madeline, you takin' me down right here?" Cale's eyes, measuring his drunken state, gazed at me through the boozy heaviness of half-closed lids.

"No, I'm thinking you're so hammered, you won't remember this later," I corrected, "and therefore, you'll never be too embarrassed to speak to my father again."

"I'll drive you home, Cale," said Kevin, downing the remainder of his drink, and putting on his leather motorcycle jacket.

The asphalt scars down the back of Kevin's leather jacket called to mind a spill he took as a high school senior, when his rickety Virago 1100 lost a front wheel, and sent Kevin sliding for five hundred feet along the uphill grade of a freeway off ramp. The motorcycle was trashed at roadside, while Kevin, probably the luckiest son of a bitch I know, lay in the middle of an intersection upon the top of the overpass. Drivers, too stunned by the lone man in leathers and full-face helmet shooting into the intersection, stood down behind the limit lines, saving Kevin from certain death beneath their wheels.

"See you, Maddie," Kevin grinned, leading poor drunken Cale Benchley outside.

Now that I was alone, I finished Cale's contribution, the shot of tequila, and started on my second beer. I'm adamant about not heading home impaired, and will walk up and down the main drag to sober up before getting behind the wheel.

Doris, noting my decisiveness to intoxication, quickly arrived at my part of the bar.

"You know that guy I told you about, Maddie?" she asked.

"The one who's been looking for my dad?"

"Uh-huh, well, he's here."

Twisting on my stool, I attempted to see whom Doris was referring to. The stage lights were hazy with cigarette smoke wafting inward. From the direction of the thrumming stage, a man emerged, framed by the bar lights.

I felt like a casual driver on the overpass who'd witnessed Kevin shoot through in his leathers, as though smacked between the eyes. The response was instinctual, and should have served as my first warning.

"Yep, that's the guy," Doris was saying, but I barely heard her.

He made it to the bar, and sat down on Cale's former stool. I smelled leather and wood smoke, and *God, he looks fine* unfortunately began to in my head. I knew better; it's just that when I've been drinking, I can lose my reserve. That radar is always in place, what those with functioning eyes deploy when sizing up another human being, an inherent prejudice.

"Hi, Doris," the man said, in a voice that was absolutely crisp and succinct, without a trace of any accent. "Any chance Mitchell Benités is here tonight?"

"No, sorry," Doris smiled, apparently softened by the man's beauty. Doris was usually such a hard-ass, distrustful of every comer to the bar, and a shark to collect on tabs. "But you know, it's funny, because this here is Mitch's daughter, Madeline."

I could have slapped her for indiscretion. At least if she'd held her cards, I might have been able to determine what he wanted of my father.

"Oh?" His eyes swung to me. "You're Madeline Benités?"

"Sure," I nodded, tongue-tied by sudden shyness, which is almost never an issue if I'm doused in alcohol. I felt exposed, not a good sign, as I tend to put up defenses when I feel cornered.

"Wow." He laughed, and studied me closely.

I hate scrutiny, especially from an attractive man. I am about as plain as a woman can be, my face devoid of makeup, and hair usually secured in a ponytail. And my hands; let's just say that they are definitely a reflection of my career choice as a general contractor.

"What're you looking at?" I asked harshly, to divert his attention. I have a hot temper once I get going, and his examination was goading me. I could feel the blood rise to my cheeks, and my hands twitch reflexively.

"If I'm right, I may just be looking at my sister."

* * * *

When I think about that night, I should have owned the strength of retrospection, rather than impulsive stupidity. I wasn't prepared to handle the about-face, because somewhere after claiming I might be his sister, I popped this unnamed individual across the face with a closed fist.

There are bar brawls, but they are events of television fiction, with chair-beatings and jagged bottle ends. This was less a brawl, than a striking out at invasion. That's how I acquired blood spray across the front of my sweatshirt. My fist vibrated upon impact with that beautiful face. After my assault, I sat on the stool with Harold Tolliver, one of Dad's musician buddies, holding my shoulders to prevent me from leaping into the fray. While Doris called the police, I observed the man I'd slugged hold a wad of paper towels to his nose to staunch blood, heavily staining his button-front shirt.

Apparently, he'd decided to remain on speaking terms with me.

"What a way to meet family," he said, though I knew he was only trying to piss me off, since he'd already pressed a hot button in me.

"Fuck you!" I snarled.

Three San José cops sauntered in with batons in hand, ready to break somebody's ribs. Luckily for me, I knew one of the officers, who played saxophone in his off-duty hours as a member of a local horn band, *Taco Stew*. Harold released me, assigning responsibility to licensed authority.

Officer Randy Garcia studied my victim and the blood-soaked pile of paper towels, shaking his head.

"Whew, Madeline, does Mitchell know you're in trouble?"

"I'm an adult," I defended. "I don't have to run to my dad."

"Did he come on to you?" Randy asked, perhaps leading me.

"No, he said I might be his sister, so I punched him in the face. But he'd already pissed me off, so the rest was easy."

Randy sighed.

"I decline to press charges, officer," my victim said. He had withdrawn the paper towels, but his nose looked tender, the curve of each nostril outlined in blood.

"What's your name?" Randy used his Maglite to shine into the man's face, which, according to the bar's lighting, was totally unnecessary, just a simple means of law enforcement intimidation. "I.D. too, if you don't mind."

The man handed over his driver's license, unaffected by the flashlight beam. "Jesse Ibarra," he said. "You can run my license, officer, you'll find I'm P.D. in Los Banos." He brought forth a badge for Randy to study.

"Los *Baños*," I corrected fiercely, aiming to call his employer's city a toilet.

"If you don't mind," Randy waved the badge and driver's license in hand.

"By all means, go right ahead," said this Ibarra character, and Randy headed out the door, to his cruiser and laptop.

"Geez, Madeline, you slugged a cop." Doris scolded.

I studied her with a carefully neutral expression, as I was nearly sober now.

"I don't have a brother," I insisted, glowering at Ibarra, while the other two cops stood back about fifteen feet, conversing with some of the musicians, who had stopped playing and waited in suspense for the outcome.

"Maybe you do, and you just didn't know it, Ms. Benités."

"So, who do you imply is our common parent?" I intentionally

19

colored my voice with disgust.

"Your father, Mitchell Benités."

I scoffed. "Well. That'll be the day."

Ibarra stood, as Randy returned with his personals.

"Yep, you check out." He handed Ibarra his license and badge, and then clapped me on the shoulder. "Are you really sure you're not going to be pressing charges against this female perp?" he asked Ibarra.

"I'm sure," Ibarra assured. "I would characterize this event as a misunderstanding."

"Did *I* misunderstand you?" I asked, in an attitude not typical of me. Under normal circumstances, I would never posture, or defy authority.

You're too steady, an ex-boyfriend from high school once told me, a preamble to breaking up, as though it were a defect, instead of a gift. *There's no ups or downs with you, Madeline.* Apparently he'd never seen my nasty side.

"Not at all, Ms. Benités, you heard me loud and clear," Ibarra assured.

"Then I don't know why you'd lie to Officer Garcia, Mr. Ibarra. I punched you in the nose, without obvious provocation." I smirked. "And I still have my left hand, you know?"

"Madeline," Randy sounded amused, "you really don't want to set this in motion."

"It's nothing, no problem at all," Ibarra promised. "Simple miscommunication, and bad timing on my part."

I slid slowly from the stool, my right hand a bit stiff from throwing that punch. By morning, there would be a decent bruise across the knuckles to complement the cuts.

"I'll be going now, Randy," I grabbed up my jacket.

"You been drinking, Maddie?" Randy asked. "I could breathalyze you."

"Yeah, I was drinking, but I won't drive, I'll go take a walk." I headed swiftly for the door.

Ibarra caught up to me, while the three San José cops bee-lined to their cruisers, absolved of any more involvement.

"Ms. Benités." He matched my hasty stride. "I apologize for putting the truth out there like that."

I halted on the passenger side of my work truck; and besides, Ibarra seemed on the level, and most sincere. The fire of my rage had died, replaced by self-reproach.

"The truth." I scowled. "I really...don't know what to say." I jangled by keys in my pocket, while the wind bit through my sweatshirt.

"You should put on a jacket," Ibarra noted my shivering.

"I don't feel like it." I could hear that challenging tone behind my words. "Because you see, I'm not cold, just really, *really* pissed off right now."

He sighed. "Look, Ms. Benités, I'm sorry, I didn't do this right, not right at all." He waved his hand at the stretch of roadway. "Maybe we could, I don't know, go somewhere and talk, just talk."

I was squinting at him with deep suspicion.

"How old are you? Thirty-one? Thirty-two?" Because, I reasoned, if he were older than Mallory, it would make everything right.

"Actually, I'm twenty-five."

"Damn." I folded my arms, and frowned at his feet. "*I'm* twenty-five."

I began to walk toward the dark heave of the Santa Cruz Mountains in the distance, and Ibarra followed.

"What the hell do you want?" I challenged.

"Your dad, he and my mother had an affair."

"Brilliant," I paused, fuming. "You know, come to think of it, why did you wait? Huh? And your mother..."

I was tempted to disparage the unknown woman who had the nerve, twenty-six years ago, to risk destroying my family. But then, you don't denigrate a person's mother. These would be considered as legitimate fighting words. And it appeared that my father shared equally the burden of culpability.

"Yes?"

Evidently, this Ibarra was the master of calm under pressure, a trait also owned by my father. I had inherited Dad's dime-turning passion, with a fragile edge of self-control against its momentum.

"Didn't your mother know? *Didn't* she?"

"That's the thing, Ms. Benités, yes, she knew, but she was married to my father, and he wasn't what you would call an understanding person. He had a vicious temper. She couldn't tell him there was a possibility that I wasn't his son."

"Huh. You'd think a bad-tempered husband would be enough to keep a wife from two-timing. Is your father still alive?"

He shook his head. "No, he passed away two years ago."

"And now your mother wants you to know who she *thinks* your biological father is?"

"Yes."

"She waits twenty-six freaking years, and decides the time is ripe to destroy my family."

"I can't believe that's her intention, Ms. Benités. You know, otherwise she would have brought it up a long time ago, and we would not be standing here."

"My preference entirely." I found another of my father's business cards, and flicked it at Ibarra savagely. He was agile enough to catch it between thumb and forefinger. "Go to my father, you tell him yourself. I'm not anyone's messenger."

I stalked back to my truck, and leaned against the passenger door.

"Ms. Benités," he said, though I could tell there weren't any words beyond addressing my name. We'd already reached the point of no return.

"Leave me the hell alone, Mr. Ibarra." And I continued to walk, this time, with the hills at my back.

In my peripheral vision, the last glimpse of him might have been enough to inflict shame upon my actions, had I not been so disturbed. For a man as substantial as Ibarra, broad-shouldered and solidly built, he appeared less than confident, framed by the huddle of smokers lining the sidewalk, and the neon *OPEN* sign glowing in JJ's window.

* * * *

Laying on the sofa bed, with the thin mattress doing little to relieve the frame pressing into my lower back, I stared at the ceiling and thought about Mallory. If she had problems, they were simply a foreshadowing of these ripples into waves of destruction Jesse Ibarra inflicted. Mallory's rationale was self-preservation, but Ibarra wasn't due any support for his mother's transgression.

I recalled how, after walking for close to an hour, I returned to my truck, and drove home, constantly searching in my rear-view mirror for following lights. Part of me wanted him to attempt contact, so I could lash out at his hope with my own desperation, and crush it. Not until I'd stumbled out of my truck from emotional exhaustion and the after-effects of alcohol consumption, I saw the white rectangle of his business card tucked into the edge of the passenger window, sodden from rain, keeping it flush to the glass. I stared at it for a moment, thinking I'd leave it to disintegrate by morning; but then I analyzed the consequences, and instead, peeled it carefully off the glass.

When I entered the house, I stuck the distorted card on the fireplace mantel in my bedroom, beneath the edge of a lidless wooden box of obsidian. The tiny stones, collected in Modoc County when I was a girl, belong to a class of sentimental treasures I never throw away. I then lay down in my bed, and these were my last acts, aside from stripping off that bloody sweatshirt before the call came from Mallory.

I would rather endure ten years of audits with the IRS, than tangle with my explosive elder sister. Her mettle was like mine, our strength and failing, only she had been blessed with premeditated restraint. I considered setting Mallory loose on Ibarra, for predictably she would approach the man like one of Uncle Mark's dreaded pit bulls, knowing which metaphorical artery to sever.

And just before I finally drifted off to sleep, with the cheap mattress poking at my back, and the wood coals in the fire box dwindling into ashes, the room throbbed with a fatal glow of moonlight shining through a hole in the storm clouds, the singular echo of who I have come to be.

3. Family Planning

In the morning, I rolled over on the sofa bed with a groan, muscles stiff from resisting the frame beneath the thin mattress. A chill billowed up from the floor, beating back the heat from the stove. Through the sooty glass, the fire had subsided into a pile of gray ash. As I rose into a sitting position, the stiffness of my body rode the length of my right arm, fingers clutched tightly in a bruise.

I then recalled details of the previous night, and hastily set off across the cold floor to search for Mallory.

She was sound asleep in my bed, stretched out beneath a pile of blankets. Her head was thrown back on the pillow with one arm arced over, and snoring softly.

I hesitated to wake her up. This was Saturday, barely seven o'clock, and the skies were still fouled with clouds. Besides, I would rather speak with my father alone. Mallory's future legal problems would require a remedy exceeding the simpler issues of paternity.

I was feeling queasy as I showered, allowing hot water to steam away physical pain, my knuckles on fire. While I dressed, I considered my parents' schedule. At this time of the day, they would have already eaten breakfast, and would be involved in their daily habits, none of which would alter with the arrival of a blustery Saturday. My father would be teaching students in a bedroom converted to a music studio, and Mom might be working in the garden in defiance of the weather.

I set off in the truck, leaving Mallory the gift of undisturbed sleep. The streets were fresh and slick, and beyond three-story boxes of newly built high-density housing, the eastern hills were colored green, new shoots lifting through last summer's drab fuel. A freight train was at the crossing, and I awaited the blur of cars as they sent a deep rumble through the floor of the truck.

Once the crossing arms lifted, I made the left toward the neighborhood where my parents had lived for over thirty years. I note that although I live a mile from my parents, I visit no more than once a month, contingent upon my schedule, or so went my excuse. They occasionally threatened to sell the property, and yet, were prevented by the very fact that the house had evolved into a quirky family heirloom.

Our parents planned the frequency of their children's conception like old hands. My siblings and I are approximately two years apart in age. Except for my eldest sister, Mallory, who was born in a hospital, we final three were birthed in the master bedroom of their house in a neighborhood ostensibly named after professional golfers from the 1950s. A midwife supervised the births; my father cut our umbilical cords, and buried each expelled placenta in the alluvial soil of the backyard. Knowing the progression, to this day, I can't gaze at my parents' vegetable garden without realizing what once nourished the earth.

We lived in a third hand, stucco covered box built in the late 1950s for then-cannery workers, whose eventual drift thrust them into the limelight of assembly lines in the burgeoning electronics mills at the infancy of Silicon Valley. Ours was a neighborhood of solidarity, *mulattos* and *mestizos*, thick with the tongues that rattled off Vietnamese and Tagalog, and the rolling spice of Mexican Spanish. The streets were childproof, lighted with road-facing kitchen windows framing the faces of mothers straining to chaperone our security. We never thought about skin color in our children's play. The summer evenings were redolent with sautéed garlic and fried *da-ing*, dried fish, its odor dank with the release of stored molecules from the Philippine sun. The colors of clay and sky-stained stucco walls, traced by trellises of *sayote* squash, and the pocked lengths of *paria*, the Filipino bitter-melon, which my part-Native American mother learned to grow from my Filipino father.

Our home was not a reflection of affluence, but it did reveal our intellect and familial consonance. My parents stressed the harmony and strength of family. They raised us to think for ourselves, to be leaders in our community, and walk the jargon of our hearts. They taught independence and originality, and the utmost importance of cohesion. We were consciously bombarded with the term *responsibility*, and the need to own our lives. Consequently, we were well heeled in what mattered, and our parents instilled in us gratitude and patience that became our daily guides.

There was no thought then, to the substance of prosperity, or the significance of our *barrio* factions. Not until many years later, my younger sister, lipstick-lesbian Margot, declaring the stated disgust of a girlfriend's

25

mother, that members of our family were "ghetto dwellers," and I gained awareness of the borderline poverty that haunted our family's cultural richness. So absurd, that this woman who lived in a million-dollar Fremont Hills home wafted by the eastward-stealthy wind, daily carrying the stench of the regional dump, would descend her self-elevated existence long enough to determine my family's poor social lot in life.

The irony of these memories was palpably bittersweet, as I parked the truck, and trudged toward the house, burdened with my purpose.

My mother stood in the front yard, knee-deep in a pair of black rubber boots, wielding a set of hedge clippers with which she carefully trimmed a wall of Mexican sage. Her waist-length locks, what my sisters and I always referred to as her "Indian hair," was pinned up in a bun, and covered with a faded green bandana, accentuating elegant cheekbones.

"How are you, Madeline?" She dropped the clippers, and waded through rafts of cuttings in squeaky boots. Her tone was casual, as in Mallory's tendency, but her eyes were eager.

She hugged me close, as always, the muscles tight in her back. My mother is a physically strong person, which hasn't been compromised with her reach to age fifty.

"I had Mallory over last night. She's still sleeping," I added, without revealing details exclusively my sister's realm. I hid the injured right hand in my pocket, careful not to wince at the sting and ache. "Is Dad around?" I asked, though I could clearly hear the *plink* of the upright piano through the opened studio window.

"He's teaching." She shrugged. "Did you eat yet? Would you like some coffee or something?"

In the background, I could clearly hear my father's voice admonish his student to "count out loud when you play." The baritone of his speech gave me a twinge of compassion for the student.

"No, I just...I was passing by, and thought I'd check in." Overwhelmed with Mallory's revelations, and the events at JJ's, I was at an impasse, but my mother was no fool. She eyed me closely, and then just before she diplomatically withdrew, offered a last chance for disclosure.

"Anything you'd like to talk about?"

"No, nothing important," I assured, and I rubbed my nose, which telegraphed a lie, or at least my withholding.

"When you're ready, I'm here." Her eyes were bright with maternal *Knowing.*

26

"All right, Mom, just...tell Dad I said hi."

A car pulled up to the curb, and a high-school-aged boy emerged with a guitar in a soft case across one shoulder.

Mom glanced at her watch. "A bit late, are we?" she commented. My mother has always kept track of the clock for our family.

The teen ducked his head, as he hurried to the front door, obviously nervous about being tardy for his lesson.

"Dad has a break soon. You could join us for lunch." She smiled. "Mallory too."

"I can't today. I have some errands to do with a job. I'll come back another time."

I could see the hurt in my mother's eyes as she fought for personal objectivity. My throat was tight with an age-old fever, a certain awe of my father, even a hint of fear.

"It's your choice," she agreed, but I was already making my escape to the truck.

The view of my mother as I drove past the house was of her stance over the piles of sage, gathering the bones to her chest, and dragging their shattered carcasses to the green bin. And I wondered—not for the first time, I promise—how in the world a kind soul such as she could survive beneath the crushing weight of my father's dynamic temperament.

* * * *

My father is the consummate teacher, schooled by his predecessors, the *Benités* and *Cassins* who lived before. The actual elders or main characters in stories passed along in the ancient tradition of oral history, despite the desperate vortex of war that swallowed much of the universal flow of human testimony. Family philosophy is extremely important. If you're fortunate, well-tuned doctrine has been instilled into each generation.

Our father enjoyed another axiom given by his granduncle, Agapito Cassin.

Agapito was the brother of Grandpa Feliz's mother, who had been institutionalized immediately after the War. A nervous breakdown from the unyielding stress of Japanese invasion and occupation, from the death of her eldest son, and scattering of family, Cora Benitéz disappeared for good. Because of this loss, including his father, Ferdinand, from typhus, Grandpa and his two surviving siblings needed a place to live. Grandpa's younger brother, Mauricio, went to relatives in Manila. A childless couple from

Mindanao adopted the baby sister, Belen. Feliz was homeless and adrift. To that consolation, Agapito Cassin took in his absent sister's eldest surviving child.

Common family knowledge paints Agapito Cassin as a man of militaristic ideals. Grandpa Feliz had to earn his keep under Agapito's totalitarian rule. They lived in Narvacan, a rural town in Ilocos Sur, where the primary vocation was farming, and trade goods were secured via barter system. Water was fetched from wells, and *carabao*, the local domesticated water buffalo, were utilized for farm labor involving plowing and hauling. These were the highlights of Ilocos Sur, which had not been thrust into the dark ages by war, merely paused.

Agapito was a teacher and owned certain expectations. Though Grandpa was treated much like a hired man, he wasn't allowed to mentally vegetate. He was required to attend school. Agapito might have been striking the figurative whip, but he recognized the potential in Feliz Benités. Therefore, Agapito gave to his nephew the Cassin family philosophy, which was also passed along to my dad:

There are three things of grave importance in life: your church, your family, and your education.

When a person finished their schooling, the *education* directive evolved into *job*.

Dad enjoyed repeating this to us, but he didn't overuse its theme. He has always been adept at taking advantage of the moment, and in making use of Agapito Cassin's adage was no exception.

When I fled from my parents' house that wet Saturday morning, I was running from the prospect of my father's likely response to the trouble Mallory and I had created, and I dreaded the moment of truth. His tendency to weave philosophy around any life event proved he was adept and opportunistic, but also predictable. When I finally chose to get around to confronting him with the hypothetical of a twenty-five-year-old bastard son, the backlash would be painful. I just hadn't figured who was going to hurt the most.

* * * *

"You're an idiot, Madeline," was Mallory's composed reply to my emotional recount of the assault upon Jesse Ibarra at JJ's, though she hugged me close to remove the bite of reprimand. "You're going to take a stranger's word about something so important? God!" She then tipped back her head to finish her coffee.

Upon my return from the brief foray to my parents' house, there was Mallory, awake and already having addressed both the unmade bed, and three dirty dishes in the kitchen sink. She'd produced a pot of coffee, and we shared it slowly, working on a strategy.

"So, what do you think I should I do about it?"

Her gaze retained a wicked sharpness characteristic of Mallory, who should have been an attorney, instead of a fitness trainer.

"I think you should get the two of them together, father and son, and let them fight it out." She stood, and placed her mug in the bottom of the now-immaculate sink. "If you could take me home, please, I'd appreciate it. I've got an aerobics class to teach this afternoon. My head isn't quite straight, and I really need it to be."

"Let's go, right now," I offered. "Will you be all right?"

"I certainly hope so."

"You know you can call me anytime," I reminded, knowing she would. Availability was the strength of our sisterhood.

She regarded me for a moment, nodding. "You remind me of Mom."

"Why?" I took it as a pleasing compliment. Conversely, whenever someone commented how much I was like my father, I would consciously recoil.

"You're nurturing, Maddie. When you gonna get married and have kids of your own, huh?"

"You're the eldest. That's your job," I huffed, and she rolled her eyes.

"Do you want to know what I *really* think, Maddie?" Mallory held the blood-spotted jacket over one arm, as we walked out of the house.

"Of course."

"You should write a letter to this person, and tell him to hire a lawyer, and the lawyer should request a paternity test from Dad. And then, if it all pans out, the lawyer could sue Dad for back support." She laughed at this.

"Maybe I will."

In the truck, Mallory became pensive, and she grabbed my hand.

"Let's not joke about it, Maddie, I think you should write the letter and suggest the test, but don't put yourself between Dad and this guy. You know Dad, he can be extremely single-minded."

"And maybe I should go to Los Banos and have a candid conversation with Mr. Ibarra."

"Yeah, *not* a good idea. That's his turf." She shook a finger at me in warning. "Your terms, Maddie, keep it all on your terms."

This is one situation where I should have followed her advice.

4. Here, Kitty Kitty

Uncle Mark Benités lives in Tres Piños, San Benito County, in a house built in 1941 on of ten acres of oak wood and grassland. Originally purchased in a state of serious disrepair, Uncle Mark salvaged the house from further deterioration project by project, with his own hands.

But Uncle Mark, though highly proficient with *html* and *Java*, isn't that well-versed in home repair. A job that might encompass one day for me would stretch into a month, or two or three, in Uncle Mark's case.

Most of this behavior can be blamed upon the time factor; that is, the lack of it, as he commutes five days a week, and sometimes Saturdays, to his tech job in Silicon Valley. He lives alone, and has been accused of being a workaholic. Uncle Mark seldom takes the time to drop in on any of us, though he's a constant fixture at family parties, especially if alcohol is being served, and he has a relative's blessing, and an extra bed, to sleep it off. Although his employer is just down the road from my bungalow on Bassett Street, his pattern exactly matches my failure to regularly visit my own parents. This isn't a reflection of the state of our familial relationship, but the fact that his daily commute equates to nearly a four-hour road trip, morning and evening combined, unless he rides his motorcycle, which shaves up to ninety minutes off the chore, but includes a death risk.

We crossed paths one weekday afternoon, long before Jesse Ibarra surfaced, or Mallory's bad dream. I'd been taking a break from a renovation job in the Santa Clara University neighborhood, and paused for lunch at a deli, discovering I was in line behind my uncle.

Mark is the youngest of the Benités siblings, and only American-born, conceived just a month after Grandma Enida and the elder four children arrived in the States. At age forty-nine, and despite a battle to quit smoking, he has acquired the Benités tendency to delay those first subtle effects of aging. He is often confused for being thirty, and as such, attracts women from both sides of that milestone. He was married once, ten years of what he terms *unholy matrimony* to my Aunt MariLou Kabiling. The marriage viciously parted some fifteen years ago, in part due to the irreconcilable differences in their extra-curricular entertainment. Uncle Mark enjoys hunting and fishing, and wasn't averse to bringing braces of dead quail or whole feral pigs home, in the prospect of Aunt MariLou's preparation.

MariLou prefers shopping as a pastime, a euphoria that emerges when she sets loose in the Outlet stores. She keeps court with female friends, and never joined Uncle Mark on a single hunting or fishing trip.

At their conclusion it wasn't their disparities, surprisingly, so much as the run-down, antique house in Tres Piños that killed the marriage.

The Uncle Mark who stood in front of me in the deli line looked almost like any Valley programmer, except for the tattoos beneath his long-sleeved dress shirt. My favorite is the *carabao* on his right forearm that he acquired in the Philippines while in the Navy. When I was a little girl, he would twitch his muscles and claim that the *carabao* "shimmies like a dancehall girl."

Which left me to wonder what these lonely Navy men did when they went on shore leave, and couldn't find human females for entertainment.

"Maddie!" He greeted me with a hug in his wiry arms. "What've you been up to?"

I explained I was in the middle of a renovation, a circa 1889 house near Santa Clara University; and how, on Monday mornings, I would often wade across a torn-up lawn fettered with red plastic cups, smelling of traces of beer and sour vomit. I wasn't working on a frat house, but there were Greek establishments on either side, and so the lawn of my job site had been stricken by the heedless alcohol consumption of college students. I would literally spend fifteen minutes cleaning up the trash of lazy bastards whose education cost somebody over thirty thousand dollars a year, and yet who were endowed with the social initiative of a two-year-old.

Uncle Mark laughed. He laughed at everything, including his divorce, and at Aunt MariLou's frank storytelling of the low points in their marriage, even fifteen years later. His ego was developed enough to recollect to perfect strangers that his ex-wife's legs had apparently been sewn together shortly after birth, and this was why she never conceived. He called her "the Problem."

"Her new husband inherited the Problem," he'd joke, "because the Problem still ain't spreadin' those legs."

Due to my love and respect for Aunt MariLou, I never repeated Uncle Mark's satire, but I'm positive she's already heard it all.

On that day, Uncle Mark rubbed his cleanly shaven face, and wanted to know when I'd have time to fix his decrepit bathroom.

"In a couple of months, Uncle."

"Good, 'cause the bathroom floor's gettin' so bad, that now I can see the basement through the cracks."

But it was well into six months before I could finish my contract jobs, and get down to Tres Piños. When I made the move, I figured I'd kill the proverbial two birds by invoking a face to face with Jesse Ibarra.

* * * *

Often stated about the historical agricultural icon, Henry Miller, was had he not arrived in San Francisco in 1850 there wouldn't be any serious human settlement in Los Banos. Six dollars languished in Henry's pocket, modest funding for an early California start-up. By the time Miller was leveled with his ambitions, he owned a vast cattle empire, had his fingers in the pies of several irrigation companies, and gained recognition for introducing cash crops such as alfalfa, rice and cotton to the Central Valley.

As for Los Banos, Henry Miller may have instituted a need, but it was the railroad that determined where the town's nexus would be built. That the city of Los Banos attributed justification in its settlement to Miller is evidenced by a couple of street designations, a town plaza and an elementary school, which imply Henry was more of a white-man's capitalist god, than a mere rancher.

On a day over one hundred fifty years after Miller's inauspicious arrival to California, I was angling down the east side of Pacheco Pass in my gas hog of a work truck. I would have preferred to ride my motorcycle, a reflection of the nature of the terrain, but fighting the wind sweeping through the area magnifies peril. The grass is laid flat, the trees bent over, and the incessant moaning on roof tiles of new home subdivisions is enough to drive anyone crazy.

But land was cheap, and water abundant from the Aqueduct, and with these elements setting the stage, housing developments spread like festering sores atop the skin of San Joaquin Valley soil. Maybe insanity is an equitable trade-off, when the walls the wind is battering theoretically belong to you.

Arranging a meeting with Ibarra was the easy part. Going to Los Banos meant a hefty detour on my way to Tres Piños, but the extra mileage was worth the effort.

When I telephoned Officer Ibarra at the cell number prefaced by his

Los Banos P.D. business card, he offered to meet with me, and front me a cup of coffee as a prop for the conversation.

"I'm glad you called, Ms. Benités," he told me, holding off from the more familiar *Madeline*, which would have exceeded my comfort zone.

To reinforce my naturally suspicious nature, I asked for our session to be set in a heavily visited public forum.

He suggested a coffee house, and in my paranoid taste, one located along a major thoroughfare. If I had a mental deadlock about what I would say to him, at least the coffee house was simple to find, wedged into a strip mall along East Pacheco Blvd. It could have been an outlet anywhere in California, as the blight of strip malls leave sense of the unique behind, traded out for consumer convenience.

He was early for the seven a.m. meeting, seated in a brown Suburban, and dressed out in street clothes. The moment he saw me pull in, he exited his rig and headed over to my truck.

As I stepped down from the cab, I was slammed by the immutable wind, edged with a bite of winter chill.

"Ms. Benités." He approached within six feet of me, and then hesitated.

"Mr. Ibarra." I locked the truck. "I don't know about you, but I'm locking up."

"Crime isn't too bad out here," he spouted some vague assurance. "It's far worse where you come from."

"Yeah, well, I'd rather deal with the crime stats from my side of the hill, and leave out all that wind."

We ordered our coffee, and then found a table at the back of the room where our conversation would blend with everyone else.

"For the record, Los Banos is Spanish for *The Baths*," he opened. "If they meant *restrooms*, they would've called it *cuarto de baño*"

"I called it *baños* at JJ's, because I didn't think you were listening."

He grinned, but the smile didn't match the wariness in his eyes.

"That's the best time to listen to what people are saying, when they figure no one's going to hear."

"Thanks, I'll remember that."

"Tell me why you changed your mind about talking to me," he said.

"I discussed you with one of my siblings. It was agreed you should take a paternity test."

He waved that off. "I don't think it's a matter of a paternity test."

34

I smiled. "Of course, you're right," I thickened my sarcasm. "Why *shouldn't* I take the word of a total stranger?"

"A paternity test, well, that might be intrusive."

I sighed, an early release of irritation, because I had decided prior to contacting Ibarra, I would resist the temptation to feed my own flame. Evidently emotions would soon undermine me, and I suppose my body language reflected this.

"Your whole sense of right and wrong was upended when you went through the act of looking for my dad at JJ's," I said in a low voice. I often utilized this tone just before an outburst. My sister, Miranda, had long ago termed it my *Killer Voice*. "And by the way, how did you even know you might find him there?"

"I did a Web search of his name," Ibarra admitted. "There was a listing on JJ's web site. Looks like he's performed there before."

"And you took it upon yourself to personally investigate at a bar." I could hear the intensity of my voice increase ever so slightly. "He *is* listed in the phone book."

But Ibarra seemed amused, and completely cool-headed.

"Open information, common knowledge," he concluded. "I didn't do anything unethical. I haven't gone to your father."

"Huh. A cop who's concerned with ethics." I knew I was building toward *ugly*.

"If I ask for a paternity test, I pretty much think your father would have to know," he pointed out. "You can't simply take a tissue or blood sample for genetic testing without permission." He rubbed his chin. "And from the photos posted on the Web of Mitchell Benités, it's not as though I could request a hair follicle. He shaves his head."

That *was* somewhat laughable. My father ritually cut his hair every Sunday evening with electric clippers, and retained only a mere suggestion that any hair existed at all on his scalp. I have no memories of Dad ever using a comb, and my anger briefly ebbed.

"Okay. All right," I held up my hands. "You have a point."

There was a moment of discomfort, but I thought of an icebreaker.

"Just for the record, you know, in case I have to brand my father as an adulterer, you might want to give me your mother's first name. You know how words are great memory prompters."

"Clea," he said without hesitation. "Her name is Clea."

I paused, frowning.

"What is it?" he asked.

"Well...it's like this, my father is a diabetic."

"That's too bad. You'd better watch out for your health."

"Don't worry. I'm a contractor. I move around all day long," I explained.

"What's the significance of your father being diabetic?"

"He has to stick his finger to check his blood sugar level," I pointed at the tabletop.

"And?"

"Okay, how did you *ever* get hired on as a cop?" heading back to my previous state. Amazing my emotions could take such a circuitous route.

He smiled benignly.

"By letting the guilty keep talking into self-incrimination," he said gently.

"I'm not guilty of anything." The *Killer Voice* was working up to crescendo.

"Everyone's guilty of something, Ms. Benités. So, go on."

"Really?" I pushed back my chair. "Thanks, I will."

I walked out on him. I'd orchestrated a fairly simple mode of retreat. I imagined his face slack jawed as I left the coffee house, unlocked the cab of my truck, and drove away. I was on the west side of Pacheco Pass, when my cell phone rang.

I pressed the button to *speaker*, because I knew it was Ibarra from caller I.D.

"Sorry, but I can't talk on the phone while I'm driving," and I terminated the call.

A moment later, he called again. I let it ring through to voice mail. At first, he refused to leave a message, and my silence forced him to call back ten times, undiminished proof he was persistent, or crazy. I had no intention of answering. Everything that needed to be said was over and done with.

In the end, he left a message, a few words, tacked together in a phrase: "The guilty manufacture their own downfall."

I cursed myself for not taking Mallory's advice to heart. I didn't need a psycho-neurotic cop leaving me cryptic messages, even one who professed to being my half-blood brother.

* * * *

When I reached Tres Piños, it was almost nine-thirty, and Uncle Mark was still asleep, having spent the evening drinking in his favorite Hollister biker bar. I knew this, because when I pulled into the yard in my work truck, Mark's black Harley Fat Boy was parked beneath a Valley oak, leaning into its kickstand at the end of a very long skid-mark dragged through leaf matter.

He didn't answer the door to the bell, or to my insistent knocking. I peered through a window, and spotted him asleep on the sofa, still wearing his leathers.

At least the back door was unlocked, and Mark's dogs knew me well enough to greet me in the mudroom. They were happy to slip past me to the yard to relieve their bladders, and then roll in wet grass.

After all those pit bulls he once raised to hunt feral pigs, he was down to a friendly neutered pit bull male, Chauncey, and a spayed Lab bitch named MariLou.

Go figure, that he'd name the bitch after his ex-wife.

Chauncey was the last pup from the hunting pack, but had been brought into the house as a pet, not a working dog, and so wasn't corrupted by the blood-fest of pig hunting. Sweet MariLou was Chauncey's companion, and together they pursued squirrels and rabbits. One time they cornered a skunk, that mistake adding high stink to their mutual history.

Without waking my uncle, I measured the bathroom's specs, and began to list the demands of repair. There were drywall and concrete backboard to acquire, along with tile and grout, and a roll of plastic to serve as moisture barrier. The bathroom would require gutting down to the studs, as the basement could be seen, revealed by ruined linoleum and gaps in the structural floor. I included flooring-grade plywood, and floor covering to a list; and then, I made coffee.

The only sound, aside from the coffee maker, was the uninterrupted rumble of Uncle Mark's snoring in the living room.

The odor of coffee must have awakened him, because he stumbled into the ruined bathroom, and threw open the toilet lid. Eggs sizzling on the stove weren't loud enough to drown the noise of his mighty piss, due to the lack of any sort of partitioning door, as I'd already removed it from the jamb.

He eventually appeared, combed and washed. He'd taken off his riding leathers, and changed into jeans and a sweater against the chill of the house. He then sat himself on one of the dinky dining nook chairs, circa 1965, having been salvaged from his parents' former property in the Orchard Gardens area of Sunnyvale. The vintage flowered plastic was torn in many places, allowing stuffing to poke through. I thought about Aunt MariLou's immaculate breakfast nook, and shuddered at the contrast.

"Hi Maddie," his first words as he leaned painfully over the coffee I served him. "Give me the damage."

I quoted a ballpark figure, and he didn't even blink.

"I've been waiting a long time, saving up for it. No way I'm gonna pay interest to some Goddamned credit card company."

"You have a few thousand dollars in the bank?"

"I have fifty-thousand," in the conspiratorial tone he used at my twenty-first birthday party, and had smuggled a bottle of quality tequila into the restaurant beneath his leather jacket.

"Isn't that your retirement fund?"

"No, I got a 401k at work. It's what I would've paid to your Auntie MariLou in alimony, if the bitch hadn't remarried."

"*Uncle*," a reminder of my split allegiance.

He looked smug. "I gave it to myself, instead of to that *bakut*," he grinned, referencing Aunt MariLou as an "old woman" in Ilocano.

The coffee seemed to be restorative, and we talked a bit while we finished breakfast. I told him about Mallory's problem, the self-defense killing, but he already knew.

"I watch the news, *Nakong*," he reminded, calling me his "little dear one" in Ilocano. "Satellite television works great out here."

He liked to do that, speak in his California accent, and then weave in a few Ilocano words. Uncle Mark was the only American-born, the youngest of five siblings, and the most prone to tackling fragments of a language they all understood perfectly yet couldn't utilize in fluent conversation.

But I didn't tell him about Ibarra. That issue seemed remote, irrelevant and unproven.

* * * *

That Saturday, we ripped the bathroom apart and made it inoperable. If we needed to go, there was always Uncle Mark's battered hunting trailer with its commode.

With crowbars and power tools, we removed fixtures and drywall and the old linoleum, including the grainy subfloor. We took out tile that had been glued to heavy plywood for half a century, afflicted with dry rot. The refuse pile in the back of my truck quickly rose into a small mountain. We made a late trip to the county dump, and then to a home improvement store for the puzzle pieces.

By Sunday, we'd fitted the subfloor, and replaced plumbing inside the wall. In went insulation and atop that stapled moisture barrier. We then hung drywall and concrete backboard. I had a hellacious miter saw, a tile saw, a portable table saw, and other beautiful tools of the trade, upon which Uncle Mark was proficient, without nicking his flesh.

At the close of our forty-eight-hour marathon, the bathroom was complete, from new linoleum, to the tiled bath enclosure, and a toilet and sink. All it needed was paint to seal the drywall mud.

He took off work on Monday, and we drove into Hollister to buy a gallon each of paint and primer. By noon, the drywall was primed, and we sat in the sun on the back porch, waiting for the primer to cure, drinking coffee and talking about old times.

The weather had been mild the past few days, with blacktailed deer traveling regularly through the field in front of Uncle Mark's house. The dogs would bed down on the porch, and whine when the deer made their way across the grass. Deer had been the aggressors in previous encounters, and the dogs were satisfied to observe from afar. Once the deer had passed with their air of superiority, the dogs would muster up to forage in the grass for ground squirrels and gophers.

While he was in the middle of a story about one of his hunting trips, the dogs chased something up an old oak tree that loomed over Mark's house.

At first we thought it was a house cat, due to the madness of the two dogs, and their bloodthirsty snarls. There's just a certain natural hostility between *canid* and *felis*. Even jackrabbits didn't build them up to this type of frenzy.

Coming around the house, we saw the bulk of an animal substantially larger than a mere house cat in the crotch of the oak, and we figured a bobcat, maybe. By the time we stood beneath it, we realized the dogs had treed a mountain lion.

The lion lay across a thick oak limb, and gazed down at the dogs with emerald eyes. The cat seemed more pensive than afraid, sizing up two white-eyed, growling adversaries half-leaping up the side of the oak trunk. The dogs were the only obstacle between the height of the tree and freedom in the hills. If they relented, the lion might quickly descend, and then where would we be?

Uncle Mark solved the conundrum by dashing into the house, and returning with his hunting rifle, a 30.06 mounted with a scope. While he loaded the chamber with fresh cartridges from a snap-lid box, I reasoned with him to let the cat have a chance at making a run for the hills.

"Maddie," he said mildly, "do you think it won't come back?"

"It's afraid of the dogs," I argued fruitlessly, while Mark peered through the crosshairs at the lion's vulnerabilities.

"The dogs, they're stupid. They don't know any better, but the lion will, pretty quickly. It'll eat both of my dogs once it figures out they taste good, and they're easy to kill."

"We could throw rocks at it. Maybe that'll scare it off."

"Right. Hey, have you ever seen a house cat get pissed? Multiply that by a thousand, with a cougar." He laughed. "Here, kitty kitty!" he called up to the lion, which only gazed earthward warily.

"What about Fish and Game?" I listened to my voice soaring high from the excitement. I didn't want to see the lion killed.

"Fish and Game? Huh! They'll just do this."

He raised the rifle to his shoulder, and expertly shot the lion between the eyes.

Rather than its sudden death draping the cougar across the fork of the oak tree, the body rolled with gravity. I held my breath, waiting for it to hit the soft, grassy earth, but instead, it veered east, and fell onto the metal roof of the house with a squishy *thud*.

Uncle Mark looped the rifle over one shoulder.

"Damn," he cursed. "Now I gotta climb up there and move it off."

I brought a ladder from my truck, and set it against the eaves. Cautiously, with the rifle still on his back, Mark climbed toward the cat to be sure it was dead. Once he'd figured the job was done, he set to work rolling the cat off the roof.

"Damn, this is a big boy!" he called down, holding open the lion's hind legs.

With a grunt, he heaved against the carcass.

The lion must have been heavy, especially in its limp state, because Mark couldn't turn it. The roof was steeply pitched, and it slid rather than rolled, accelerating as it flew off the eaves, which acted like a chute to toss the lion through the air, and into the grass twenty feet from the house. The legs and tail flopped violently when it slammed to earth.

The dogs investigated, sniffing at the body, while Uncle Mark gingerly descended the ladder. When he joined me, I was poking at the lion with a broken stalk of thistle, but it was clearly dead, due to the monster hole in its skull. The green eyes stared out in a fixed expression of what might be termed utter surprise.

"We gotta bury it, Maddie." Uncle Mark was breathless, setting the rifle against a stack of cinder blocks. "Get a couple of shovels from the tool shed, and we'll put this thing to rest."

"Why do we have to bury it?" I asked, after finding the shovels, and setting the blade of mine into the thick earth. I'd found a pickaxe, too, and hefted that when the ground proved resistant to the blade.

"*Because*," he insisted, as though I must be somewhat of a dim-bulb. "It's not legal to kill a lion."

"No way. You could just say that it was about to attack you."

He laughed heartily. "Yeah, like anyone could get a clean shot like *that*, with a lion running straight at 'em."

After an hour, and done with the pit, we dragged the lion toward it together. The body was getting cold and stiffening, but between us we managed to maneuver it into the hole.

"I'd say about two-hundred pounds," Mark said, nodding.

A die-hard hunter and fisherman, his stories suggested a tendency to exaggerate; except that I'd seen some of his catches, and here I'd witnessed the lion in the flesh.

All the same, I offered a doubtful expression.

"What makes you so sure about that?" I asked.

"There's this skin-head biker dude I know. Well, he wants people to *think* he's a hard ass, but he's really a pussy. He weighs, I don't know, two-twenty? Got drunk as a skunk one night, and it took three of us to drag him into the back of a pickup truck so someone could take him home. That's how I figured the weight of the cat."

"Right, Uncle, another one of your fish stories, eh?"

He stared at me, incredulous that I'd questioned his character, given the subtleties of culture.

"The lion's big, Maddie, he'd have attacked either of us." He rubbed his face, tired from all the effort. "Didn't make sense to let him go."

He emptied a bag of lime onto the lion's carcass, which we buried five feet or so beneath the ground. I eyed that bag of lime, which had been inside of the tool shed, because it symbolized the fact that Uncle Mark had laid it in store for just such a possibility. When I first brought the shovels out, I had discovered four bags of lime carefully stored under a blue tarp, so

I could only presume that my uncle might have done this sort of thing before.

Later that evening, the bathroom work was completed, and I was cleaning up the job, putting the tools away in my work truck, when Uncle Mark approached me.

"You did a great job, *Nakong*," he praised, and handed me a sheaf of bills. Right in front of him, I counted out the roll of C-notes.

"Thanks, Uncle Mark," I nodded.

"Look, Maddie," he broke the strain, "it's not the first time I killed a lion."

"It's okay, Uncle, you don't have to explain. Maybe if I lived here, I'd be worrying about lions, too."

"Your dad used to take you guys out at night, remember? Up in the hills?"

"Yeah, I remember. He certainly liked those full moons."

"Once, a couple days afterward, I scouted around, and found lion tracks in the same area you and your dad and sisters had been. Tracks laid right over, and fresh."

"Wow."

"I hope you don't hold this against me," he added.

"It's not that," I shook my head; and then, I realized what had been bothering me, that the beautiful green eyes of the dead lion had reminded me of Jesse Ibarra, who was disturbing in a far-off manner. The very distance was unsettling.

I then told Uncle Mark about Ibarra, spilling everything, my assault, the conversation with Mallory, and visit to Los Banos.

"Huh," said Uncle Mark, rubbing his chin, which after three days of failing to shave had only a few whiskers on it, the product of our Filipino ancestry, as we are by no means a family of hairy individuals. "What does Mitchell say about it?" he asked.

"I haven't told him yet."

For once, Uncle Mark didn't laugh. He only shook his head.

"You know, my marriage was a joke, right?" he contended. "I figured early on, it probably wouldn't last, but your parents, they're steady people." He exhaled. "I sure hope your mom is easy on him."

When I left Uncle Mark's place, I watched the house diminish in the rear-view mirror, until, around the curve of the road, it was hidden in the slope of the hills. Like a dream, it seemed to disappear into the fog of invention, swallowed by the truth of the land. Tender grass pushed forth beneath the bleached remnants of last season's blades, and a deep blue sky arced above earth, which often rests heavily upon forgotten bones.

5. Girly

Around the downtown area of Los Gatos, the shops are upscale, catering to the perceived affluence of hill residents. On weekdays, it's bustling, especially at noon, but on a Saturday night, the demographics transform from upper-class housewives on shopping incursions, and intellectuals of the business world, to college students and young single professionals. They pour in, and the atmosphere comes to blows in the incantations of live bands and dance clubs. I know the scene well. Mallory thrice dragged me to Number One Broadway, where she feigned sexual interest in strange men, and then ditched them, a twisted expression of anti-masculinity revenge. This is why I generally fall asleep before the clubbing begins.

But more often I come to Los Gatos to meet up with my youngest sibling, Margot.

Wedged between an art gallery and an artsy wine-bar, is my sister's boutique, Butterfly Road, a take on the ubiquitous women's dress that's classic Filipino *couture*. In the narrow retail space stocked with wares from a ragtag list of local Filipino American artisans, and items from her own production, Margot sells enough merchandise to afford to pay the mortgage on a modest cottage in Saratoga.

This day, my work schedule directs me to the shop, where Margot sets me to repairing a display cabinet. The glass was smashed one Friday evening by a drunken patron of the wine bar who staggered into Margot's shop, lost her balance and fell onto the glass countertop. The paramedics from County Fire arrived to bandage the woman's bloody wounds, just in time for the police to swoop in and arrest her for public intoxication. Somewhere between Butterfly Road and County jail, the drunk's wounds were cleaned and sutured. At first, my sister, who is all consumed with business, was uneasy about potential liability, but apparently with a blood alcohol level of .22, the woman didn't recall enough to litigate.

When I arrived, Margot was standing behind a long mahogany wood counter, showing jewelry to a customer. The man, a Caucasian, was fit and well dressed, towering over my sister with apparent delight in her physical appearance. She glanced at me when I entered, without skipping a beat in the presentation. Within three minutes, she closed the deal, handling the transaction with the same pleasing tone of voice, probably offering the gentleman, who was buying the jewelry for his wife, a sense of regret in his marital timing.

"Madeline, thanks for coming," Margot said professionally. "Follow me, please." She guided me through the curtain to the back room.

The damaged fixture had been removed to the rear of the shop, its broken, blood-spotted glass gaping like shark teeth under the rows of fluorescent lights.

In the long, well-lit space, two elderly Filipino women worked on late-model sewing machines, skillfully piecing custom-designed garments, inspired by the Butterfly dress, all the while conversing in Bicolano, a Philippine dialect.

The women are sisters, Revalina and Emerilda Cassin, related to Grandpa Feliz by way of Agapito Cassin. They are daughters of Agapito's younger brother, Nobilio, who fled Ilocos Sur during the war, and migrated straight to the Bicol Region, hiding in the volcanic highlands near Mayon Volcano for refuge from genocide. His respite came in the form of a seventeen-year-old girl, Rosalita Gascon, whom Nobilio married.

Nobilio resurfaced in the late 1960s, when Rosalita had been deceased for ten years, and he was close to death, yet still working his modest farm. To care for their sick father, these two daughters postponed matrimony. Nobilio lingered in Bicolandia, until his death in 1997. The lengthy deferment from male companionship left the sisters with a bleak, childless future, but at least disclosure of these so-called lost relatives added them to the already heavy roster of Benités relations.

Margot had sponsored Auntie Reva and Auntie Emy, referred to as The Aunts, on H-2B work visas. According to Margot, it was more reasonable to pay family, even for work that would be theoretically cheaper to produce in Chinese forced-labor camps. Margot was considered by the sparse politically conservative members of the Benités family to be a left-wing nutcase. She despised initiating trade with a communist giant, while a regime as inconsequential as Cuba was politically squeezed. Margot is a registered Democrat, and always manages to reveal the liberal colors of her political leanings in all capitalistic ventures.

I hugged The Aunts, received the standard pat on the cheek, as I gave them each a kiss; and then took control of the repair of the display cabinet. In no time, I had removed the broken glass, cleaned off the dried blood, and replaced the glass panel. All the while The Aunts were listening to Raul Sunico croon *Manang Biday* in Ilocano over the CD player. I understood nothing, except for The Aunts' croaking attempts at joining Sunico's siren call. Deciding that moving the cabinet into the shop was out of my realm, I struck off to find Margot.

She was behind that wooden counter once more, shop-talking politics with a middle-aged Vietnamese woman. Evidently Margot could poke her politically leftist sword at a right-wing dragon, and then faithfully conclude a financial transaction without risking the alienation of her customer. The concept was baffling, and yet appeared to be the high point of their brief encounter. The woman waved happily to Margot as she exited, shopping bag in hand.

"You are hell on wheels," I told my sister, as I wrote out the invoice.

"No, I'm not, Madeline." I could hear the debater's inclination heating up.

"Okay." I handed her the invoice. "Hell in high heels," I amended, and this seemed to please her.

"That's more reasonable," she agreed as she read the amount.

She found her pocketbook, and wrote me a check in her loopy scrawl. As her personality implied, the check amount exceeded the invoice by twenty dollars, her way of tipping me. Margot tipped everyone, even slipping tokens of appreciation to her customers, such as packets of free stationary or a business calendar. People tend to adore Margot on sight. She has been the focus of at least four serious marriage proposals from male admirers, all generated by awkward misunderstandings.

But none had any promise of hatching, as my sister Margot, with her five-inch heels and flowered silk dresses, is a lesbian.

As though to reinforce her sexual identity, she married her girlfriend, Julie Fife, in 2004, when San Francisco Mayor Newsom opened marriage licenses up to gay couples at City Hall. At one point the marriage was ruled by the courts to be an illegal union, however, the act conveyed their solemn purpose.

"You look stressed out," Margot commented, peering at me closely.

"I *am* stressed out," I agreed, because I know it's fruitless to lie to any of my sisters. The general good health of our relationships is testament to our adherence to truth.

"Let me buy you a drink," she suggested, powering down the cash register, and locking certain items behind thick glass.

"I'd like to, but I'm not what you'd call *dressed for success*."

"Hmm." She considered my paint-spotted blue jeans, the steel-toed work boots, and my dark blue work shirt, with its corresponding cloth nameplate, *Maddie,* stitched onto the chest like a cross-dresser's badge.

"I'll take you to Black Watch," she mentioned a bar on North Santa Cruz Avenue, not far from Butterfly Road.

"No way," I rebuffed her. My tools were already in hand. "Besides, what about The Aunts?" The women lived in an apartment space above the shop, which Margot had included in the lease.

"They'll close up their area, they always do. Come home with me, then." She bolted the front door, and dimmed the lights.

"Why, so you can dress me up like a girl?" I taunted, good-naturedly

"You know, you should dress like a woman from time-to-time, Madeline, instead of putting on your bull-dyke ensemble," she scolded.

"You're right, maybe I'd get laid more often." This disarmed her.

"Well." She scooped up her purse, hitching it over one shoulder daintily.

"We need to talk, Margot."

"Oh." She frowned. "I guess it's not going to be about politics," and she sounded disappointed. "Is it about sex?"

"Yes, just not mine."

"Too bad for you," she lamented; and we kissed The Aunts good-bye, before slipping out the back door and heading off to Margot's home.

* * * *

At the kitchen table, Margot stirred up a batch of fettuccini. While I uncorked a bottle of cabernet, I broke the story about my encounter with Jesse Ibarra at JJ's.

"And you didn't end up in jail?" Margot was aghast.

Julie, home from work, and cutting up salad material, choked back her laughter. Julie is a gangly white girl with the body of a marathon runner, a good six inches taller than my prissy sister, which explains Margot's heels.

"And that red wine isn't a good match for this pasta," Margot sounded cross.

"Well, I found it in *your* wine rack."

"Hush," Julie said, "don't you get it, dear? Maddie just told you that your father had an extra-marital affair."

More strangled laughter from Julie, but I only sighed.

"Yes, I know, difficult to comprehend, isn't it?" I mused. "There's that vision of Dad as a dignified teacher, and then, *poof!* He's a thirty-year old bimbo, banging some hot Hispanic chick."

"Madeline Lucia Benités!" Margot admonished me in parental fashion, her beautiful face flaming red beneath creamy brown skin.

"Wow. You need children, so you can yell at them." I poured out three long-stemmed glasses of cabernet, and then took a healthy pull from the one I considered mine.

"Why would I have children, when you try me so much?" Margot rolled her eyes. "Besides, the thought of Dad... Yuck!"

"Does Mitchell even know you've been contacted?" Julie swept the organized vegetable cuttings into a large wooden bowl.

"I don't know, but I sure didn't tell him." I shrugged.

"Who else knows about this?" Margot's pasta was ready, and she placed the serving bowl onto the table.

"Mallory." I pondered. "Uncle Mark. Maybe Doris-the-bartender at JJ's, if she overheard."

"That means Mitchell will know about it fairly soon," Julie concluded. "Pardon me for saying this, but your family simply can*not* keep a secret."

"She's right, Margot," I nodded. "Just think about our cousin Darwin, and his mail-order bride."

Margot lost the modesty that implored me to toe her line, and began to laugh.

"That's a hell of a lot better." I made certain to sound relieved. "You had steam coming out of your ears for a while."

Margot sobered. "It is possible Dad won't find out anytime soon," she said thoughtfully.

"Why?" Julie took a chair.

"Would you go out of your way to tell our father something like that?" I asked.

"Of course not," Julie smirked. "It's not any of my business."

"Why not ask for a DNA test?" Margot said, as though I had been too dumb to think of it for myself.

"Ibarra claimed that it's not necessary," I told her.

"Huh!" Julie snorted. "That's his way of saying he knows he isn't your brother, Maddie. Now you have to figure out what his true motivation is."

"Do *you* have a brother, Julie?" I asked, out of the blue.

"What? Why?" Margot wanted to know.

"Because. You're hot, but my sister found you first. I was hoping there'd be another *Fife* for me, one with a penis."

Julie threw a balled-up napkin at me, bouncing it off my forehead.

"Don't listen to her, Jules," Margot warned, "she's a virgin. She wouldn't know what to do with a penis if it hit her between the eyes."

"I am *not* a virgin," I flashed, to prove my debauchery.

"*I* certainly wouldn't know what to do with one," Julie smirked.

"Neither would I," Margot agreed.

"No brothers, sorry. I do have a cousin, but he lives in West Hollywood," Julie supplied. "Too far away to matter, I suppose."

"Why would anyone live in West Hollywood?" Margot wanted to know.

"He's a painter," Julie explained. "Houses, commercial property, that sort of thing." She wiggled her eyebrows. "Apparently business is really good down south."

I was tempted to make a sideways comment about *business down south*, but figured I'd be pushing it with my little sister, who tends to show her teeth when her tolerance level has been exceeded.

"Not biting at that one, huh?" Julie prodded, bouncing another tightly wadded paper napkin off my head.

Margot grabbed it up, and tossed it at Julie, hitting her right between the eyes. There were a couple minutes of scuffling, and napkin wasting, which ended with a napkin ball lodged in the bowl of fettuccini. My sister, who was laughing so hard that tears streamed down her cheeks, delicately picked the offending article out of the food, and put it on her plate.

"Really, Madeline, grow up," she pretended to reprimand.

"You should ask for a DNA test," Julie returned to the subject of our father.

"I've been trying to figure a way around both of them," I nodded. "I was thinking if I could get a sample of blood, you know, after Dad checks his sugar level for his diabetes, I could send it off for confirmation at one of those testing labs."

"You can buy a kit from a drug-store," Julie informed. "You get the sample, and mail it off to the lab, prepaid."

"How do you know?" I asked pointedly.

"I *read*, Maddie," Julie scoffed. "Haven't you ever heard of a newspaper? Aha! To you, the *New York Times* is like a penis, isn't it?"

"How would you get a sample from that guy?" Margot ignored Julie's comment. "If he already said it wasn't important, maybe he's hiding something."

"I'm not sure yet." I poked my fork into the food on my plate, pushing at it.

"I can't fathom telling Dad anything about this, unless you have some sort of proof," said Margot.

"Then, I'll just have to make it happen, won't I?"

"Madeline." My sister placed one hand on my shoulder. She is so feminine, that I often see myself as a linebacker type when I'm next to her, even though our bodies aren't really that different. It's probably due to my clothes. I'd never be caught dead in a pair of heels.

"Yes?"

"Be careful." She patted my shoulder. "Be *really* careful."

"Sure," but I had doubts.

When the wine had burned off, and I was ready to leave, Julie handed me a brown bag of leftovers, a plastic box of salad, and a zip-bag of fettuccini. I'd settled into my jacket, and accepted the food, followed by a hug from Julie.

"Madeline, come back more often," Margot squeezed my upper arm with her little hand. As though mooching dinner a couple of times each month from my sister wasn't too much.

"You'll get tired of me," I warned, hugging her close.

"I'll let you know when I'm tired of you," she promised, and I carried my precious brown bag to the truck.

* * * *

By the time I hit the freeway it was eight o'clock. I had intended to drive straight across the Valley, but somewhere between Saratoga and Santa Clara, I made a detour, and found a drugstore open twenty-four hours. Before I lost my resolve, I hurried inside and purchased a DNA paternity testing kit from the pharmacy. The entire transaction seemed furtive and uncomfortably illegal, as I returned to my truck. I felt like I'd bought some real nasty porn, for the way the clerk judgmentally studied my face.

Sitting alone in the parking lot, I knew I hadn't the faintest idea how

I was going to leverage a sample from either of the two men. With this thought in mind, and feeling frustrated, I headed home.

I was about to pass the turn for my parents' street, when, at the last minute, I swung a left, heading cautiously toward their house. The crinkly drugstore bag lay on the seat, a companion to my guilt.

But that notion fled as soon as I spotted a brown Suburban parked in the pool of streetlamp across from the house. As I drove slowly past, I studied the license number, which matched my memory of Jesse Ibarra's plate. I have a photographic memory and a knack with patterns, which is why Dad was disappointed I didn't choose music as a profession.

Ibarra was sitting behind the wheel with his window rolled down, and the cold air on his face.

"What are you doing here?" I asked, approaching on foot.

"Sitting," he replied.

"How long have you been sitting?"

"I dunno. Maybe a-nour."

His speech was slightly slurred. This reminded me of my normally even-keeled mother, who, once behind the wheel, assumed her alter-ego, *Roe Draje*, and often berated rude or overly aggressive drivers by use of what she called her "ventriloquism". This only meant that she spoke her mind without moving her mouth. Thus involved, she would state, through barely parted, smiling lips, "Son oth a ditch, you cut ne oth! Muzzer thucker!" Fortunately, this was the only revenge Mom would bother to inflict.

"Great." I stared at him sternly. "You've been drinking, I can smell it." I kept my voice intentionally low, as there were plenty of busybodies along this street.

"So?"

"Are you a fucking idiot? Do you want me to call the police?"

"D' ya wan' me ta tell yer Pa?" he countered.

I opened his door, and out came a nearly empty fifth of vodka, which clanked as it hit the step, and fell onto the pavement without shattering. What little vodka was left in the container, maybe one mouthful, streamed downhill beneath the Suburban, toward the gutter. I shoved the bottle further out of sight with one foot. Even as my foot contacted the bottle, I had a sudden inspiration.

"Come on, I'm taking you home."

"Nah, ahm a'right."

"Either you come with me, or I swear, I *will* call the cops."

"Ahm a cop," he informed, as he unsnapped his seatbelt.

"That makes it an even *better* idea for you to come with me."

He stood, nearly falling, and then, giggling, leaned on me for support. Outweighing me by fifty pounds and shaky upon his drunken feet, I was at least strong enough to get him to my truck, and shove him in.

"Goo' girl," he groaned, closing his eyes, head lolling on the top of the seat.

I drove away, hoping the commotion hadn't created a scene that would attract the cops, or that my parents hadn't been curious enough to poke their noses through the blinds.

Ibarra moaned and bitched unintelligibly for the entire three-minute drive. I figured it was the burn of his indignity. Just when I'd parked, and came around to open his door, he proved to have absolutely no shame at all, just a bad stomach, because he leaned out and vomited onto the dirt alongside the railway bed.

"You are one miserable jerk," I complained, guiding him into the house.

I settled him onto the couch with a blanket and an empty five-gallon paint bucket at his side for a catchall to his spills. But he had passed out, and was snoring more forcefully than Mallory's tune, which I chalked up to him being drunk. For a few minutes I stood and studied his face. There was nothing at all familiar in his features to cause me to suspect my father had contributed to this man's conception. My father would not resort to stalking or drink to forget his troubles.

I removed the kit from the drugstore bag beneath the overhead lamp, and read the printed insert. The collection system consisted of simple long swabs in sterile packaging. The leaflet instructed me to scrape cells from the inside cheek of the individuals targeted for testing, and ship the samples off in the paper envelope provided.

Standing over Ibarra, the room was tinged with the odor of vomit, which probably landed as droplets on his shoes, or dribbled down his chin. Ignoring the pungent wind of his breath, I took advantage of the fact that his mouth was wide open, and forcefully rubbed the swab along the inside of his cheek, counting off the allotted twenty seconds in my head.

He struggled for a moment with the swab, bearing down on it with a wrench of his jaw, and then released, without rousing from his drunken stupor. Sweating bullets, I removed the swab, and slid it into the protective envelope. When I was finished prepping it for mailing, I concealed all traces of the test kit, and locked myself into my bedroom.

* * * *

I may drink when I'm of a mind, but I never exceed my determined limit. One hangover in this lifetime is enough of a deterrent. Unlike certain minor offenses, you can't escape your consequences from alcohol.

In the morning, Ibarra was still there, quieter now.

Around nine, he stumbled into the bathroom. I could hear him retching into the toilet, then the sound of flushing. Soon the shower was running, and kept going for a good fifteen minutes. When he was done, he blundered into the kitchen with my blue terry-cloth robe tied at his waist.

"Ms. Benités," he said, feeling for a chair. Fortunately, he was able to keep his knees together, but he was shivering, even though I'd loaded the wood stove. I rummaged in the pantry, and found a tablecloth, which I threw across his bare shoulders.

"Your *serapé*," I proposed. The tablecloth was striped red and gold, and garish against the sickly pale of his face.

"I feel kind of ill," he groaned, eyes closed.

I filled a glass, and placed it on the table before him.

"Drink water. It's the quickest way to get rid of a hangover."

"Hangover's not so bad. It was vodka."

"It was almost a whole fifth," I reminded. "Drink the water." I included a couple of aspirin tablets on the tabletop.

"Okay, but I'd really prefer coffee."

I put together a pot of coffee, and after he was full of water and had visited the bathroom again, we sat and talked.

"What were you planning to do last night?" I had made plain toast, and we shared the plate between us.

"I decided to talk to your father." Already the toast appeared to be making him feel better.

"Why were you sitting inside your truck drinking then?"

"First I was having a drink to get up the nerve. I kept drinking, because it wasn't working."

"And what were you going to do next, just drive away?"

He grinned, and his eyes matched his smile.

"No, I probably would have passed out. That's what I did, isn't it? 'Cause I don't even remember coming here."

"What's the last thing you do remember?"

53

"I, uh, was getting into your truck. I don't recall anything after that."

Finished with my coffee, I rose from the table and put my cup in the sink. "Well, you threw up when I opened the truck door. "

"Oh." He seemed resigned. "Maybe that's a good thing." He rubbed his face. "I should get going. I've got to clock in tonight at six."

"Fine. If you get yourself dressed, I'll take you back to your rig."

"Thank you, I appreciate it."

"Look." I sighed. "I really don't want to get to know you."

"Why?" He stood, and was neatly folding the tablecloth.

"I don't like you."

"You don't have to like me, Madeline," he said kindly.

This was the first time he'd used my first name, and I was almost hoping he was my brother, not because I wanted to continue with some sort of platonic relationship, but quite the opposite.

"There's no danger in that, it won't happen," I promised.

"Well, I'll get dressed." He cloistered himself briefly in the bathroom.

When he reappeared, he followed me to the truck. I said only one thing, some advice to avoid him stepping in his own vomit, which was clearly splattered on the hard earth beside the truck. We didn't converse, even when I dropped him at his Suburban. He mounted the cab and drove away, while I sat in my truck watching him make the turn in the direction of the freeway.

"Madeline!"

A knock on my passenger door, and I jumped. There was my mother, lifting one hand in apology, as I leaned across and unrolled the window.

"I didn't mean to scare you, Madeline. I saw you parked out here. Did you want to come inside? I can make coffee."

Already swimming in coffee, I agreed, and followed Mom into the house.

Dad had gone for the day to his teaching commitments, and Mom had folded a load of laundry on the kitchen table. The blue painted walls felt like warm water, hung with framed photos of family, including a delicate black-and-white print of Granny June, dressed for a Powwow.

Granny June is Mom's birth mother. Mom located her in 1994, using a clever private investigator that used to be a cop. With that sort of corrupt mentality, it required less than twenty-four hours to locate June Gage Oddam in Rio Vista, having lived there for twenty-six years. Before that, between Mom's birth and relinquishment, June lived in the eastside *Avenues* of San Mateo, a few miles from the house Mom grew up in.

I motioned to the Granny June photo, while Mom removed laundry piles from the table to make room for our tryst.

"What tribe did you say Granny June is from?"

"Rosebud Sioux," Mom reminded me. "She said her father, my Grandfather Lawrence, was born in St. Francis, South Dakota. Granny lived there until she was twelve, and then the whole family came to Lone Pine, California. Her father was a truck mechanic."

She studied the photo, Granny June at age eleven, before leaving St. Francis behind, and heading into the chaotic mists of California, where she would soon be impregnated by a high school acquaintance. That child would be my mother's elder brother, Darcy, raised in the San Fernando Valley by a family of Mormons. I'd met Darcy, who wore his hair long like a '70s rocker, in defiance of the LDS. My sisters and I always thought Darcy was cool and youthful.

When June was twenty, she met a man in a bar that was owned by her maternal grandmother, Petra Soares. Petra was a divorcée, and had been married to an Irish sailor, Patrick McCarthy, who skipped town so often, that Petra divorced him *in absentia*. The man from the bar was Petra's lover, probably thirty years her junior. According to June, Rudy Søerlle used Petra for his liquor stop, and then cornered June for sexual service.

"Just think." Mom brought out the coffee and sugar and cream, and a plate of her home-baked chocolate-chip cookies. "If I could prove that I'm one-fourth Sioux Indian, you and your sisters could've received scholarships."

"We did fine, Mom." I took a cookie and held it in a napkin to catch the crumbs.

"Yes, you have," she smiled, patting my arm. Something caught her eye, and she gave a sigh. "I forgot," and she stood to pick up a napkin, briefly stained with blood. "I meant to throw that away."

"What is it?"

"Oh, blood-sugar measurement, the lancet and test strip. Used blood." And she laughed.

I watched her intently, as she rolled the napkin in yet another fresh napkin, and tossed the whole package into the trashcan. This was an opportunity, and now I felt completely wired from coffee and intrigue.

"I didn't tell you, but now's a perfect time. Dad and I want to hire you to do some repair work."

"That'd be great." I had a mental picture going of that napkin ball.

"It's not here, it's in Susanville. There was ice damage to the house, and the insurance wouldn't pay the claim. They say the fix is financially up to us."

"Out of your own pocket?"

"Yes." There was that optimism my mother always carried, evident in her face. Bad news never kept her down for long.

"Gee, I mean, why even have insurance, when they don't pay for a catastrophe?"

"Because. Insurance is a racket."

"I'd think it's a possibility you have mold."

"Yes, probably. We can't fix it ourselves, we're too inept, and you know how protective I am about Dad's hands, but I'd love to pay you, Madeline. I always favor nepotism."

"I'll take the job, Mom. I don't have another contract starting for a couple of weeks."

I finished the coffee, and went to put my cup in the sink. *Too much damned caffeine,* I was thinking. Opening the trash, I pretended to shove in my napkin with its cookie crumbs, but snuck the packet of what I assumed was my father's genetic material concealed in the palm of my hand. Mom wasn't looking anyway, her eyes on that photo of Granny June.

June was sixty when she had a debilitating stroke. She'd been left with aphasia, and was partially paralyzed on her right side. She lived now in a convalescent care home in Stockton that smelled of soiled adult diapers and geriatric sweat. When we visited, you could see in her eyes she knew you and understood everything you said, but couldn't sort out her own vocabulary to express her thoughts, and was limited to a droop-mouthed rambling of chaotically-mismatched phrases. Losing the precious commodity of communication seemed starkly worse than death.

"Did the insurance people give you any paperwork?" I asked, my voice rousing Mom from the photo.

"They gave us an estimate." She went off to find it, while I tucked the ball of contraband into my jacket pocket. She returned with a stack of papers, which I thumbed through quickly.

"Okay if I take this with me?"

"Of course. Here's a check, Madeline, to cover the initial material expense." She pressed a personal check upon me, written out for one thousand dollars. "Remember to bill us just like you'd bill anyone else."

"I always do, Mom," I assured, and kissed her.

When I had assumed she'd forgotten to wonder why I'd been sitting in my truck in the first place, I was already standing by the door with my hand on the knob.

"Madeline," she said, touching her chin, "do you know the man who owns that Suburban?"

"What?" I could feel my face getting red. I'm a terrible liar when it comes to my mother, though in my adolescence, I never had a need to withhold, because Mom was discreet with all secrets.

"The young man who owns the Suburban. It was here all night." Her eyes read right through me. "I saw you pick him up last night, and drop him off today, so I gathered you knew him."

"Well," I hedged. "He's a friend of mine."

"Oh?"

"We...stayed together. Last night." That was true, but the sexual connotation combined with a lie was excruciating.

"Just let me know when you want to bring him for dinner."

"Well," I scrambled for some excuse, but Mom is intuitive.

"Ah, okay." She waved her hands. "Don't worry, your secret is safe with me."

"What secret?"

"It's not a serious relationship. I mean you met him at a place other than your own. I assume you don't want him to know where you live."

"Right, the motel thing does the trick." I rubbed my nose furiously.

"No need to say more, Madeline."

"Sure, that's right. Listen, I'll go home now and get my gear ready. Tell Dad I said *hi*, and I should be in Susanville by tonight."

She hugged me. "I'm sorry, Madeline," as she patted my back.

"Mom, don't sweat it."

When I got into my truck, I realized I'd been the one sweating.

At the house, I packed my truck, and luggage, being sure to include the damage estimate from the insurance adjustor. Searching for my cell phone, I came across the napkin ball in the pocket of my jacket, and recalled my haste in buying the kit.

Carefully, I unwrapped the paper, revealing the used lancet with its plastic cap, the blood-dotted test strip, and a crinkled piece of torn napkin smeared with blood. This, I was certain, was my father's blood, and I

57

carefully slid the entire section of bloody napkin into the separate envelope provided by the kit. Before I left town, I dropped the mailer into the slot inside the post office. The release from my hand vowed a radical change in expectations, and in relationships. Better to have incinerated all of the evidence, and just keep driving on.

6. Under the Badge

Miranda is my elder by two years. She and her husband, Gilbert Snead, live in Susanville, in northeastern California, where they both have separate careers in law enforcement. Gilbert is a Lassen County Sheriff's deputy, and Miranda works for the California Highway Patrol.

When they married last August, their reception was held at the Bidwell House in Chester. The wedding was sophisticated, and catered by an outside firm, but that didn't prevent the elders of the Benités family from bringing in Filipino-style potluck. I may have once warned my sister away from involving herself with a man whose surname, Snead, is suggestive of nose-snot, but the fact is, my brother-in-law is a classy guy. He never even blinked when grand Uncle Rodrigo Cabezon, a very elderly man from Galt, and a distant Benités relative, brought a whole roasted pig, *lechon*, as a wedding contribution, using a hand-truck for transport from his vehicle to the reception area. Imagine that swine, cooked into permanent open-mouthed surprise, nestled on crisp white linen amidst the blanched organic arugula salad, herbed parchment salmon and high-end Napa Valley goose-liver *paté*.

Our parents own a property in Susanville near the foot of Roop Mountain, which figures into Miranda's love of the region. From an early age, we were raised to fish and ride dirt bikes, although most of us never quite acquired the enthusiasm our parents manifested. Without fail, every dirt-bike trail ride, hike foray, and bicycle trip, was a mind-bending marathon that seemed to last from dawn to dusk. I exaggerate, because at the crack of dawn we were up at Eagle Lake fishing, until it was hot enough to fry a brain beneath the rarified sky.

Somehow, the hardship didn't scar Miranda the way it damaged us. She steered her course strategically from college into employment with the CHP, to start her professional life in Susanville.

At the beginning, Miranda lived in our parents' mobile home, which is set back on ten acres at a little over five thousand feet. This makes for deep snow in the winter, where one is greeted by the county plow's driveway-blocking berm at the end of a long workday, when it's pitch-black at six p.m., and you'd prefer to crawl into bed. But, hell no, there's a wall of snow to scrape away with either a shovel or a snow-blower, take your pick; and then a wood stove to fill to keep the mobile home closer to fifty degrees, instead of the ten degrees the porch thermometer is reading. You use wood for heating fuel, because for the price of a ten-dollar permit you can cut and gather it yourself, making it dirt cheap, while the price of kerosene for the furnace can be a deal-breaker.

I'm not saying my parents' Susanville mobile home suggests unending torture, but it does require a dedicated measure of physicality to live there fulltime.

After a couple of years, Miranda bought a 1922 Craftsman home situated in town, a thousand feet below the cruelest of winter's punishment. The house stands in the *Uptown* section, on North Gay Street, ironically a target of sibling ridicule from our sister Margot's lesbian corner.

Miranda's story was that she first met Gilbert Snead at the Lassen County Fair, between the Haunted House and the Tilt-N-Whirl. She had been making a pig of herself with a casual date, eating too much cotton candy and chilidogs, and then shaking it up with a ride on the Giant Zipper, where she puked in the cage. Needless to say, her date, a Correctional Officer from High Desert State Prison, took the low road, and abandoned my sister, who was stuck in a kneeling position, drooling in the grass for the entertainment of all passersby. I can only suppose the poor C.O., accustomed to threatening felons with bodily injury, couldn't stomach having vomit spewed upon him, even by an attractive woman.

An off-duty Lassen County Sheriff's deputy, enduring an unpleasant date of his own, caught wind of Miranda heaving in the shade of the Tilt-N-Whirl, and came to her aid. With all that coddling, the deputy's date took off running, but what the hell, my sister Miranda is a stunning woman. There's something magnetic about *Island* girls that white men seem to find irresistible. Miranda, with Granny June's straight dark hair, Mom's cheekbones, and Dad's eyes, sets a lot of testosterone into motion, though the interest is often deterred by the crude reality of my sister's occupation. Not many men willingly agree to their woman in uniform on a daily basis.

She admits that she had wanted to laugh at Gilbert's last name, when he introduced himself—holding Miranda's purse, to prevent theft—but she was feeling too ill to bother. I do note that while Miranda honored Gilbert by marrying him for perpetuity in the Catholic faith, my sister retained the name of *Benités* for what she claims to be "professional reasons."

Hanging over the front porch of the North Gay Street Craftsman, is a carved wooden sign Miranda bought from an artisan's booth at the Lassen County Fair. The plaque reads, *SNEAD & BENITES*, their marital logo.

* * * *

Miranda was seven when she first aspired for a career in law enforcement. The subsequent pathway to this goal carried her through the severity of our father's sarcasm.

During our formative years, we had been taught in school that *the police officer is your friend.* To reinforce this axiom, don't stare at the television set revealing a scene depicting the brutality of law-enforcement, as a man of color is being pummeled beneath the white cop's baton, or killed with bullets to the back. Rather, fixate upon the shiny free stickers that designate you as an honorary member of the local police force.

Miranda collected these stickers the way some children accumulate Major League Baseball cards or school certificates for outstanding behavior. She taped the metallic badges to her bedroom wall in an orderly pattern of compliance.

Being a rational man, my father attempted to justify his skepticism of law enforcement. Most often this practice of unequivocal trust applies if one is irrefutably Caucasian, otherwise known as "white privilege." A person of color had better be damn sure to follow the law absolutely, as ethnic scrutiny and racial profiling are unavoidable realities of law enforcement behavior.

A classic challenge from Dad is tied into the *Jobim* song title, "Watch What Happens."

Now, I'm not sure whether my father *meant* to break the law when he drove twenty miles over the posted speed limit, on a damp spring morning, while on our way to church. Maybe it was because we were going to be late for mass, if we didn't shoot up the highway in a screaming blur. This wasn't the first time, just a nasty habit my father repeated. But the California Highway Patrol officer who rode the fast lane ahead of our vintage Corolla station wagon sure didn't seem very pleased about it.

Of course, Dad decelerated, as he's no fool. The cop wasn't an idiot, either. Once Dad meandered slowly past, the CHP cruiser slid into the lane behind us.

"Watch what happens," Dad said, while we sat paralyzed like cornered mice, except for Miranda, who told our father he "deserved a ticket."

"Really?" Dad asked. That tone implied a challenge. "I'd have to get caught first, don't you think?"

"He's still behind us," said Mom, as Dad headed for the slow lane, the CHP right on our tail.

"It's the license plate," said Dad smugly. "It confuses them."

Even on surface streets, the cruiser followed, until a quarter mile from church, the cop veered left into a turn lane, presumably to head back to the freeway.

I had no idea what my father was referring to, until a few weeks later we had a flat tire. While Dad was changing out to the spare, an approaching CHP cruiser pulled up behind us on the wide highway shoulder. I watched while the white officer conversed with Dad, and then, leaving Dad to wait in the midst of the change out, headed to his cruiser, Dad's driver's license in hand.

"Hey, kids," Dad said to us, where we stood in a row alongside Mom in the ice-plant, uphill from the disabled car. "Watch what happens."

Five minutes passed, and the cop, with an odd expression on his face, returned Dad's license, and then got back into the cruiser. Without so much as a wave or nod, the cop scudded onto the highway again. We could hear the sucking whine of the cruiser's surge as it leapt ahead of oncoming traffic.

"It's the license plate." Dad blamed the metal identifier. "Cop sees a commercial plate on a car, he thinks it's stolen."

Why there was a commercial plate on an economy car was anyone's guess, though it probably had to do with the fact that Dad used the vehicle for business.

And now he let loose with the clincher: "No, wait, he sees a nigger with a commercial plate, and he thinks the car's stolen!" He laughed wickedly, and went back to finish the task.

We were stunned, as the *N* word was banned from our vocabularies, both at home and at school, guaranteed to impart in each of us a disturbing sense of agony at its pronouncement. And here our father had just blatantly used it, even if to serve a life's lesson.

I might have been ever more confused, except that, as we went off to get the flat tire fixed, Dad explained what it means to be a person of color.

"Cops will check you out, even if you're not doing anything suspicious," he said, though I doubted this. I was ten, and we lived in a diverse multi-ethnic community, where our neighbors consisted of whites, Filipinos, Vietnamese, Hispanics, Indo-Asians and a handful of African Americans. I had never seen a police officer bother anyone in real life, unless it was a situation on the television series *Cops*, and then I figured, even at my tender age, perps of any ethnicity probably asked for it, being disgustingly drunk or peddling a girlfriend's flesh for drug money.

None of Dad's prolific speeches dissuaded Miranda from entering law enforcement.

"Cops are stupid," Dad tried reasoning. His prejudice might have seemed just as vulgar as that which he attributed to law enforcement, except for the life experiences he carried.

His was a classic tale of confusion involving a misinformed cop, and a disingenuous boy, who in the story, happened to be our father at age twelve.

* * * *

Mitchell Benités was raised in the Santa Clara Valley in the era of apricot orchards, strawberry fields, and the last great Japanese-American farm in Sunnyvale. As a child, my father rode a cheap department store bicycle through the orchards, with a pack of boys close to his age, including his own brothers, leaders of this Sunnyvale troop. The group was comprised of white boys, except for the Benités brothers, from one of only two Filipino families living in that particular neighborhood.

The boys instigated minor thefts of cherries and other stone fruit, which would occasionally prompt the orchard owner to arrive wielding a shotgun loaded with rock salt. Often the slowest member of the group, a lumbering giant by the name of Wade Woolridge, couldn't pedal swiftly enough to keep up. This was the same concept as being chased by a bear, you don't have to outrun the bear, you just have to be swifter than the slowest member of your group as you beat a hasty retreat. Wade earned the nickname of "Baby Hughie". Poor Wade was shot twice in the buttocks with rock salt, before they learned to post an alert boy at sentry while on these raids.

Grandpa Feliz worked for the City of Sunnyvale's Parks & Recreation Department, tending landscaping at city parks. There was a small-town attitude about Sunnyvale, and as a consequence, the Sunnyvale cops knew Grandpa Feliz, and continued with the assumption that they were familiar with Feliz's five sons, although the only name of prominence any cop could readily recall was *Michael,* the eldest. If a Benités brother happened to be on foot, or riding a bike down the street, and a cop spotted him, they would wave and call out, *Hey, Mikey!*

Dad relates a story about a day when he was in junior high school, and decided to skip out on classes. Whiling away the hours, he walked around town, pilfered a fall orchard or two, and generally just pissed away the day. He admits that this was not his common theme, but a flagrant error in judgment.

Walking toward home, the school day technically in session, he gambled that he wouldn't be caught. Feliz was still at work with the city, and his mother, Enida, had started her shift at Teledyne. Just as my father supposed he was assured a clean getaway, standing at the base of his parents' driveway, a Sunnyvale city cop rolling down the street spied Mitchell Benités, and, cranking down the window, called out,

"Hey, Mikey!"

Dad, of course, waved. He wasn't going to correct a cop.

That evening, elder brother Michael received an ass whipping from Grandpa Feliz for cutting school.

This placed my father in an awkward position. He couldn't help his eldest brother, because that would involve telling their father that the punishment is being meted out to the wrong son. You have to understand Filipino culture in my father's era, where questions from elders were rhetorical, complicated by the rule that you didn't correct any elder, especially your father, even in the middle of disciplining your brother for your truancy. Talking back to an elder or making eye contact was considered the ultimate in disrespect. This would reveal that your father is blatantly wrong by default, and you'd be facing even harsher penalty.

My father never forgot this lesson, not so much the injustice of the punishment, but the illumination that cops are somewhat dimwitted, hasty to finger their suspect before the facts are straight and the proof aligned. Never mind Grandpa Feliz's reaction, *that* was simply good old-fashioned Filipino parenting.

Miranda was in high school, when Dad decided to reveal this secret he carried for forty years. The intractability we all inherited from our Grandpa Feliz had focused Miranda with severe tunnel vision upon her career goal, and Dad wasn't too happy about it.

He did, however, feel obligated to make a statement. At the dinner table on a Sunday, following another event just that morning of racing to make it on time to mass, Dad had yet to receive a speeding ticket for his rash practice.

"If you're going to be a police officer, Miranda, make sure you go to college," was Dad's advice. "The world doesn't need any more stupid cops."

Miranda smiled evenly. Our father didn't raise us under the restriction of the unanswerable statement. We were actively encouraged to participate in discussions, to form opinions and to voice our thoughts, within reasonable limits of respect to your elders. Therefore, Miranda, who is a calculating person, replied,

"Just don't let me catch you speeding to church, Dad."

* * * *

Although Miranda has never cited any family members, I am mindful of the lengthy speed trap between Reno and Susanville. CHP drive with dash-mounted radar, and can verify your lawless habits as they bear down on you from the opposing side of the yellow line.

I rolled into Susanville at eight-thirty that night. Dark had been the rule for a couple of hours, with the distant glow from the state prison puny against the weight of mountain sky. As I drove up Main, I called Miranda's landline on my cell. Her husband, Gilbert, answered the call.

"You're in town?" he repeated my utterance as a question.

"Yeah, to fix my folks' place."

"Oh boy, I guess this means you haven't seen it yet."

"No, I just got here."

"Let me tell you, it probably isn't as bad as it seems," he said quickly. "When Miranda comes home from her shift, I'll tell her you called."

Feeling rebuffed, and irritated because he hadn't extended hospitality, I continued up Main Street, and drove straight through to the property, ten miles of dirty, ice-crusted asphalt. Snow edged the highway, and private access roads faded into the darkness, scraped down to patches of ice and gravel by plow or Bobcat.

One of these was my parents' long driveway, marked by a reflective address placard, the surface dusted with five inches of snow on top of old tire tracks. Using care, and four-wheel-drive, I negotiated the slight grade, until I was traveling in a cushion of darkness. Between spears of trees, sky showed through, bright with stars I could never view in the Bay Area.

After a few moments, the motion detectors on the garage activated lights, and beckoned me into a yard churned by what appeared to be the tires of a fuel tanker that probably visited earlier in the day delivering red-dyed kerosene for the furnace. I parked, and used a flashlight to pick my way to the front door, floundering over an irregular berm of snow, which appeared to have been sourced from snow methodically removed from the roof. Climbing over, I slid down a skin of ice, and managed the lock in the beam of flashlight.

As soon as I entered the mobile, I knew I'd have to ask Miranda to put me up for the night. The furnace purred, set at a temperature just high enough to prevent the pipes from freezing, but also making the air sharply pungent with the smell of mold. My eyes began to burn. On the initial walk-through, turning the beam on ceilings and walls, there were no visible indicators of mold, as it probably grew in water-damaged carpeting, or inside walls. Ceiling panels bulged downward, water intrusion evident from dark stains.

The damage was bad, but salvageable. I locked the mobile, and drove back to Susanville. I didn't bother phoning my sister's house, I just showed up on the doorstep.

I'm guessing they were both in bed, because Miranda cruised out after ten minutes of my doorbell ringing, dressed in a hastily tied silk robe, her hair a mess.

"Did I interrupt something?" I asked.

"What do you think?" Miranda was openly annoyed. "Could you come back in say...fifteen minutes?"

"Is that *all* the time you two need?" I moved past her, and dropped my luggage onto the tiles of the entry. "It's cold, and I can't sleep in the mobile. It reeks."

She pulled the neck of the robe closed. "You could stay in the basement," she offered, pointing at the floor. "Gil put a bunch of firewood down there for the stove," she added, to my expression of disbelief.

"Thanks, see you in the morning." As soon as I headed for the basement door, she was running up the stairs to resume whatever I'd torn her from.

Miranda hired me to finish the basement when she bought the Craftsman. The concrete walls and open-beam ceiling were transformed into living space. Because she had intended the studio for extra income, she hired me to outfit it with a wood stove on a stone pad, a kitchenette, and a full bathroom. The basement became their *Party Room* when she met Gilbert. Soon it gained a pool table and a wet bar. To suggest I was comfortable would be too modest. I had wood heat, a flush toilet, and a decent Scotch stashed in the bar to lull me to sleep.

* * * *

In the morning, I was up early to feed wood to the embers in the stove, and to find out if my sister was awake. Their shifts are different, Gilbert's beginning sometime around the fishing hour, and Miranda working swing. During winter, she covers a lot of Interstate mileage in darkness. The misfortune for me during the repair was that I consistently crossed paths with my brother-in-law, but never spoke with my sister, who returned home when I'd already staggered down to the basement to sleep off the day's excesses.

Their basement owns three access points, a hatch to the backyard—the fire escape—a staircase that descends from the foyer, and yet another that climbs to the kitchen. When I emerged from underground that first morning, my brother-in-law was predictably seated at the kitchen table, dressed in his dark brown Lassen County Sheriff's Department uniform.

The time was five-thirty, which he verified by glancing at his watch with the most obvious turn of the wrist.

"You're the early-bird," he commented.

"Hello, Gilbert," I greeted, as I helped myself to coffee.

"I hope I didn't wake you up."

The floor is thick, and the basement well insulated. I saw to that when I put in drywall. A major explosion upstairs would be required to register even faintly in that warren.

"Don't worry, I couldn't even hear you and Miranda getting busy last night."

He laughed, as he always does when he's embarrassed. The difference between a simple joke and his shame in torment is his red face.

He flipped the newspaper in front of his eyes to block me from view.

"What do you have there, the *Sacramento Bee?*"

When he ignored me, I thumbed through the stack, which turned out to be the *Great Basin Register*, a hick-town newspaper. Not much of the world outside of Lassen County exists when it comes to the reporting in the *Register*, as it attempts to persist with the delusion that Susanville is an isolated haven. Yet it publishes a weekly police blotter filled with countless incidents of vandalism, public intoxication and petty theft.

At least all that illegal activity ensures Gilbert will remain on payroll.

"You see your folks' place?" he asked, from behind the paper.

"Duh, that's why I came here and performed *coitus interruptus*," I jabbed. "It's not safe to sleep there."

"Ahem." A readjusting of the paper. "Yeah, it's bad all right," he agreed, as though I'd said that very thing.

"I didn't say it was bad." I got up, rummaged in the fridge, and found bread where Miranda stashed it inside of a vegetable bin. I passed a couple of slices into the toaster. "It's fixable, it's just going to be a big job, that's all."

He let the paper drop onto the tabletop. "You'll need a helper," he said for direction.

"I don't know, I haven't thought about it." The bread popped up, barely toasted, and I pushed the handle down again.

"My brother Duke is living in Susanville." As though he were being sly to mention his younger brother. "And two people can hang drywall better than one."

I knew Duke. He was twenty-nine, and worked as a seasonal ranch hand, or a handy man, performing odd jobs in Reno when employment was lacking in Lassen County. He was tall, hard muscled and slim, not thick in the middle like those characters you see tilting back their chairs on porches in rural communities, a dog at their feet and a beer in hand. Duke liked his beer, but he never excluded food in favor of alcohol. He outfitted himself in faded blue jeans, a ratted denim vest over a sleeveless t-shirt, and a pinch-front hat, and wore his sideburns like muttonchops, with a soul patch under his lower lip. He drove a two-tone 1985 Ford F-250 diesel 4x4, and like all boys in the county, he tied his dog out in the bed. The dog, Rascal, a mongrel with a hint of Rottweiler, was a typical happy, slobbering canine. Besides his dog, Duke loved fishing, line dancing and the local radio station, KSUE, for its conservative drivel. He had once talked about establishing a Lassen County campaign to elevate Rush Limbaugh to the office of U.S. President. *Hannity Up!* was Duke's personal slogan, which he'd scrawled in black paint on the tailgate of the F-250.

"Who names their kid Duke?" I asked, certain what was going to come out of Gilbert's mouth.

"If you think you'll need a helper, Duke's your man."

"I mean, come on," I said, sidestepping his request. "You have a regular guy name, Gilbert, but *Duke?*"

"You know, it isn't a dog's name," he scolded, and he shook a finger at me. "I know what you're going to say, Maddie, that Duke's a dog's name, and why in the hell would someone name their kid Duke!"

Now Gilbert's face was *really* red.

"I'd be willing to hire him, just as long as I can say, *here boy,* and whistle. Do you think I'll get his attention that way, Gilbert?"

"Anything but undressed, Maddie," he advised, heaving up from his chair. "He likes women, you know? But *you* naked just might scare him off."

I knew he was irked, because he'd crossed the line with the usage of the word *naked*. He was only trying to dig at me, so I smiled.

"Don't worry, Gilbert, I don't do dogs."

"Yeah, neither does my brother."

Gilbert, hurt and edgy, made a move to clean up his mess, but I quickly removed his bowl and mug. I may at times intentionally act like a jerk, but I was raised within the parameters of Filipino social protocol, and know when a *manong* deserves respect.

"I'll call him," I promised, before Gilbert left. Duke *was* a dog in some respects, but he wasn't lazy.

Gilbert mumbled his thanks, and fled through the side porch door to his truck. I kind of felt sorry for him, because as always I did an excellent job of playing with his mind.

After I washed dishes, I fulfilled my word, and dialed up Duke's number. I had no trouble at all finding it, because it was posted next to the kitchen telephone extension, appearing suspiciously fresh, and in Gilbert's handwriting. Duke didn't answer, though I left a message on his voicemail anyway, intending to head up to the property to begin the demolition alone.

Just as I closed the front door behind me, there was Duke rolling up in that ugly-ass Ford truck. For once, Rascal wasn't tending the bed. I was relieved, because Rascal acted like a toddler-aged child, and would wander onto the highway if left on his own accord.

"What's up?" Duke asked, as he swung out of the cab.

Sporting the excessive sideburns, he had also failed to shave, so the soul patch was integrated into a bristly face warmer. I give him credit for wearing a long-sleeved t-shirt under the denim vest, but now a Confederate flag patch was stitched to the breast pocket. For his personal safety, in a region where he shared space with an Indian *Rancheria,* the members affluent enough from their casino endeavor to pour financial support into the community, you'd think Duke would be sensitive enough to forgo the redneck motif.

"Gil said you were hiring." His tone was expectant.

"Oh, I see." *Blind date*, I thought, a bit irked at Gilbert's presumption. The more I thought about it, the more practical it seemed, and by the time I got into my truck, I once again appreciated my brother-in-law's initiative.

Duke climbed in beside me.

"Aren't you hiring?"

He smelled like soap and toothpaste, and had a rucksack of gear, which he had tossed onto the rear bench.

"Yep, Duke, I believe I am."

"Maddie, if you ain't hiring, just tell me." He could wiggle around bad grammar, as easily as the worst expletives.

I started the engine. "Duke, I couldn't ask for better help," I assured, and smiled to soften my facial expression.

And it *was* true, Duke was better than most, except for my pal Kevin. Duke took instruction without holding his credentials beneath my nose. As his reward, this would mark the fourth time I'd hired him.

"That's a relief," he sighed, and we headed out.

* * * *

That first day, we worked for four hours straight on demolition, removing carpeting and pads, ceiling panels, insulation and wallboard. Hauling it piecemeal to the truck, the mobile began to lose its taint of mold, which had been trapped in floor covering. The heaviest portion was the insulation from the damaged ceilings, which was so saturated that it dripped as we carried it out, cradled in a tarp.

With nothing substantive to hold back the cold, now that the plywood under the roofing had been bared, Duke stoked up a fire in the wood stove, while I began to take measurements.

"If you're hungry, lunch is on me," he offered, as I recorded the figures in my notebook.

"Thanks." I didn't waver from my task.

"Cause *I'm* real hungry," he elaborated.

"Maybe there're potato chips in one of the cabinets." I wouldn't raise my eyes from the paper.

He muttered something under his breath that I didn't catch, and turned down the air intake on the stove, as it was roaring by now.

"I'm professionally gratified that you were available to hire, Duke," I told him sincerely. "I don't know anyone who works as effectively as you."

Of course, it was a partial lie, because Kevin is more efficient, but he charges a hell of a lot more. I just wasn't familiar with the labor force in Lassen County. My biggest concern was that I might hire some lazy fool with a work ethic bordering on incompetence.

"You sure? Cause Gil told me you might take some talking into it."

I glanced at him. He seemed worried, and his face was puckered up through his whiskers so tightly, that they all stuck out straight.

"I'm *positive*," I spoke forcefully, more inclined to believe I was persuading myself, rather than Duke.

"Gee, thanks, Maddie." He grinned in relief.

We visited the dump, before stopping for food in town. Sitting down to a couple of burgers, it seemed as though everyone in the joint knew Duke. Some elbowed him, in one of those surreptitious congratulatory motions. One burly fellow even gave Duke a bald-faced high-five.

"What's that about?" I asked, when we were driving out to Johnstonville Road to buy materials.

"What?"

"The pushing and shoving. The high-five."

"Huh?"

So clueless.

"You know, the winking, Duke." And I winked at him.

"Maddie!" and he proceeded to straighten me out. I was his boss, he was my hire, and there shouldn't be anything improper between us.

"Unless, *hah*!" He laughed, almost revealing himself unconsciously.

"Yes?" My face was, I'm sure, very hard, and Duke pressed his wiry body into the seat.

"Nothing." Sobered, he shook his head.

"Are you sure?" The same dark stare. My father is a master at this, and I would oftentimes use a mirror to perfect the expression.

"Nothing," he repeated, as assurance.

To me, that was clarity.

* * * *

We were busy for two days, replacing insulation, tacking up moisture barrier, and screwing in the fitted gypsum boards which I'd cut to measurement on the miter saw. The mud patch was the most tedious, all the texturing, but it was completed in such a way that we could let it cure before sanding and painting. In the interim, we reframed several windows, which allowed me to inspect interior walls that turned out to have been impervious to water intrusion.

During this period, it seemed that Duke was working some routine on me, though I was too diverted by the job to put my finger on it. He was absurdly courteous, and deferred completely to my instruction, unlike the very first time I'd hired him to assist me in building a deck at my sister's place. On the first hour of that job, it seemed like he questioned every cut and measurement, until I pointed out the fact of my contractor's license. Fortunately, Duke was agreeable to being told what to do, although I doubt he'd ever be the whipped type.

At the close of each workday, when I'd decided we'd done enough for ten or twelve hours, Duke and I would hustle up dinner in town— usually the standby burger—and then I would return to my sister's house, where I slept through the night. I was often too tired to harangue Gilbert, or make troublesome remarks to Miranda, had I seen her. Her CHP uniform was often compelling enough to shut me up. Mostly it was the length of the job that put my witty remarks to bed.

I also hadn't broached the subject of Mallory's iniquity of the assault upon her stalker, or the matter of Jesse Ibarra. Both of these stressful issues had faded in the tedium of the mobile home repair, temporarily reprieved by a distance of three hundred fifty miles from their scene of villainy.

* * * *

On the fourth night, following a day spent painting I dragged myself into Miranda's kitchen, and discovered Gilbert at the table, playing cards with two men. One of these, a strapping hairy guy, built like the back end of a barn, was smoking a cigar. He wore bib overalls, and a billed cap with the logo of a Monster truck trailing flames. Under the denim overalls were what appeared to be bright red, one-piece long johns, as the edge showing below his hiked-up pants cuffs matched the color of the long-sleeved shirt.

Standing at the fridge, and washing down the flavor of my most recent hamburger dinner with a cold beer, I studied the back of the cigar smoker's head, and considered my attack.

"Madeline." Gilbert was glaring directly at me. I'm sure he could read my mind.

"What?" I feigned innocence, but my brother-in-law knows me very well.

"Nothing," he said, and shook his head, but I retired to the basement, thinking how lucky we all were that I was too bushed to follow my wicked inclinations.

* * * *

Nearing the close of repairs, I was awake extra early, waiting for Duke to arrive. Seated at Miranda's kitchen table with a cup of coffee and my laptop, I was compiling receipts and Duke's labor over the last week to both pay Duke and invoice my parents. While I frowned down at the keys, in came my brother-in-law, wearing his dark brown uniform. He headed straight to the coffee maker, and then sat opposite me at the table. He sat there for so long in silence, sipping his coffee every now and then as his only motion that I finally looked up from the laptop with disgust.

"Good morning to you, too, Gilbert."

"Has Duke said anything to you?" He got right to the point.

"Nooooo...what about?" I was instantly intrigued, and too poor of an actor to hide it. "Is Miranda pregnant?" I shut down the laptop. "Are you ill?"

He smiled wanly.

"I gather Duke hasn't said anything, then."

"Jesus, Gilbert, isn't it unlawful to lead people on? Where're the cops when you need them?"

"Madeline," he said earnestly, so I figured I'd better cut the crap.

"Go on."

"I can't tell you, it's not my place."

"I'm not sleeping with your brother, if that's what you want to know."

He shrugged. "I told you, Duke, like yourself, doesn't sleep with dogs."

I laughed, though it was more for defense, because I am not what you'd call a delicate woman, as I'm lined with muscle, though I am small framed. Not that I've ever been mistaken for a man—at least, I don't recall, if I have—but I almost never trick this body out in anything aside from work clothes. Maybe it's because I'm usually working. When my mother's aunt died a few years back, I wore a black pantsuit to the funeral, because I knew a dress would contradict who I feel I am.

"Well." I cradled the laptop under one arm, and stood up to end this fruitless conversation. "If you won't tell me, and by God, Duke hasn't told me, I don't know why you bothered to say anything."

"He's likely too scared to say anything to you, Madeline."

"He says what he thinks."

"No, he *doesn't*, and you know it. You're so—", and here, he shook both hands in the air.

"Impossible?"

"That, and really, *really* confrontational." He sighed.

"It's not my intention to act like a pain in the ass one-hundred percent of the time."

"But that's the result, Madeline. Maybe you think you're funny, I don't know. I do like you, even though you seem to go out of your way to be difficult."

"Well, I apologize if I've been difficult." I tried to make it sincere, but it only came out sounding wounded.

"Madeline, don't get me wrong, you're my wife's sister. You have fine ethics, but sometimes, I think, you're too much like Mitchell."

I was shocked. "You think I'm like my father?"

"Every time he visits, it's like he goes out of his way to make fun of me. Pokes at Miranda, says off-colored things. Maybe he's trying to be funny. But you act just like him."

My eyes burned now, though I wasn't going to cry in front of my brother-in-law.

"I'm sorry, Madeline, but who else would tell you?"

"I was kind of thinking I'm more like my mother," I said in a small voice.

He laughed at me then. Oh, I know, he didn't mean to. I wasn't trying to be funny, but I'm sure he saw the irony in my statement. I am nothing like my mother. She nurtures, she's the peacemaker, and I had known all along that Mom is my father's harness. She represents a certain limit that's not exceeded just by being with Dad.

"I'm sorry," he repeated. "Look, can we get back to my brother?"

I nodded, staring down at the floor. I noticed that floor looked damned good. I'd floated the linoleum the year Madeline bought the Craftsman, and I recall being meticulous with each small job. To me, it is extremely important my professional integrity continue to remain very high.

"I'm listening."

"Duke looks up to you. But I think he's also a little intimidated by you."

"Okay."

"Can you remember that, Madeline?"

"Sure."

He patted my arm, his cue to leave for work, and after I'd stood in the kitchen like an idiot for a few minutes, I finally decided enough was enough. I put the laptop away in its case, and was cleaning up the coffee maker, when Duke pulled up in his truck. Standing in the kitchen window, I could see Gilbert and Duke were having a conversation. Gilbert kept turning toward the house, and Duke was nodding like a bobble-head on the dash of a ranch truck. The scene was so humiliating that when Duke came through the side door, I was bent over the sink, elaborately rinsing the glass carafe to avoid meeting his eyes.

"Morning, Maddie." Duke scratched the back of his head. I could hear his fingernail against the pinch-front hat.

"Hi, Duke, are you ready to go?"

"Sure, yeah."

I stashed my laptop in the basement, and when I came back up, Duke was already in my work truck waiting for me. I got in and started the engine, and we were silent, as I let the engine warm up.

As soon as I turned around in the street, he spoke.

"Before we go to the house, I have something to show you."

"Okay, then." I nodded. "Where to?"

"River Street," he said, and guided the way. Our silence was punctuated by his request for a left turn on Main, and then a right on South Osage Orange. When we came to River Street, I paused.

"That way." He stabbed left with one finger.

"Park over there," he instructed, so I pulled to the curb, beside a weather-beaten house from the era of the 1890s, with an odd, double-keyhole chimney keeping watch above an ancient, corrugated metal roof. Formidable rust stains ran from roofline to eaves, formed after decades of snow and rain.

"What do you think?" he asked, though I hadn't the faintest idea what he was referring to.

"About which?"

"That." He pointed his chin toward the beat-up house.

"*That?*" I shook my head. "I apologize in advance for being blunt, Duke, but that house looks like a piece of shit."

He grinned. "Come on, let me show you."

We got out, and I followed him with concealed irritation, itching to finish my parents' mobile home, so I could get out of Susanville. I was merely humoring Duke at this point, keeping Gilbert's advice in mind.

We passed through a gate, and into the backyard of the faded house, which owned a scabby lawn patched with snow, and assorted heaps of demolition. I could identify asbestos ceiling tiles wrapped in plastic, wallboard and coils of electrical cable, as well as miscellaneous cabinetry and molding. Among these mounds, Duke's dog, Rascal, apparently left to guard the refuse, leapt about in exuberant play. I had to shove him off with one foot to keep him from jumping on me with those big muddy paws, while dodging colossal dog turds.

The trash explained what came next, since it was apparent that the garbage had come out of that banged-up house. The inside looked so drastically different from its exterior, it almost felt like a farce.

"See, I've been fixing it a little here, a little there," Duke said, as he marched me through the rooms. They were clean and bright, with new beadboard and crown molding, and refinished fir floors. On the main level were two beautifully refurbished fireplace mantels strategic to separate rooms, which explained the fantastic double chimney.

"What do you think?" he asked.

I *was* thinking about Duke's behavior on the day Miranda married Gilbert. Duke had been quite drunk, and I suppose for some people, that would translate into magnified anger or hostility. Not Duke. His misplaced angst, if it ever surfaced, bubbled out as exaggerated affection.

"Pull my finger, Maddie," he'd instructed, one hand wrapped around a Bacardi and cola.

Of course, I pulled his finger. I'm not too stuffy to accommodate another person's attempt at fun.

He farted audibly, and laughed with glee.

"What the hell was *that*?" I asked, a huge mistake.

He winked coyly, and smiled.

"That's what's known as pre-copulation arousal."

Now, in Duke's habitat, I left that bizarre memory behind. "Am I supposed to have an opinion?" As soon as I spoke, I knew I'd said the wrong thing.

"I figured you would have an opinion." He was clearly frustrated.

"Well." I touched the sitting room mantel carefully. "It's...nice. From a woman's point of view, I'd say it's all happening."

"Nice. All happening." He hung his head, shaking it as he looked down at his feet. "C'mon, girl, what'll it take? What does your contractor-sense say?"

"All right," I relented. "It looks like a hell-hole, Duke, on the outside, a piece of crap, if you ask me. But inside, it's beautiful. You performed a lot of the restoration without losing a feel for the period."

He grinned, slowly. A light seemed to switch on in his eyes.

"Madeline," he started in. I figured I was in for something serious, because Duke rarely uses my full name. To deflect the moment, I stuck out my index finger.

"Pull my finger," I dared.

He stared dumbly at it for a moment, and then purposefully tugged.

I made an awful face, but not a sound.

"Nope, still cooking," I announced. "Sorry."

* * * *

The last chore at my parent's mobile was installing carpeting, now that painting was completed. The coach had been manufactured in 1975, with sickly flowered kitchen wallpaper and marbleized yellow countertops, though the kitchen linoleum had been replaced five years ago. Our painting project had covered the wallpaper, and the cheap wood paneling, hiding some of the tackiness.

"Wow. It looks like a Goddamn coffee shop!" That was Duke's opinion, roaming around the salvaged pressboard subfloors on kneepads, as we stapled down carpet pad.

"That's a positive," I told him. "It's better than *Brady Bunch*."

"Dude. Maddie. *Brady Bunch* had avocado and red-orange." He laughed. "And one hot mama."

If he'd had his way, there'd be murals patterned after those in the Black Bear Diner in Susanville, the silhouettes of paw prints and pine trees, and obese bears with huge, bulbous asses strolling across the walls.

We walked around inside the finished renovation, and inspected everything, walls and ceilings, fresh paint, and new carpeting. A summer of opened windows would be necessary to rid the mobile of the stench of fire retardant and assorted chemicals. We completed the small touches of rehanging curtains and blinds, and putting the furniture back into place, restocking the wood-rack next to the roaring-hot wood stove, and eating three rib steaks from my parents' freezer. There was a case of cold beer in the fridge, and we drank some of that too, to celebrate. On the icy front porch, we barbecued steaks on my father's gas grill, and tipped back Coronas, complimenting each other on our efficiency.

"You are a special kinda girl," Duke claimed. "None of this nail-polish bullshit."

"That would be my sister, Margot."

"Yeah, what a waste." He adjusted, at my hostile glare, "Well, for a man." He nodded his whiskered chin at me. "You're not a shop-a-holic, are ya?"

"Only when it comes to power tools," I assured.

"Ooh, my kinda gal." He rocked on his feet. "Unless you already have a boyfriend."

"I don't have the time."

"You must get lonely, Maddie."

"Never. I *like* being alone."

"It gets old, Maddie." He fiddled with his whiskers. "I mean, ya gotta settle down sometime."

"Not in the cards." I continued to resist the direction of the conversation.

"You and me'd be perfect together, Madeline," he persisted. "I think we should get married," he stated out of the blue.

He didn't declare it in his bumbling, skinny white-dude manner. This emerged from the mouth of a man who had discovered an ease and sincerity in my company.

"Ex*cuse* me?" I was appalled, and didn't bother hiding it.

This last day, he brought Rascal, traveling as a passenger in the cab instead of a dog in the bed. I had restricted the dog to the back, on the floor, beside the bench seat, because he smelled like shit, what with running around in River Street backyard. While we were laying carpet, Duke tied Rascal in the garage for safekeeping, as I wouldn't dream of letting the dog loose to wander off.

Watching Rascal busy on my parents' lot, made me realize that the dog's Rottweiler blood hadn't spoiled him for honest play. All the mixed-breed dogs in Susanville seemed afflicted with Rott in their lineage. You'd see them in the *Register*, photographed as vicious sheep killers, or on the Shelter ad available for adoption. The genetic revealers were eyebrow marks and beefy muzzles.

This dog was as happy-go-lucky as its master regarding the simple aspects of life. A beer for Duke, and a smelly mound of shit left behind on the property by a mystery canine for Rascal. Rascal ran around in the brash of the yard, chasing Steller's jays. Next to the garage, the hulk of my father's old offshore fishing boat sat, huddled under a layer of snow and a roped-down blue plastic tarp, in permanent storage. Being as the boat would probably never see the open ocean again, it wasn't a problem for me when the dog urinated a couple of times on one of the galvanized trailer fenders. I suppose it was only fair to assume that other dogs had been here, walked by neighbors who violated fenced property lines, accompanied by their canine guards, which explained the lone stool, kept fresh by low temperatures. Only natural these dogs peed their markers in the same places as a kind of signpost for their kind.

I recalled Duke's proclivity to peeing in the snow behind the mobile, once we'd shut off the water, emptied the on-demand water heater, and then flushed the system with an air compressor. He said he had tried to pee his name in cursive, but ran out of urine before he was finished. You'd think that four simple letters wouldn't be such an unattainable goal, until I noted, with some disgust, that he'd written *D-U-k* with a six-foot reach.

"Well." Duke removed his pinch-front, and scratched his head. "I think we work good together. Marriage don't seem that far off."

"No, it's very, *very* far off," I corrected. "And anyway, I hired you for work, not for...for...*that*!"

"Right." He displayed no ego issues, and laughed loudly at mine.

"I don't think it would work out, Duke." I tried to soften my distaste in his suggestion, all the while brainstorming on a way to extricate myself from *The Question*.

"You ain't even slept with me yet, how do you know how it'd be?"

The very thought of having sex with Duke was preposterous. I was reminded of that finger-pulling incident.

"I couldn't even begin to address that." I tipped back some more beer, although I had begun to suspect that the alcohol was the culprit in this screwed-up marriage proposal.

"There ain't any decent women here," he confessed. "They're all...I dunno, trying to get out of Susanville, so they can go shopping. You're different, Madeline, you do things that men do. It'd be like marrying my best friend, only with benefits."

"I don't live in Susanville, Duke," I reminded, trying to ignore that last suggestion, repulsed. The steak I'd consumed was beginning to make me gag, in conjunction with Duke's lame wooing. "I have a house and a business in the Bay Area."

"Yeah, I know." He rubbed his whiskers. "I figured you'd like the

River Street place, anyway."

"It seems real nice." In my own ears, I sounded like an idiot.

There was a long period of silence, and then I cleared my throat.

"Actually, it's a beautiful house. What are your plans for it? Are you going to flip it?"

"I ain't sellin' it, I'm livin' in it, Maddie."

"Oh."

"I'm gonna stay in Susanville. There's enough work to get by."

"That's great. Duke. Don't get me wrong. It's just that I have a lot on my plate right now."

"I know. Miranda told me about Mallory's problem."

"What?" I wasn't sure I'd heard correctly.

"C'mon, Maddie, I figured you knew, or else maybe you didn't want to talk about it, so I never mentioned anything."

"What did Miranda tell you?" I was starting to wonder if my sister also knew about Jesse Ibarra.

"That Mallory beat the crap outa some dude. Y'know, hey, if I ever do get married, I hope she's tough like your sister."

Take the real thing; Mallory is single, I wanted to point out.

I was fighting to digest the fact that Miranda knew all about the assault, but hadn't said a damned thing to me when I unexpectedly arrived the first night. I blamed it on Miranda's sexual needs of the moment, because what *else* had been on her mind when I hauled my gear into the house? Our constant separation due to her work schedule hadn't helped matters, either.

"What else did Miranda tell you?"

"Cops aren't charging your sister. Must be nice."

I didn't ask any more questions, just started to silently close up the mobile. When I was finished, I herded Rascal back into the cab, admonishing him in low tones to keep to the floor. Rascal, clearly distressed at being scolded as though he were a bad dog, whined softly, and dropped his face to his folded paws. I scratched his ears for a moment, and Rascal forgave my human rudeness, whacking the floor with his broad tail.

"Rascal likes you," Duke approved, when we left the mobile behind, driving through the messy snow to the main road.

That's it! I thought, knowing how much Duke loved Rascal. Easy enough to open my mouth and insert a heavy, thoughtless foot.

"Rascal likes everybody," I disputed. "He'll even like the shelter worker with the euthanasia syringe."

"Wow, Maddie, that's fuckin' harsh! I mean, what's Rascal ever done to you?"

We arrived at the River Street house in record time, and Duke departed without a word to me, just a kind of infantile babbling to Rascal, to shield the poor dog from my evil aura. Duke slammed the truck door too. I watched him negotiate the trash-dotted yard, dancing once or twice when he encountered a phenomenal shit pile, and then he disappeared around the back of the house.

I drove away, feeling like a jerk. All the way to the Craftsman, I kept stealing glances at myself in the rear-view mirror, thinking I might sprout horns at any moment. When I pulled up, I noted Miranda's Jeep in the driveway. I thought it was odd, until I realized that it was two o'clock, and my sister hadn't yet departed for her shift.

She was in the living room when I entered the house, or as Miranda liked to call it, the *Parlor*. Dressed in her uniform, she was sifting through a pile of mail. To one side was a stack of garbage, with neatly incised envelopes and junk mail inserts, and to the other, a couple of unopened bills.

"Madeline." She shot to her feet, with the letter opener, which was fashioned after a Samurai sword, held in one hand like a stabbing tool.

"Miranda." I cautiously leaned in to hug her.

She held the blade of the letter opener sheathed in her hand, while she patted my back with the other.

"This is the first time I've seen you since you came up here," she accused, as we took our seats.

"No, I saw you the first night. Remember? I barged in on something."

Miranda recalled my intrusion, and her face changed.

"Anyhow," I hurried past that awkward moment; "we have to talk."

"Oh, yeah?" She swept the paper garbage into a small wastebasket, which was already mostly full of the same. "I gather there's nothing new you should tell me, right?"

I leaned forward. "You *know* there is." I could feel my irritation begin to rise.

Miranda regarded me casually. "It's a good thing I don't get easily annoyed, Maddie. Unlike you, a person in my position could find herself in the middle of a civil rights lawsuit."

"Miranda, you know all about Mallory's little problem, what else do you want from me?"

"I'm just confused as to why you'd stay in Susanville for an entire week, and not say anything to me." Now her glare proved she was capable of an equal level of anger.

"Out of all due respect, I haven't seen much of you," I said for my defense. "Just like your husband, you and I have different shifts, so to speak. I know what a grouch you are when someone wakes you up before you're ready and willing. When I actually *did* see you, you were in a hurry to get off. So, if you just cool it, I'll tell you more."

I could see she was fighting it, but eventually she sat back in the chair. I wasn't convinced until she allowed the letter opener to slide onto the carpet beside her.

I described it all from the beginning, from my association with Jesse Ibarra, Mallory's emergency telephone call, and up to the moment I'd stolen cells from Ibarra's cheek to ship away in the DNA test kit. I included the part about stealing our father's blood sample from their house garbage can.

"You really have some nerve!" Miranda fumed, but now I could see she was impressed, not annoyed. "Do you realize it won't stand up in court?"

"Who gives a damn? All I want are facts, and since this so-called brother of ours isn't being forthcoming, I just took matters into my own hands."

"That's just like how cops act," said Miranda simply, "like they're above the law. How ironic."

I motioned to the uniform she was wearing, and she waved me off.

"I live for the day when Dad is speeding on 395, and I'm aiming that radar gun right at him." She inhaled sharply. "Wouldn't that be something?" She pantomimed writing a citation. "Here's your fucking ticket, Dad. Have a nice fucking day." Her brazen use of the *F* word might have surprised me, had I not sensed the depths of an obsession.

"Miranda, listen to yourself, get a life. Anyway, Dad uses cruise control."

"Then I'll get him in a construction zone," she expounded. "You know how incompetent Cal Trans contractors are in Lassen County, they *never* post the 55 zone correctly."

"Miranda." And here I buried my face in my hands.

My sister began to laugh. She laughed until tears poured down her face, and she had to hold her sides, to avoid peeing her pants.

"Oh, look at *you!*" She pointed in triumph, bobbing one finger up and down. "Look! At! You!" She clapped her hands. "I sure got you, didn't I?"

I suppose I must have appeared grave, as I rose out of my seat.

"I'm gonna get you back someday," I promised. "Wait and see, I will."

Of course, revenge isn't my strong suit, as it leaves a rather nasty flavor in my mouth. But Miranda didn't have to know that. Pathetic enough that I believed, even for a moment, that my sister was preoccupied with retribution against our father, and that she would ride her entire law enforcement career on the prospect of one citation.

"You should've taken up acting," I commended, hugging her stiffly, and then descended to the *Party Room* to claim my luggage.

While I threw my clothes into the bag, I saw, through one of the ground-level windows, my sister back the Jeep into the street as she left for her shift. For a moment, I could view the profile of her upper body in entirety seated behind the wheel, her crisp uniform, her dark hair pinned up in a bun, and her full lips pulled into a line of irritation. I didn't want to part this way, but Miranda often dug her demon's pitchfork deeply beneath a person's skin.

Which left me wondering just who is more like our father, Miranda or me? Gilbert's accusations about my shortcomings seemed feeble in the aftermath of my epiphany, and I realized their marriage had been temporarily preserved by their disparate work shifts. The moment they are stuck in the same God-awful room for retirement, they'll reconsider matrimony.

You'll see.

7. Beach Queen

During a period of three days following my return to the South Bay, the weather turned unusually cold. An arctic air mass settled across the northwest, rather than the humid breath that usually springs from the Pacific Ocean. The temperature plummeted, and my *Green* neighbors, who usually take me to task for burning wood, now eyed my purring stovepipe with what I can only describe as wood-fuel envy, a feral emotional condition caused by living in suburban California. While they paid their steep bills for natural gas, I was using my ten dollars a cord stash I'd cut up in Lassen County last spring. Split by hand with a maul, and dried in the backyard of my Basset Street property, even including the fuel cost to haul it nearly four-hundred miles, I still came out ahead.

Three weather fronts worked their way through, bringing rain to the Valley, and dusting the heights of the Mount Hamilton range with snow. Whenever the clouds cleared off the summit, there sat the domes of Lick Observatory, color-matched to the snowcap.

I thanked the weather, because my next job was a kitchen renovation in a Palo Alto home, a referral from my normally grudging Grandmother Beth McKracken. Not that I dreaded the job, which meant building from a prefabricated kit, and fitting custom-cut countertops, probably the easiest ten-grand of my career. Since my return from Susanville, I was experiencing a lapse in physical energy, as though my body were recuperating from jetlag.

I could have spent seventy-two hours confronting my issues with Miranda, Gilbert and Duke, with Jesse Ibarra and even with my father, the Crown Jewel of why a person ends up on a psychiatrist's couch late into their adult life. Instead, and except for one brief telephone conversation with the client to delay the project until the weather cleared, I curled up next to the wood stove. I faked a secret illness, doing nothing to expose myself to the cold, short of retrieving the daily newspaper. The mail slot had been strategically built into my garage door, and therefore I never really had to leave the house to claim the mail. The post was dropped daily into a monster bucket that could be categorized as a child's toy-box, or often used to ice beer at parties. This was where I'd legitimately swiped the great blue bucket with its frayed rope handles, from a party at my grandparents' house.

"Nakong, you take all the drinks,*"* my Grandma Enida had commanded. While I began to empty the great cache of sodas and beer into the limited space of my arms, Grandma solved this nonsense by yanking the bucket toward the front door, which moved a few inches, but I got her point.

Jammed beneath the mail slot, it became a collection receptacle. I could leave town for a month, and that reliable old bucket would have mail reaching barely halfway to the rim.

On the first day of my return, I e-mailed the completed invoice to my mother. Her electronic reply voiced great joy in the repair, and her suggestion that when she and my father returned to Susanville, it would "feel like Christmas." I had attached a couple of photos of the repair to the email, so as not to involve my parents in unacceptable surprise.

I saw my mother arrive in her car to handle the deed. On the second day, she parked in front of the driveway (which made me think about Miranda, and would she be willing to give our mother a ticket for blocking my driveway?) and ran up to the slot to push through the envelope, dodging raindrops, her breath a long stream of white in the frigid air. For a moment, I figured she knew I was watching, but my truck with road dirt was hidden inside the garage. Unless I moved the blinds, no one would be the wiser.

I completely forgot about the smoking stovepipe.

On the third day, when the storm clouds were breaking up, and I lodged expectations the illogical fatigue would vanish, Mallory telephoned me.

I knew it was my eldest sister ringing me up, and this is why I enjoy caller ID, which allows a person to use their best judgment about whether to accept a call. Some calls might lead to conversation that, depending on the parties' temperament, could deteriorate into a shouting match. I tend to speak aggressively to telemarketers, hoping for a blacklisting. Family is a separate matter altogether.

At the last moment, I picked up the call.

"Mom says you've been at home," Mallory claimed.

"How would she know?"

"Mom's clairvoyant, you know that."

"I've been sick." But my voice didn't reflect illness. I coughed a few times for effect.

"I'm coming over. I won't take *no* for an answer."

"I'm taking a shower," I said, and roused from my sofa perch, on my way to the bathroom.

"Funny, I don't hear water running."

I turned both shower knobs on full blast.

"*Fine*, I hear water."

"I just started." I tried to sound inconvenienced.

"Take your time. I'll just wait in your driveway."

Now that I was irrevocably committed, I stripped off my clothes and took my second shower of the day. I was hurried, because I don't enjoy keeping uninvited company waiting, even somebody I'm not too keen to visit with. While I dressed, I tried to put my thumb on my misgiving, but the only thing that came to mind was an image of my sister Miranda, and her obnoxious laughter.

Look! At! You!

I have never experienced ridicule thrown like bricks from a sibling. Heading for the front door, I was feeling downright put out.

Mallory was standing on the porch, tapping one foot. The rain was gone, but three days of intense cold had killed the *vinca* in their redwood planters. They drooped, frost-burned and pitiful, scattering bright flower petals on the porch boards in drops of blood.

"About time." Mallory was already promoting sarcasm as she entered the house. Knowing her way around, she found the bar, and poured herself a Scotch.

"Kinda early, don't you think?"

"It's four-thirty, Madeline." She thrust her wrist toward me, flashing her watch. "Must be nice."

"What?"

"Sitting on your ass." She downed some of the Scotch.

"I work hard to sit on my ass," I defended.

"We all work hard, Madeline."

I pressed my hands to my temples.

"What *is* your problem?" I imagined I heard capillaries sizzle in my ears, as they burst from my swiftly elevated blood pressure.

"Relax, I'm just joking." She set down the tumbler, and although she hadn't finished her drink, I possessively removed the glass to the kitchen sink.

"You and Miranda should've been roomies," I said when I returned. "You're so much alike."

I was referencing our childhood in a four-bedroom house. We sisters were placed in pairs as our father utilized the largest non-master bedroom as his teaching studio. The argument had been it was the only room, aside from the living room, where the upright grand piano had sufficient space to occupy without shoving students out the door. Since Mom refused to concede communal living room space, Dad simply used the self-adhering law of *Parental Domain* to acquire the bedroom we all coveted. In the end, when the last of us had flown, Dad knocked down a wall, and expanded his turf. I know. I was the contractor he hired for the evil deed.

Mallory, the eldest, had been my roommate until she graduated from San José State. I was seventeen when I finally owned my own space, and in that brief period, I realized that I was probably better off in the long run if I lived alone.

"Speaking of Miranda, she told me about your job."

I sat on the sofa, with one leg hooked over the armrest, and twirled a finger in the air.

"Mom and Dad's property," I confirmed. "I fixed their mobile home."

"Yeah, I saw the pictures. Very impressive."

I eyed her closely. She seemed as unruffled and cool as ever.

"What about you? How's everything?"

"I can't complain."

"Have you—" and I paused, considering my approach. "What about counseling?"

She laughed. "For whom, Madeline? For *me*?"

"Why not? I'd be haunted if I assaulted someone, even if it was a matter of life or death."

"Well, then that's the difference between you and me," she said dismissively. "I don't dwell on it."

"Did you tell me why you came by?" The tired feeling still permeated to my bones, and I hadn't even had a drink since the beer with Duke Snead.

"I came to ask if you got the test back."

"What test?"

"Miranda told me you'd sent off some genetic material?" she cued.

"Ah! *That* test!" I shook my head. "I don't know, haven't checked."

Mallory, who knew my habits well, frowned.

"Haven't checked *today*?"

"Not since before I left for Susanville."

"You lazy bum, Maddie."

She tossed a throw pillow at me, but I caught it handily, bouncing it off her head, reminiscent of the napkin fight at Margot's house, which seemed so long ago, but in fact, was less than two weeks past.

"How long does one of those take to get test results?"

I walked over to my desk, and found the instructions. *"Three to five days from receipt by the lab,"* I read the documentation aloud.

"And when did you mail it?"

I stood, calculating. I had dropped the package the night I left for Susanville, ten days prior. That sudden revelation, and I was off like a shot, heading for the garage, Mallory on my heels. We clattered down the wooden steps, pushed past my truck (shining off its road-dirt with our backsides), and concluded on either side of the mega-bucket, crouched above the pile of mail tangled in the bottom. Sticking out was Mom's envelope containing her payment, and that's when I remembered the smoking stovepipe.

Leaning down, I scooped the entire mass into my arms. Held tightly against my chest, I ferried the mail into the house, and dumped it onto the kitchen table.

Mallory immediately located the manila envelope from the testing company. She found herself a steak knife, and slit the top of the envelope.

"That *is*, uh, addressed to me," I reminded.

"*You* read it, then." She passed the envelope with its potentially damaging contents into my hands.

"All right."

Removing the paperwork, I read it slowly. I had asked for verification of paternity between the two samples, which I'd designated as *paternal* and *offspring* with the accompanying test kit stickers.

Mallory read over my shoulder.

"Wait," she said, and pointed to the paper, "why do the results refer to *maternal sample*?"

"Huh?"

"Look, Maddie." And there it was, the sample which I'd assumed was our father's, clearly revealed it had sprung from a *female, blood type A pos*. The results concluded that the two samples in question were from completely unrelated people.

"Maybe...they got the gender wrong," I said doubtfully.

"*Maddie!*"

Mallory was starting in on me, with that reverberation to her voice. I recalled it from our days as roommates.

Maddie, clean up your part of the damn room!

And then you would hear her thunder roll into the distance.

"What did you do, Maddie?"

"I sent two samples," I reasoned.

"And one was from a woman?"

I pressed my palm to my head, which was getting to be a common gesture, as though keeping my brains from leaking out.

"I...it *couldn't* be." I was adamant.

"Maddie, did you draw Dad's blood or Mom's blood?"

I didn't draw anyone's blood, I thought. *I stole it.*

"Wait, what was that?" I perked up.

"The sample, Maddie, was it from Dad's blood sugar test or from Mom's?"

"Mom tests her blood sugar?"

"Geez, Madeline!" She threw herself violently into a chair, and the legs creaked upon impact, threatening to snap from the force.

"Mom's not diabetic," I reasoned, as though it would instantly change the results.

"She's obsessive-compulsive, Maddie, she checks her blood sugar more often than the real diabetic in the household does."

"I had to be underhanded, Mallory," I explained. "I hijacked the sample from the kitchen garbage."

"So, how did you conclude it was Dad's, did she *say* it was Dad's?"

"Not exactly. I just assumed, you know, because Dad's the diabetic."

She exhaled sharply.

"Not Mom, she's not diabetic," I repeated, which did nothing to relieve her ill humor.

She began to curse, but then I put my foot down.

"*You* go ask Dad for his blood, then," I dared. "I paid my dues on this one already."

I left her there, because she was too immobilized by the physical expression of her rage to speak, and I wanted to get away from my sister. I puttered around the house, in any room, except the kitchen, where she sat like a steaming lump in the chair, staring down at the results.

Finally, hauling to her feet, she tucked the stressed chair in, and wandered out to locate me in the bedroom, where I was building a fire in the hearth, after yanking open the chimney damper. I guess I figured if Mallory was pissed at me, a few disgruntled neighbors observing two sources of airborne particulates spewing from my house couldn't hurt my status.

"Use that fireplace very much?" she asked, contrition in her voice.

"Not much. All the heat just goes up the chimney. But it's very cozy-looking."

She cleared her throat. "Listen, Maddie, I'm sorry for getting so pissed off."

"It's all right, like you, I don't give a damn anyway."

I stood, and looked for the butane lighter on the mantel, finding it tucked behind the open wooden box of obsidian stones I'd gathered many years ago near Alturas, on one of our Susanville jaunts. I remember *that* marathon, climbing around the rubble of Little Glass Mountain with the wasteland of the lava beds spread out below like remnants of a bombing range.

The rough facets glittered their tiny eyes. Something was amiss, and I stared back at the stones, distracted.

"I've been getting telephone messages from Jesse Ibarra, that's all." Mallory's words should have raised a red flag.

"Well." I turned away from the stones with their sinister gleam. "He's *all* yours."

Crouching, I set fire to the starter block. The flame licked up slowly, found a foothold, and rounded thin pieces of kindling. Satisfied, I replaced the fire screen, as the flames backlit the soot-worn bricks of the fire box. I remained in my stance, staring at the fire slowly burn into the fuel.

"What is it about you and fire?" Mallory asked, searching for something, anything, beyond the huge block of Jesse Ibarra that had suddenly choked our conversation. She stood behind me, and I imagined that she glared down at my shoulders as I hunched before the fire in pyromaniacal savagery.

"I like fire. It's cheap heat, and a cheap thrill."

She squatted down beside me. I suppose she'd figured out I was just down there in the hopes she'd get fed up with me, and leave.

"What do I do, Madeline?"

When I finally looked at my sister, I softened immediately. Mallory is no pussy, she's a hard sell, and her fame to barbarism she'd stretched out half-dead beneath her own hand. I'd had it by then, with Jesse Ibarra, with my father, maybe even with Duke Snead, because despite his weird marriage proposal and my deliberate undermining, I hadn't heard a peep from his direction since we'd parted. That spelled the answer as to why I don't trust a man until I know him well, and why I despise when a man assumes he can dictate to me what I can or cannot do.

I blinked to clear my vision of the odd shadows cast by the glowing fire.

"Screw them all. They can all go to hell."

Mallory, as though the intent were dawning in ratio to my spoken aggravation, smiled slowly, until she grinned, her lips stretched wide, the fire reflecting off her strong, white teeth. Above us, on the wall, the framed text of one of my favored poets, Hasty McNair, was symbolic of the frieze of our lives:

> *Inspire me so that I may grow the strength to move mountains;*
> *Humiliate me so I may be worthy of the inheritance of the meek;*
> *Indulge me, for my heart to remember the ease of childhood.*

Maybe my ill-considered words gave her strength, or fresh ideas for her usual tricks, that taunt of men. When she departed, I walked her to her car, a sleek gray Infiniti coupe, which is the manifestation of a modern muscle car in heels and eyeliner, and wielding a .45. She drove away, the tires shredding the shabby leaves of the pear trees into tatters against the roadway.

* * * *

The weather was predicted to clear, so I contacted the client again, and made arrangements for access to the rear of the property. I rented a rubbish bin, and a portable toilet, one of those sickly green bunkers, and then stopped at the closest home supply outlet to hire a couple of day-laborers.

I know enough contractors Spanish to get by, but I'm exempt from understanding more complex conversational language. It's a blessing, because I often imagine my hires talking me down in front of my face, nodding and smiling all the while:

Miguel, the woman who hired us owns the face of a horse.

Yes, José, but she has a rear end that cancels out any unpleasantness demonstrated by her features.

I have never hired a man who proved directly insolent. Respect seems easily earned by the almighty U.S. dollar, and as many of these men are my elders, I give them deference dictated by culture.

On this day, I find Juan Jiminéz, a trusted repeat contractee, and his cousin, Humberto.

"*Buenos dias, Señora Benités,*" Juan salutes me, as I roll into the parking lot.

I advised Juan during one of the earliest jobs, when I'd busted him sizing up my womanhood, that I was *Señora,* not *Señorita*, to keep him from pursuing any closeted ideas. I advised that my husband, Vito, was *muchos grandé.* Later, Miranda, who speaks Spanish fluently, told me my rudimentary attempt at the language had been incorrectly structured, that I'd referred to my poor fictional Vito as *many large,* but I know Juan at least received the gist of my message.

And besides, very few men desire a woman with *la cara de un caballo.*

"I have a kitchen remodel," I announced, not simply to Juan, but to all the men lined up in their groups like meat at the market. In a moment of weakness, I imagined Mallory walking amongst them like a snake, sinuously rubbing against their bodies, wrapping them in a stranglehold of erotic cynicism, and then striking out with poisoned fangs at the first hint of an erection.

Juan took hold of the man to his right. His cousin, Humberto, Juan explained. Though I'd never hired Humberto, Juan had gained personal integrity through his own attitude and workmanship, so I always trusted his referrals were reliable.

I squinted. "What happened to Alejandro?" I inquired about the man who'd worked three prior jobs due to Juan's recommendation.

"He go back to Guadalajara," Juan said.

Which meant, in all probability, that Immigration & Customs Enforcement had ejected poor Alejandro from the States.

"On his own?"

"*Si,* by his self."

"Was he taken by ICE?" I asked, and Juan looked puzzled.

"No, Señora, *en un autobus.*"

On a bus. I sighed.

"Come on up, Juan," I invited, waving one hand. "*Por favor traiga Humberto.*"

I could hear them talking softly in Spanish as they sequestered themselves on the truck's passenger bench seat.

La mujer que contrato a nosotros es el propietario de la cara de un caballo.

Oh, yeah, I was waiting for it, but it sounded more like they were discussing *un juego de béisbol.* There was a mention of "Barry Bonds." Humberto made a fierce expression, and Juan laughed.

"You like *béisbol, Señora Benités*?" Juan addressed me through my rear-view mirror. In the loaded truck, that particular mirror was good for nothing except for making eye contact with a back-seat passenger.

"Unless it shoots nails or saws a two-by-four, I have no interest, Juan," I assured.

Juan clucked his tongue, and the two fell back to their private conversation.

* * * *

In Palo Alto, we were finished with the kitchen demolition in half a day. Situated at the top of a very long driveway was the dumpster, which we filled with kitchen cabinets from the 1950s, and Formica countertops. Curled sections of linoleum entertained slabs of underlayment.

I'd asked the homeowner, who happened to know my Grandmother Beth McKracken, if she wanted to give away any of the cabinets. The renovation ordinance is strangely convoluted in Palo Alto. Had there been a taker for the cabinets, the homeowner would have received a *Green* exemption to the permit.

"Goodness, *no*, dear," she said very firmly. "I don't want a bunch of strangers tromping around my property."

I'm guessing she wasn't counting Juan or Humberto in that equation. The two men worked amicably and efficiently, removing flooring, and taking measurements to cut and place the concrete backboard used as underlayment.

The woman's name was Linda Bell, and she had known my grandmother from long ago, when they raised their children simultaneously on a cul-de-sac in the high-snob community of Burlingame Hills, adjacent to the border of neighboring Hillsborough. Who knew that those mammoth homes built in the 1950s would be worth over a million dollars fifty years down the line? Pricey, even with backs chilled by the fog and wind coming straight over the tops of the hills from the sea.

Linda was smart. She sold her house in 1980, and moved to the pleasant warmth of Palo Alto, before land values shot up during the era of Hewlett & Packard. The modest *Eichler* home along Embarcadero was buttressed from the street by ivy covered stone-faced wall, and great sheltering oaks. No matter the lush nature of its surroundings, the house gasped through the antiquated boxy styling of post-World War II *Americana Suburbia* design.

Within two days, the men and I had transformed that cold, drab kitchen into a work of art, a place where even boiling a pot of water is a delight. The earth-toned walls breathed with light, while the granite countertops and their hint of green complimented birch cabinetry, and pale tile floors.

At the close, when all that was left undone was to test the new gas range, Linda Bell approached me with a smile and an envelope.

"Here you are," she said, seemingly anxious to pay me before I'd even finished the job.

"I can't take that from you," I balked, but she pushed it on me anyway.

"It's not the total fee, it's a tip," she explained. "Take it now, because in twenty minutes, my daughter will come back from work, and she'd kill me if I expressed any sort of appreciation in a monetary sense."

"Thank you," I said, nodding gratefully. "That's extremely generous of you."

When she was gone, I opened the flap of the envelope, and stared down at a thousand dollars in cash. I tucked it into my back pocket, stunned, because I was thinking about the magnanimity of this woman who'd trusted me enough by word of mouth to hire me for such a personal job. After all, a kitchen is often a place of sanctuary, and for some, a base for their culinary art. If they are anything like my mother, the kitchen represents a certain nurturing that can't be produced in any other room in a home.

"It beats me why you like tools, Madeline," Grandmother Beth McKracken had said to me, when I was fourteen.

Normally such a comment proffered during the era of my father's childhood would rank as rhetorical, as it was cultural violation for a child to speak back to an adult, even if the rhetoric contained the upward lilt of query. You didn't even look a grownup in the eye, because your own were cast downward at the ground.

But our parents encouraged us to become outspoken if we utilized tact and respect with every statement. In these contemporary times, even Grandmother Beth, who is Mom's adoptive mother, was not exempt by virtue of race from the subtleties of Filipino culture.

"I'm an artist, Grandmother," I told her. "Tools are the same as paintbrushes."

This kitchen joined that definition.

On the third day, just as at the end of every workday we cleaned up the premises. This time, it included the removal of the dumpster by the trash contractor, which I'd built into the fee. Linda joined us on the driveway to watch the process, and waved happily at the retreating contents of her former kitchen.

I walked Linda through the renovation, and she delighted in every touch, the hanging café lamps, the subway tile backsplash behind the sink and stove, and the fact that every cabinet had been installed flush to the low, eight-foot ceiling.

Eichler homes are traditionally open-beamed, but sometime in the last twenty years a previous contractor had framed an attic space to accommodate a forced-air furnace to avoid mounting it ponderously upon the roof. As a result, the kitchen was transformed into the only room that seemed finite by comparison to the rest of the house.

For a moment, I vacillated on how to address the cabinets, which had meant to be mounted with a gap of about a foot between the tops and the ceiling. These were right up to the ceiling, the crown molding an airtight connection. Juan, in his wisdom, had listened closely to my instructions, and then quietly disagreed, suggesting the alternative, and therefore I'd given him leeway to install the cabinets as he saw fit.

"Just perfect," Linda marveled. "I hate the thought of dusting up there, and who ever stores anything in such a place? It would've been a dark space for spiders, *I* say."

I nodded, and in the patio, where the men were wrapping electrical cords and laying my power tools in their cases, Juan sent me a knowing glance.

Later, on the drive home, I eyed Juan in the mirror.

"*¿Cómo lo supiste?*" I asked him. How did you know?

He laughed and nodded sagely.

"*Sé lo que las mujeres quieren, Señora.*"

I know what women want.

That, and their work ethic, earned each of these men a two hundred fifty-dollar cash bonus, straight from Linda Bell's golden envelope.

Humberto savored what he presumed to be a wisecrack, but it seemed to me Juan was speaking with sincerity. He really *did* know what women wanted, and if it meant as little as installing an entire kitchen cabinet system with connectivity to the ceiling, then bless Juan Jiminéz. Somewhere in the world there is one hell of a lucky woman.

* * * *

I remember when Juan was unwittingly exposed to my Grandmother Beth McKracken, and the consequences of that painful encounter.

I was finishing a double-paned window installation at my parents' house in Santa Clara, and had hired Juan as my helper. While I was in the backyard out of earshot, Grandmother appeared in her Buick to partake of lunch with my mother, as a way of continuing their flimsy truce. Inside the room my father had converted to his original teaching studio, Juan had been jimmying out the aluminum window frame, when Grandmother clicked up the driveway in a fancy dress, low-heeled pumps, and glittering heirloom jewelry, announcing herself to the Mexican with the pry-bar.

"Do get Moira for me, good man, and hurry, will you?"

Juan blinked at her, and then smiled, his two front teeth, which are gold-capped, really digging into my Grandmother Beth's sense of propriety. Her own father had been an oral surgeon, and gold teeth that could actually be seen when one smiled she considered a serious social *faux pas*.

"I am here for Moira, you must announce me at once!"

Juan set down the pry-bar upon the windowsill, tipped his sweat-stained cap, and went off to track down my mother, leaving Grandmother Beth alone and locked out on the doorstep.

Later that afternoon, Juan kept referring to Grandmother Beth as *Puta Reina*.

"Her name is Beth McKracken." I tapped my chin thoughtfully. "Though she still likes her mail addressed to 'Mrs. William McKracken'." I smiled professionally. "How about *Señora* McKracken?"

But he kept insisting that he would refer to her from that moment on as *Puta Reina*. Somewhere in the depths of my sparse internal Spanish language dictionary, I figured that I *must* know this phrase. Not until I returned Juan to The Home Depot parking lot in the evening that he translated it to me in heavily accented English.

"Beach Queen," he said cryptically. I was six miles away and fifteen minutes gone, when I'd realized he'd christened my Grandmother Beth as the *Bitch Queen.*

* * * *

I can list the ethnicities of my mother's people with the same level of interest that beguiled me at age eight. *English, Irish, Norwegian, Portuguese, Scotch and Sioux Indian.* This was a neat trick at such a tender age to be able to quote the ponderous liability of my heritage, then adding in my father's *Filipino*, for a dash of exotic flavoring.

There's no riddle, that my mother, adopted by a middle-class, homogeneous Caucasian family at the close of the Baby Boom era, would wish to completely cast off the shackles of her adoptive family's schema. There was an adoptive grandfather who referred to nonwhite people as *coloreds* or *negroes*, and the adoptive mother, who, upon being informed that Mom was actually part Native American, declared in indignant resonance when faced with a supposed deception, "Oh, no you're *not!*"

For my adoptive maternal Grandmother Beth McKracken, denial is the technique to keep your gene pool unsullied, even to those adopted into the circle with its darkest secrets.

But you must understand the engine driving Grandmother's racism to read between the lines. A life of black and white, of categorized humanity, a sense of caste and orderly documentation, they kindle a seemly preoccupation that does not weather as rough as that *run-for-your-life* through a moonlit jungle with death on your heels while your feet are bleeding.

I was thirteen, when I spent a week with Grandmother Beth at Yosemite, just the two of us, a 'girl's week out', as Grandmother claimed. We played nine-hole golf at the prestigious Ahwahnee Hotel, eating in the luxurious restaurant, and hiking trails to Vernal Falls, and upward to Nevada Falls, then back down, no feat for me, as I was conditioned to the outdoors, while Grandmother complained of sore feet and achy bones.

Still, our mutually shared experience had been better than tolerable. Grandmother silently acknowledged my athleticism, and I conceded to her generosity in gifting me such a week, when I was not her only grandchild, and certainly far from her favorite.

At the Visitors' Center, a woman, who was a member of the Miwok tribe, gave a demonstration on how to make ground acorn flour palatable, by washing out the tannic acid with cold water. This absorbed me, because I am connected to cultures I am completely ignorant of. I could have sworn that Grandmother muttered under her breath, "a heathen occupation," but I was in the bliss of the moment, and refused to let what I perhaps imagined hearing ruin our stay.

But it was during our lunch at the Yosemite Lodge's cafeteria, that the force of Grandmother Beth's racism floored me. While we were in line, a woman in front of us struck up a conversation with Grandmother. The woman was obviously intelligent and well educated. She claimed to be a pediatrician from San Francisco.

"Such a small world," Grandmother said pretentiously, for she had been raised in that vertical enclave, though all the while of bombastic politeness, she was working up for an outburst.

We made it to our table, and then Grandmother dropped both shoes.

"That woman, thinking she can be just like us!" she hissed.

I gawked at my grandmother for a moment, as the fluff cleared from my mind.

"Why?" A rise of an epiphany, yet I wanted so badly for her to explain.

"Those people, they try, but they'll never be like us."

I swallowed, sick to my stomach. The doctor, with her brilliant quips and charismatic manner, was African-American.

"I think what matters is what's in a person's heart, not the color of their skin," I said, in my precise diction.

Grandmother stared at me, with what I later realized was loathing. For the moment it appeared she had forgotten—or, possibly, remembered—who I truly was.

"You talk too much, Madeline," she said acidly. "We're going home tomorrow," a pledge to cut short the vacation one day early.

And that was our final close of frank personal dialogue, the release of my childhood fantasies about being loved by Grandmother Beth. I recognized buried warnings in the conversation between my parents, before departing for Yosemite with Grandmother:

"If you think she should go," my mother, reticent of the idea of the trip, which would interrupt a week of school.

"Yes," my father, in strength of certainty which is his trademark. "It's imperative, Moira, imperative!"

Now I understood *imperative*. I understood that my Grandmother Beth had been coerced by her late husband into adopting a female infant she had wanted nothing to do with, a child from a failed woman's uterus; a *colored* child, who she had been duped into believing was indisputably Caucasian. Grandmother embraced her twisted racist philosophy keenly, while any semblance of compassion withered from neglect.

That final night in the Ahwahnee Hotel, my Grandmother Beth slept like blank stone. The woman didn't snore, nor did her dreams bring her subconscious to life beyond the reach of her command. I shared a double bed with a stranger who despised what I represented, and therefore, had elected to underwrite my transformation, rather than accepting me. I might have wept for the death of potential, had she not been who she was.

I remember leaning forward, and parting the curtains. The moon wasn't full, yet bright enough to define every detail of the grounds outside of the window, the shape of trees, the granite profile of the valley rim, and the sheen of autumn frost on the little nine-hole golf course, where Grandmother Beth had delighted in my antics. I thought about Grandpa Feliz, and the Philippine jungle. I brought to mind those retreats up in the hills at Tres Piños. For a moment, I became the elder to my grandmother's pitiful, self-limited world. Rather than embracing my frustration, I forgave her ignorance. This was instantly healing, and endowed in me a strength and independence from negative opinion I have carried into my adult life.

* * * *

Because I had reconciled to Grandmother McKracken's bizarre notions on humanity, it was an easy task to swing past her house in Burlingame to thank her for the job referral.

I apparently caught Grandmother in a tricky situation, for she was dressed in old clothes, a bandana and dust mask, and explained that she had been cleaning out her narrow climb in attic with a gargantuan vacuum hose. She was in no mood or shape to welcome visitors. Finding me standing on her front porch with a childlike expression, she couldn't exactly turn me out. But I read her discomfort, and for me, it hinted of payback for all the nasty phrases she'd invoked in regard to my parents, and my Filipino relatives.

"Madeline," she said uncertainly, the dust-mask hanging around her neck. "Why are you here? You should have called."

I didn't require verification of my grandmother's narrow requisite of *Distant Early Warning*. Knowing I could always bank on that personality deficit of hers, I could drive her nuts and still remain innocent of scheming.

"Hello Grandmother," I replied formally, leaning in to kiss her wrinkled cheek. "I apologize, but I was in the area, and wanted to extend my appreciation for the renovation referral. Your friend, Linda Bell?"

"Oh." She blinked, blindsided by my polite tone. Sighing gustily to reflect how put out she felt, she nevertheless stepped aside to allow me to enter. "Come in, I guess."

She made no effort to hide her disgust in being inconvenienced, which only added to my feeling of power. That's a flaw I have, the need to discriminatingly grate the raw nerves of a person's vulnerabilities. With Grandmother McKracken, I could disguise my attacks with civility, as respect toward an elder is so inherent to our family culture that open contempt is unthinkable.

"Hurry up," she grumbled, leading me to her kitchen, a holdover from the resplendent 1950s. Grandmother's electric range, a Frigidaire Flair, installed in 1961 (which was the last time her kitchen experienced an upgrade), had survived the modernization of succeeding decades. I had always admired the pullout drawer that hid the cooktop, and the beautifully crafted visual imbalance of the double ovens with their thick, heat-resistant glass.

Grandmother, who is always the perennially grudging hostess, pulled out the cooktop, and set to boiling a kettle of water.

"May I help you, Grandmother?" I stood on her immaculate linoleum floor in my clunky, scarred work boots.

"No, you may not, Madeline," she said crossly, even a mite bitchy, but still resigned to entertaining me.

She puttered with a dish of applesauce from the refrigerator, set it out with cottage cheese, two bowls and four spoons, and then left the room briefly to divest herself of the dust mask. I could hear her in the garage, climbing the wooden stairs to the attic hatch, and slamming the door closed with the force of her annoyance, which only served to make me smile in self-satisfaction.

But the fun wasn't over yet.

The kettle was starting its wail, and Grandmother, dust mask put aside temporarily, hauled it off the cooktop, and proceeded to pour hot water over two mugs of instant coffee. Muttering something about the inconvenience in having to let the cooktop cool, she carried the steaming mugs to the table in the breakfast nook, and set them down with enough force to get her message across, yet without sloshing a drop.

"You are the perfect hostess, Grandmother," I complimented. "You always remember how much I love cottage cheese and applesauce."

Grandmother grunted, but smiled a bit at the corners of her downturned mouth.

Oftentimes Grandmother's poor attitude, bordering on rudeness—and occasionally just blatantly uncivil—was ignored in my parents' household. During my childhood, her behavior had been the subject of how *not* to deport oneself. In the later years of their marriage, post-childbearing, my parents managed to laugh at Grandmother surreptitiously without taking her conduct personally.

"You are a polite young woman," Grandmother allowed. "Tell me, how did Linda Bell like your work?"

"She professed to loving it very much, Grandmother," I told her honestly, even with the tinge of well-concealed sarcasm. My words and demeanor were unimpeachable, as I retained a facade of esteem toward my grandmother.

The old gray mare, she ain't what she used to be, went the story, about how Grandmother Beth, when she was twelve years of age, known then as Elizabeth Curry, had taunted her spinster classroom teacher with the song, in the suggestion that Miss Brody was too old and dry to marry, and would consequently pass into death unloved, her proverbial cherry intact, which would shrivel up from disuse.

As my mother, Moira, related from the archives of her teenaged era, Grandmother Beth had required three years of regular psychotherapy to either accept what a jerk she had been as a preteen, or permission to strike the event entirely from the annals of her personal history. This served as hallmark to Grandmother Beth's habit of the passive/aggressive, lashing out viciously, and then retreating with a callous *I don't want to talk about it* shoved down the victim's throat, turning the tables to redefine Grandmother as the injured party.

"Linda Bell, I could tell you a thing or two about that woman, whoo-hoo!"

She sipped the caustic brew from her mug. She eyed me as I used my best table manners to partake of the cottage cheese-applesauce mixture, one hand in my lap, napkin across my thighs, and spoon carefully balanced. Unable to determine any fault in me, she proceeded to malign Linda Bell with twisted vignettes of the woman's shortcomings, when they were raising children in proximity of one another on this selfsame cul-de-sac.

I smiled, thinking how pitifully shallow my grandmother was, and that once she died, her life would be rendered meaningless by the acid spilled from her bitter words. I imagined, right then and there, leaning over Grandmother Beth's casket and whispering in her waxy, embalmed ear, "Who's shriveled now?"

Before I left, I asked permission to use her front bathroom, coffee being the ultimate diuretic. As I passed through the hallway, I happened to glance at an old black-and-white photograph of Grandmother Beth and her deceased husband, a man I never knew, the late William McKracken. For as long as I could remember, the photo had hung upon this wall, a reminder to all who passed, including my grandmother, I'm sure, that she had once been young and vibrant and beautiful.

Pondering my adoptive maternal grandparents' dynamic kept me awake on my drive down to Santa Clara. Their story was alternately tragic and hilarious, though I'll bet Grandmother Beth would find no humor in any of my thoughts.

Grandfather William McKracken died from a massive heart attack when my mother, Moira, was only eighteen. Due to her unexpected single status, and the marital "friends" who flew the coop when Grandmother Beth was optioned to widowhood, she has always tried to encourage my mother into obtaining friends outside of her marriage to my father.

"You know, Moira, you should join a women's support group," Grandmother Beth liked to nag. "Your husband is going to die before you, and you'll need something to fall back on."

My mother would only smile. She'd been bombarded with this concept for years; an idea Grandmother Beth had latched onto after her own husband *kicked the bucket* many years before any of Moira's children were born.

When I first heard the abstraction, I was seven, and I wasn't certain what *kicked the bucket* meant. Mom seemed to enjoy the terminology, and since it made her mouth twitch in dread of laughter, I decided that I liked the phrase as well.

I imagined some old, wrinkled white man, a mirror image of Grandmother Beth, kicking over a white five-gallon plastic pail (which is what we kept at home, and used for multi-purpose functions such as carrying fish bait to a pier, mixing wash water for the kitchen floor, and hauling weeds to the recycling bin). Once this wizened man thrust out his foot and knocked the bucket down, rolling it wildly, he stomped away, never to see Grandmother Beth again.

Not that I didn't blame Mom's father for having *kicked the bucket.*

What man in his right mind would be married to a pesky woman such as Grandmother, anyway? If he were crazy enough to marry her, he was likely sorry enough to have *kicked the bucket*, too.

Mom's reply to Grandmother Beth in relation to women's support groups was, "If my husband is going to die before me, I'm thrilled to spend all the time I can with him while he's alive."

This kind of mindset was really irksome to Grandmother Beth, and my mother knew it.

Grandmother Beth even tried to cajole Dad into persuading Mom into joining one of those groups.

We had taken Grandmother out to dinner for Mallory's fifteenth birthday. Mom left the table to accompany my sister, Margot, to the restroom, which Grandmother advantaged as a leveraging moment to buzz into Dad's ear.

"Mitchell, you really need to tell Moira that she must attach herself to a women's support group."

My Dad may not have appeared amused, because his face was straight, but there it was at the edges. He has this mannerism of keeping an evenly keeled expression, though there's something about his eyes that indicates just what he's up to. You have to know him, or at least feel that you're in his good graces, to avoid the burn of his serious guise.

"Why?" Dad seemed baffled. "So she can sit around with a bunch of Betties who have nothing better to do than complain about their dysfunctional husbands, and their dysfunctional marriages?"

As a silent witness to that theme, I came to realize many years down the line, that my Grandmother Beth wanted to prevent my parents from enjoying each other. Grandmother had been an unhappy wife in a miserable marriage; not because my late grandfather was an unforgivable bastard, but because he was spontaneous and apparently sexual, and liked to eat dessert after dinner each night. Grandmother Beth was desperate to do all she could to retreat from those elements in her marriage, unplanned activities, emotional and sexual bonding, and the daily grind of baking.

"I don't want to talk about it." Grandmother subsided into her standard statement, which often shut the door to intriguing conversation, and sadly, to reconciliation.

8. A Family That Preys Together

If my Grandmother Beth McKracken unintentionally portrays herself as a heartless Harpy who enjoys playing cat-and-mouse with the emotions of everyone in her life, then my Grandma Enida Benités is as generous and forgiving in equal measure.

Let's add to the mix Agapito Cassin's third, handily made and extremely portable axiom, which holds true to any generation.

No money, no honey.

The words describe how a lack of income eventually becomes the dearth of romantic fever, and falls somewhere between those *three things of grave importance* and *collect and select*. Without money, it's a given that for a man, a woman will leave his sorry ass behind.

This tenet readily explains why the Benités family holds such long sustain of endurance for my Uncle Miles's weird behaviors. There's plenty of familial compassion for this man, who by no fault of his own, scrutinizes life from a skewed vantage. Without money, Uncle Miles has been reduced to hooking up with partners who have been similarly diagnosed. Nobody wishes loneliness upon another person, even Uncle Miles, who has been so harshly dealt a hand in life that he looks out consistently for number one.

* * * *

Miles Benités, four years older than my father, was twenty-two when his mental illness began to manifest. Fresh out of Cal Poly from which he'd graduated with a degree in engineering, Uncle Miles proceeded to exhibit the tattered edges of paranoid-schizophrenia.

At first, it was the straightforward nature of five locks installed on the front door of the Milpitas house he shared with his wife, my Aunt Sherrie, and their infant daughter, Millicent, my cousin. With Uncle Miles's security clearance gained by his employment at Westinghouse in Sunnyvale, the paranoia and underlying auditory hallucinations bloomed in superabundance.

Eventually Miles's affliction became so grave, Aunt Sherrie was forced to throw a chair through a picture window to escape the house, since Miles decided one night to seal all window frames and doors with wood screws to prevent access by some entity known only within the crannies of his seething mind.

Uncle Miles spent the next thirty years roaming, both physically and psychologically. Sometimes he existed within The System, as it's referred, his finances and daily needs managed by a court-appointed conservator. Deemed mentally incompetent, he has been forced into the group-home setting with others afflicted in like manner. He has survived as a bona fide homeless man, the type that uses a shopping cart for a carryall, and spends the day ranting to inner voices along the Guadalupé River Trail. There, the mentally ill homeless congregate in their informal society on the tranquil parkland near San José's downtown, bumming cigarettes and money from pedestrians and cyclists, holding court with an invisible entourage, and overlapping uncertain lives to perform sex acts or other types of barter for food or drugs.

Strangely, Uncle Miles has preferred the self-administered freedom of the homeless life, rather than to being pinned beneath the control of The System. Even when his shoes were literally stolen off of his feet in the middle of a brutally cold winter, Miles would not denounce his hobo inclinations.

But more often, Uncle Miles has lived in the home of my Grandma and Grandpa Benités, the same house where my father and his siblings were raised from preadolescence to adulthood.

This living situation has been difficult for my grandparents. Their experiences during the War equipped them to survive within the parameters of challenging circumstances, even parallel to a state of madness, though stress-related, and not of the sort afflicting Uncle Miles. You can reason with violence and genocide, and enemy-measures placing transitory duress upon the will to survive, induced by warfare. Miles's malady, once released in a gesture not unlike Pandora's box of human ills, is open-ended, without cure. The selfish grasping of his auditory hallucinations precludes mediation. War owns eventual closure, but Uncle Miles's state of affairs enlists a flicker of Hell, as its contents leak from the infirmity of his troubled brain.

Miles lives through a steady cycle of institutionalization and release. His shaky periods of freedom guide him back to the locked mental wards, stuffed with meds that alienate him from the familiarity of the voices. He has learned to do what the doctors in hospitals direct, until he is released, and then he immediately halts drug therapy. Surrendering to the comfort of voices has become Miles's fulfillment. The silent patches in between bode an intolerable absence of normality.

The blessing is my grandparents seem to have a reason for living, a meaning in life. If nothing else, besides their function as matriarch and patriarch at the top of the ladder of honor by family, they are at least oddly benefitting psycho-socially from Miles's insanity. In no way can they give themselves permission to pass from this life, if Miles is constantly in need.

* * * *

I know we hesitate to admit it, but there is a sense of both drama and intrigue that drive our family. We talk about one another, not with disdain, or hyped-up with overt pride, but more of a rambling interchange not unlike a backwoods newspaper. Grandma Enida refers to the habit as *salawasaw,* being gossipy, a tactless loudmouth.

Fortunately, the Benités family members are prone to generosity, and unselfish assistance, instead of bashing one another. We may talk, but we're always searching for the positive, the means to uplift. If someone stumbles and falls, then we're offering a hundred pairs of hands as an alternative to disaster.

Our familial tapestry was tested when Uncle Miles was living with his parents, and decided to steal their car, an impetus to create an uproar.

I was working on a construction quote at a client's site, when Grandma Enida's birthday snuck up. Despite my schedule, I made it to Sunnyvale on that Sunday in March to celebrate Grandma Enida's seventy-ninth birthday with immediate and extended family.

What omen foreshadowed the day? Was it when I stopped for mass, arriving during the second reading, but at least before the homily, securely entrenched in Filipino Time? Was it the moment the priest, placing the Eucharist upon the altar, and bowing deeply in reverence, that a faceless cell phone burst into life somewhere in the sea of the assembly, playing the first four bars of a tune sounding suspiciously like the score to a soft-core porn movie?

I fumbled reflexively at my back pocket, but the cell tone wasn't mine.

In my car, a tray of deep-fried eggrolls, *lumpia*, now cooled by my pause at church. A birthday card with its corresponding poem dedicated to love and appreciation for one's elder, and a dozen nursery-cut purple iris, matching Grandma's favorite color. Pulling up the street, I noted the clutter of vehicles belonging to family members, the indication a party was afoot.

106

But the abnormal were four Sunnyvale Public Safety Department's black-and-white cruisers, double-parked or shoved amongst the *Benités-mobiles*. On the bottom of Grandma's driveway, six uniformed officers were hunched over her diminutive height, while members of the family hovered on the outskirts. I could easily read the reticence in family members' body language, an understated mistrust of law enforcement.

I parked my work truck down the street, and trudged to the scene, food and gifts balanced in my arms.

Margot, huddled with our mother and several cousins, gestured to me with her hand.

"Hi Margot, hi Julie." I hugged my sister, Julie, and then Mom, despite the bunch of flowers I gripped in crinkly cellophane, and the foil-wrapped tray of *lumpia*. "What's going on?"

Margot pointed with her chin, lips pursed with the motion. "The cops are talking to Grandma."

"Why?"

"Uncle Miles took off with Grandma's Mercedes," Mom simplified.

"But Uncle Miles doesn't drive," I reasoned, as though thickheaded. "Did they say he could?"

"Duh, of *course* not!" said my cousin, Jianna, Uncle Michael's youngest child. Her daughters, Liana and Laura, ages three and five, leaned close to Jianna, shocks of dark corn. "But you know Uncle Miles." She shook her head.

"So...Uncle Miles *stole* the car?" I truly needed clarification.

"Maddie, just why *do* you think the cops are here? Hmm?" Margot slapped me gently on the back of the head.

I observed the police officers as they took the report from Grandma Enida. My grandmother is tiny, and her many years spent in the garden are evident, but so is her university education from the Philippines, though even after nearly fifty years in the U.S., she retains a strong Ilocano accent. Often, I have noted that people immediately shut down their ability to receive information when confronted with any accent, more of a habit of laziness than actual miscommunication.

In Grandma's case, because she tends to sail off on a tangent when she speaks, a family member is occasionally enlisted to supervise the conversation, much in the way a determined Border collie muscles a flock of skittish sheep.

This time was no different, as my father listened closely to

Grandma's flow of words. His deadpan expression concealed any emotion relating to the cops' presence.

"I know Miles, he says she wants to drive, but he's got no license to drive, so I ask her, does he take the bus all of the time? But she says she gets tired of the bus, and that your Daddy, she's not giving the car, because Miles has got no license! And then he buys a bike, and she puts the bike on the bus, and forgets to take it when she leaves the bus!"

The Ilocano language owns no derivative for *he* and *she*, and therefore these pronouns can become interchangeable and highly fluid in English by an Ilocano speaker. Grandma Enida waters her pronouns down with a generous dose of detachment to the subject's gender.

My nearly deaf Grandpa Feliz is standing at the top of the driveway, allowing Grandma to handle in words what he cannot readily comprehend, though his eyes hold fast to the view of Grandma's gesticulating hands.

"And then," Grandma resumes, "she says he was supposed to get his license, but that the doctor would not give the permission to her!"

"Ma'am," one officer frowns, face contorted in the sheer effort to keep the threads of Grandma's story in an order that made sense; "are you talking about your son, or your daughter?"

My father's lips twitch. I'm guessing he's trying *not* to laugh.

"Huh?" Grandma asks reflexively.

"The perp, is it a man or a woman?"

"Shee!" Grandma throws her hands up in frustration, the closest she comes to profanity. "Miles, his name is Miles, she's my son!"

Grandma's hands are quieted as she holds her arms around herself, due to the cold. Beneath her hat, Grandma is fighting with the habit of protecting her mentally ill son, and the necessity to lodge the complaint.

"Mommy," my father is saying. Even as a man over age fifty, Dad still calls his parents *Mommy* and *Daddy*. "Mommy, the insurance company won't pay you for your loss of the car, unless you tell the police it was stolen," he explains.

"Shee, I know!" Grandma Enida curses once more. "Where do I sign?"

With trembling hands, she carefully places her signature upon the complaint of auto theft against her adult son, and the police begin to wrap it up. Already two of the cruisers have been mounted, and are rolling away.

The only cop remaining is talking to Grandma in a kind voice, a woman, *Sgt. J. Jones,* by the glinting nametag. She is relating to my grandmother how wonderful it was to visit the Philippines last year with a friend.

"We stayed in Baguio City," the officer was saying. "I just loved the countryside, and the hospitality."

"You want to come inside and eat?" Grandma invites the cop. "It's my birthday, you could come celebrate with us," she adds with an expectant smile. Despite the sorrow of being ripped-off by her own son, Grandma is true to form in legendary Benités geniality.

"Thank you, I'd really love to, but I'm on duty." *Sgt. J. Jones* says gratefully. After a handshake and another joke, she departs, the family milling upon my grandparents' driveway.

Grandma and Grandpa don't lose a moment. They go into the house and complete their cooking. While they warm up *dinaguan* and *cincochar*, pure meat dishes to the accompaniment of rice, which hisses away in the steamer, Dad tells the story of how Uncle Miles took off with the car.

"Maybe someone else stole it," Margot suggested, despite the earlier conversation, perhaps to negate the uneasy *Karma*. Though it was more plausible to believe Uncle Miles was the culprit, it was almost too painful to empathize with the self-torture our grandparents must be experiencing.

"No sign of forced entry," Dad shook his head. "And besides that, Grandpa's keys were gone from the hook inside of the foyer coat closet."

"Come and eat," Grandma says, as she sticks her head around the corner of the wall. "Come and eat," she reiterates, as though by compulsion.

As in many situations, we expect to repeat ourselves. There's the shaved-ice dessert, *halo-halo,* which means, "mix-mix," and the phrase in English my father uses, "Good Time-Good Time," when we were children, and he set us loose in the arcades of Reno's Circus-Circus (perhaps a name concocted by Filipinos?) a pack of excited children armed with rolls of quarters. There's even a family joke, on how to keep warm on cold nights, you lay *bukut-bukut,* which is 'back-to-back', and tuck your cold feet behind your partner's knees, eliciting mutual pain and shared comfort.

My all-time favorite is *labos-labos* (naked-naked), which oddly brings to my mind the sound that bare flesh creates in motion.

As we sit around the table or in the family room, eating hot food from plates endowed with curling steam, we converse. In our exchange, we tend to use terminologies that defy white American logic. In the middle of the banter, it suddenly occurred to my father that my cousin, Lorilei, who lives with Grandma and Grandpa in an upstairs bedroom, might have been aware of what transpired the previous night.

"Hey, Lorilei," Dad opened. "What happened last night?"

"I don't know, Uncle." Lorilei shifted uncomfortably in her chair.

My cousin Lorilei is the daughter of Dad's eldest sibling and only sister, Marianne. Lorilei evidently felt pressured by my father's unwavering tone, but was reluctant to argue, due to family culture.

"Well, what *did* you hear?" Dad persisted.

"Just Uncle Miles talking."

"*To* someone?" Dad's voice was hard and direct.

"It sounded like he was talking to lots of people, Uncle. He kept saying that he had to stop his family from being killed."

"Why didn't you call the police?"

Lorilei shrugged. "He's my elder, Uncle. It's difficult to call the cops on my own uncle."

The telephone rang, preserving Lorilei from further grilling.

Dad lurched to his feet to answer the telephone, since Grandpa can't hear well enough to conduct a conversation, and Grandma is still standing at the kitchen stove.

"It's Auntie Jacinta, Mommy," and Dad handed the receiver to Grandma, so that she can converse with her cousin. "She says she's taking you to the casino for your birthday."

His face was straight, as was his tone, and there was no humor in his eyes, because we all knew what sort of birthday this was for Grandma Enida.

The house very soon filled with many members of our extended family. Grandma Enida concluded her telephone conversation with Jacinta, and announced that they were going to take a trip to an Indian Casino. With her offspring and grandchildren filling the house, Grandma puts together a light suitcase for a lengthy bout of sleep deprivation, one hand attached to a slot machine button, which would hopefully ease troubled thoughts preoccupied with the traitorous car theft of her second eldest son.

Grandma Jacinta and Grandpa Emilio arrived to spirit Grandma and Grandpa away to the Indian casino. Their black Mercedes is a perfect twin to the vehicle snatched by Uncle Miles.

Just before Grandma crossed the threshold, Uncle Mark arrived, carrying a deep cooking pot of *kalding*. Goat meat smells of singed hair and scorched flesh, flavored with red onions, vinegar, black pepper and fresh ginger root. Between the teeth, *kalding* pops pleasantly as the mouthful of finely chopped ingredients assuage the tongue.

Grandma returned briefly, and scooped a Tupperware container full of jasmine rice and *kalding*, to be consumed on the way to the casino. Uncle Mark, the man who butchered the goat the previous day, kissed her on the cheek, and sent her off, his fingernails still evenly stained with goat's blood.

Uncle Mark got a kiss on the cheek from me, too.

"How's the bathroom?" I inquired, as though in a coded language, and he winked.

"Still looks brand new. You know, I was gettin' tired of staring down at the basement." Looking around, he was making a mental headcount. "I see Margot. And Julie. Where's Mallory?" he asked. "She *never* misses a party."

"I don't know, Uncle." I was as puzzled as anyone else as to the status of my eldest sister.

* * * *

After my grandparents' departure, the family gathering flows and ebbs. The feast spread out upon the table is visited in succession, until most of the food is seriously diminished. In the habit of our family culture, we heap Styrofoam plates with extras, topped with a sheath of foil wrap to hold the hefty chunk in place while on the road. By late afternoon we say our farewells to one another, and the ranks of vehicles curbside and on the driveway thin.

I drove away with thoughts of my Uncle Miles swirling in my head, and a plate of jasmine rice, *kalding* and pork *adobo* on the floor of the front passenger section of my work truck. A Styrofoam bowl of *dinaguan* flanked the bulging, wrapped plate.

When I reached my house, I was subdued. I carried in my portions balanced on one forearm, while I negotiated the door lock. Once inside, the plate and bowl found sanctuary inside of the refrigerator, and in the manner of our Filipino buffet, I will visit the mini repast several times before it's entirely depleted.

Still pondering Uncle Miles and his eccentric crime spree, I pulled in a stool to the breakfast bar, and let my mind wander. My introspective silence allowed me to hear the squealing chains of the porch chair swing on the brick terrace at the rear of the bungalow. Without giving it much thought, I automatically picked up the fireplace poker, and peered through

111

the laundry room window.

I could see my Uncle Bill McKracken seated on the swing with as much ease as though my house were *his* property,

I recall a conversation between my parents, and Dad, expressing about his elder brother Miles, that there's "one in every family." To which Mom replied, "That's nothing. There are three in mine," in reference to her adoptive brothers.

"Uncle Bill!" I opened the door, and shouted to him, making no effort at all to hide my irritation. "What are you doing here?"

He laughed, as though he's a charmer, but since I've experienced a lifetime of observing my mother's suspicion of this youngest of her elder adoptive brothers, I am not inclined to let him into my house.

Instead, knowing I can get back inside with a hidden key, I turned the lock, and shut the door behind me.

"Please, don't get up," I advised, pulling up one of the retro metal lawn chairs, with its slick turquoise paint.

"Aren't you gonna hug your Uncle Bill?" His appearance was scraggly, with an overgrown shock of strange blonde hair, and lines etched deeply into his sunburned face. His entire guise screamed of a hard-luck existence, earned through meticulous indignation, and mind-numbing unconventionality.

I twirled the poker. "No thank you," I declined politely. "So, why did you break into my backyard?"

"I came to visit my favorite niece," he lied. We both knew he was a quiet sneak, but that's another habit of the McKracken clan, you desperately ignore the thirty-ton monster, even as it's drooling corrosive digestive fluid down your neck.

"There *is* such a thing as a front door," I reminded him.

"I came a couple of hours ago. No one was here, so I figured I'd just wait."

"Funny, I didn't see your car outside."

Uncle Bill's rendition of *car* was a rusty green Ford Fiesta straining to retain its structural integrity as it rattled down the road sounding like a bucket of loose bolts.

"That's because I rode my bicycle." He pointed to an ancient ten-speed leaning against my sun-faded fence.

I was sure my uncle was probably going to ask next if he could throw his bike in the back of my work truck so I could drive him home, though in the diminishing afternoon light, I couldn't uncover any defect that might prevent him from rolling northbound on two wheels.

"Uncle Bill, you live in San Mateo. That's a long way to come."

"So what? I can ride my bike anywhere."

This was true, as Bill had become famous in a minor fashion for having ridden his ancient bicycle more than a dozen times between San Mateo, and his former haven of college fudging, UC Davis. He was still a member of the *Delta Omega* fraternity, and would bully a stopover in the frat house in Davis, so he could reignite his addiction to young women and free-flowing beer. Maybe he wanted to revive his youth. I presumed he was handled like an innocuous has been, excused by his cycling caprice to lie about for twenty-four hours and experience brief elder adulation. The noun proscribed to Uncle Bill by his much-younger frat brothers was *eccentric*, which is the expletive undiagnosed mentally ill white people are often assigned.

"Your grandmother was asking about you," he said, referring to his mother, my Grandmother Beth McKracken.

"I saw my grandmother today." I spoke of Grandma Enida, as the poker lay meaningfully against my leg.

"Your *real* grandmother, Madeline."

"I saw her today," speaking to him as though he were an idiot.

"The one who raised Moira." As though I just didn't get it.

"I understood you right away. And I corrected your faulty information." I shrugged. "Anyhow, I saw Grandmother Beth recently."

"Your *real* grandmother is on her way out," he claimed, in his usual pigheaded manner. "She has heart problems."

A lifelong illness, I thought. How could anyone have "heart problems" if they didn't possess a heart?

"She's dying, Madeline."

That'll be a relief to somebody, I wanted to say, but hesitated to tempt *Karma,* as the powers-that-be were already doing an excellent job at producing mayhem.

"We're all dying, Uncle Bill."

His face changed. Normally, my Uncle Bill carried a whimsical expression, as though he trained his features to assume childlike forbearance. But beneath that farce, lies the truth in Bill, a savage anger that's easily aroused. My mother was well versed in Bill's policies of denial and rage, and made a point in her adult life to avoid confrontation by

113

limiting contact.

"I should *make* you go and see her!" he threatened.

"Are you deaf?" I tilted my head. "Did you not hear me when I said I saw Grandmother Beth recently?"

"You go and see her *now*, or I'll *make* you!" He stuck to his orchestrated rudeness, which was when I figured we were done with this uninvited conversation.

"If you aren't out of here in the count of twenty, I'm calling the cops," I promised, rising to my feet, and *thunking* the poker meaningfully against the palm of one hand. I was having difficulty finding parity between my inherent suspicion of Uncle Bill, and a cultural supplication to respect elders.

Without so much as a backward glance I fled through the side gate, sped out with the poker balanced over my shoulder, and located the extra key inside the peat mulch of a redwood planter. Flicking off the particles, I unlocked the front door, and shut it behind me, turning the deadbolt.

In the spot of the orange streetlight, Uncle Bill jetted angrily out the gate opening on his rickety bike, launched into the street, and headed south, toward the crossing.

While I stood in the window, catching my breath, an Amtrak wailed along the stretch from the north, sleek metal skin reflecting rust-hued streetlights and their halos of illuminated mist. Trains are supposed to match the speed limit of the adjacent thoroughfare, but the passenger trains often fly past at over fifty-five miles per hour. I know because I've clocked them while riding my motorcycle. The trains bellow before each crossing, announcing their imminent arrival, then pealing the Doppler Affect before they vanish down the line. This time, racing along the rails, the operator sounded the engine's horn in earnest, shrieking at the night and the crossing.

I paused, washed with the type of expectation that evolves from a moment smoothly guiding its own fate. I knew before the eventuality occurred and passed, and I wasn't surprised when the train squealed brakes, attempting fruitlessly to stop as it slid along the rails. This was followed by vehicles zooming past, and people trotting in a southward projection, capped with sirens that amassed fire trucks, police cruisers, and an ambulance, soon sent off in favor of the coroner's van.

I even knew when to open the door, and head toward the crowd, leaving behind the poker and my fear. As I glimpsed the mangled ten-speed along the cinders, and the body parts strewn by the force of the train engine's impact, I pragmatically noted that the clothing, neatly excised in the collision, was the checkered button-front that had been worn by Uncle Bill as he tried to chew me out in my own backyard, less than ten minutes before.

* * * *

I was in a distant frame of mind as I spoke with the Santa Clara police investigators, reluctantly laying claim to the deceased. The feeling was surreal, with the ever-present backdrop of yellow tarps shielding disjointed sections of Uncle Bill's body from public viewing.

When I first joined the crowd, there were spectators with cell phone cameras held high above heads, bobbing for better visual traction, snapping photos of poor Uncle Bill's severed torso, and the splash of innards embedded with gravel along the earthen footpath that traced the rail. A handful of news teams erected portable transmitters atop vans to get a juicy byline for the evening news. Before too long, the police had herded the rubberneckers aside, fumbling with seven pieces of tarpaulin to prevent anyone other than the coroner's people from photographing the remains.

Even with the tarps, I was queasy.

To dispel the images in my mind, I approached one of the plainclothes cops, and mechanically explained my affiliation with the severed parts of Uncle Bill. He noted the unsteady rotation in my stance two minutes into the conversation—or was it an interrogation? The coroner's photographer was carefully gathering a digital record of the accident scene, which distracted me. He would pause beside each of the seven tarp-draped sections, and, aided by a stoic Santa Clara cop lifting the tarp edge, would shoot an array of high-speed pictures beneath the steady wash of the camera flash.

"Ms. Benités," interrupted the cop, who'd earlier identified himself as Lt. Ben Chappell. His street clothes might suggest he was a well-dressed, random observer, except for his law-enforcement attitude. "Would you care to discuss this somewhere else?"

I mentioned my house, and then immediately turned away, trudging back to the bungalow, not giving a damn whether anyone followed. Behind me, I could hear the railroad company working with the police and Coroner to clear the tracks.

At the house, I was surprised to find the cop had tracked me, watching silently as I obsessively wiped my feet across the mat. There wasn't anything to wipe off the soles of my shoes, except that the vision of Uncle Bill's disarticulated arm kept popping into my mind.

I let him in, and found the familiar comfort of my leather flea market recliner.

"Mind if I sit down?" he asked, shutting the door firmly.

He was not quite as old as my father, maybe halfway between my age and Dad's, but his unlined face had acquired the taint of law-enforcement suspicion that seems to etch deeper than scars or crow's feet.

"Go ahead." I sank into the crinkly leather, and pulled the handle to prop my feet. "If you want a drink, the bar's stocked with all the important things."

He looked up from a notebook, which he had been scribbling in all along.

"Thanks, I'll rain-check you on the drink."

"I'd have one, but I'd probably throw it back up." I wanted to sound as unappealing as possible.

"You were saying? About your uncle?" Lt. Chappell was relentless to his duty.

"What *was* I saying?" After all, it was his responsibility to keep track of my page.

"'Uncle Bill had a hell of a temper,'" quoting from his notes.

"Yep." I nodded. "Mom called it Intermittent Explosive Disorder." I laughed without any sense of mirth, but just the need to release nervous energy. "I used to think it was a crock, though then when I was thirteen or so, I actually looked it up in a psychiatric encyclopedia that belonged to my dad. There *is* seriously such a thing."

"Any reason your father owned a psychiatric reference book?"

"Any reason that would relate to this incident?" I snapped.

He considered his notes for a moment, and then wisely changed his tack.

"Did he seem depressed at all to you?"

"I don't know, I never saw him enough to gauge. He said he came to tell me his mother is dying, and that I'm supposed to go see her, and then I kicked him out." I stared at the man briefly. "He was starting to become agitated, but I think he was more frustrated than depressed. So, I think he was more likely trying to go around the crossing, not throw himself in front of the train."

"You believe it was an accident."

"Yes, I do."

"I looked up William McKracken on the State database. Were you aware he had a recent conviction for child molestation?"

I fell silent, and just stared at him. He finally cleared his throat, as I guess I was making him uncomfortable.

"Which meant he would have had to register as a sex-offender for the rest of his life," he went on. "Were you aware that a restraining order had been filed against him in Davis, California, by both the university and *Delta Omega* fraternity? He was bringing underaged girls into a frat house, and serving them alcohol."

"How underaged? Under twenty-one?"

"Two were sixteen, and the most recent was thirteen."

"Was there any hanky-panky?"

"The fact that he'd have to register as a sex-offender certainly indicates that, Ms. Benités."

"No, sir, I didn't know about any of that," I replied evenly. Suddenly Uncle Bill's demise seemed justified. "Like I said, I've never had much of a relationship with him. My mother was very...she became somewhat anxious when he came around. She tried to keep space between us and Bill."

"Who's the next of kin, besides you or your mother?"

I hesitated, thinking about Grandmother Beth, and her alleged decline. Not that I ever wanted to push someone over the edge, but nevertheless, it was a fitting tribute to a woman who was more destructive than nurturing.

"Elizabeth McKracken. *His* mother, she lives in Burlingame." I frowned. "There's a brother, Patrick, who's in Seattle, and another brother, Gene who lives in Topeka, Kansas."

"Kansas," the cop snorted, as though I was supposed to glean irony from that.

"What's the problem?"

"Oh, you know, Dorothy and Toto, that sort of thing. I don't think we're in Kansas anymore," quoting the last line in falsetto, which was ridiculous for a man who presented himself as an authority figure.

"And?"

He waved me off. "Never mind," but I was a dog with a bone, ready for a fight.

"What did you mean?" I was really enjoying this.

117

He stood now, either satisfied with his findings, or smart enough to get the hell out of my sights. "Bad attempt at a joke," he assured.

"You must be from Kansas." I nailed it on the head.

"Yeah, that's right."

"Go talk to Elizabeth McKracken, and you'll know why her sons live so far away."

"Except for William," he said. "He stayed fairly close to his mother."

"Well, that's easy to explain. Uncle Bill was dependent upon his mother financially."

"Very common, in this day and age. Okay. I think I've got enough for now." He tucked away the notebook and pen.

I flipped the lever to close the recliner, and showed him the door. On the stoop stood a uniformed officer, who retreated to his cruiser as soon as we emerged. A brown Crown Victoria sat across the street, piloted by a fidgety Asian cop, also in street clothes.

He produced a business card, scratched down the incident number with the resurrected pen, and handed the card to me. As a second thought, he also supplied me with a pamphlet for the County's division of mental health, in case I needed to talk to someone about being scarred by Uncle Bill's horrific death.

I must have appeared antsy as he had an expression of impatience difficult to conceal.

"You know, I was wondering something," I said.

"What?"

"Do you think it hurts to get hit by a train?" And right there, I laughed, as Uncle Bill's incised body parts were vividly swirling in my mind.

He regarded me for a few seconds, and shook his head.

"Probably not," he said with a shrug.

I'm sure he'd been asked some off the wall questions, and had developed a method of fielding them. I was considering defining Uncle Bill's accident as the crowning justice of fate, but Chappell seemed to have had enough of me for one night.

"Maybe it's like hitting a fish with a stick," I suggested.

"I think we're finished here, Ms. Benités. You can call me if anything else comes to mind."

He trudged down the steps, and then bolted off the sidewalk to the Crown Vic. As soon as he was in, both the brown car and the black-and-white headed off in opposite directions, and I was left to the chill of the March night.

The telephone rang behind me. My feet were very heavy as I dragged myself back indoors, reluctant to join up with the world beyond my walls.

"Hello?"

"Madeline," the voice of my father. I reminded myself he probably hadn't heard about Mom's brother yet.

"Hi, Dad."

"I just wanted to call you and let you know that Uncle Miles has been arrested. For the theft of the car, and for meth possession, too."

As though Uncle Miles required the enhancement of being chemically revved-up.

"Okay, Dad. Thanks."

"Is something wrong?" he asked.

As much as I tried, it was impossible to conceal tension in my speech.

And I remember his voice, because the tone would be repeated in the days and weeks to come. His voice suggested edginess, suppressed pain and a desire to break free of self-pity. My father's historical defiance lent the perception he didn't give a damn what the world thought of him. He'd been married once, long before wedlock to my mother, though he stubbornly described the Catholic annulment as having concluded the first marriage never happened. He often created his own rules by spinning off established norm, and spouted precedent to bolster argument in his favor. And yet, he's a generous man with time and possessions, if he determines it will benefit the recipient. This describes my father in a nutshell, a strange benevolence, combined with incessant defense of family.

In a rush, I told him about Uncle Bill's visit, and the stunning accident at the tracks.

For a moment, the line was so heavy with silence I thought he'd hung up. And then, he breathed deeply.

"I'm sorry, Madeline. I'm very sorry you had to experience that."

I felt it was evident that he, as always, wanted to prevent my pain, to protect me. Not that he wished to ever hinder adulthood or the trauma preceding growth, however ominous, but the residue of anguish that leaves behind bottomless thirst.

I managed to say something about how I'd be okay, and he promised to tell Mom, and that's one of the last times I spoke to my father, before meeting up again with Jesse Ibarra, his so-called son, and my so-called brother.

9. The Drama Club

Behind me, lay the burden of the last few weeks, while I avoided the inevitable. I attended William McKracken's funeral, as did my parents, and my sister Margot, but for the most part, it was sadly empty of McKracken representatives. Scheduled on a weeknight in a starkly non-denominational funeral home in San Mateo, Grandmother Beth seemed to ensure any last-minute reprieve by relatives on behalf of Bill, who'd been so clumsy and errant with the train, barely deserved attention from her closely held personal life.

That evening, following Uncle Bill's memorial service, I went out to dinner in Saratoga with my sister, Margot, and Julie, at a cozy high-end joint, and still, I could eat. Even with the hazy portraits of Uncle Bill's separated body parts rummaging around in my mind, I could negotiate a plate of spinach fettuccini, and a soufflé complete with gleaming raspberries that mimicked blown guts in the dish beneath the charming candlelit aura of the restaurant.

"Neither of you are worried about skipping out so fast after your uncle's funeral?" Julie asked, expressing mild shock.

"He, apparently, was a pervert," I told her. "There's no feeling sorry for *his* baggage."

"I didn't know him very well," was Margot's polite reasoning.

"Grandmother Beth put together one of those funeral home celebrations," I added, which meant to Catholics such as myself, Bill McKracken's soul had been shortchanged at his valediction. Being that Grandmother wasn't even remotely religious, it probably never occurred to her to position Bill's eulogy in a house of any sort of god.

"Mallory's still free," said Julie. My sister-in-law seemed to want to dredge every last point of contention in our conjoined lives.

"And why not? The man isn't dead yet," Margot grimaced, working through a plate of old-fashioned spaghetti and meatballs.

I paused knowing that the stalker Mallory had fended off with the concrete and rebar weapon was still technically alive, languishing in deep coma at Stanford Hospital.

"Funny, it could go either way," I mused.

"That's *funny*?" Margot could find no humor in the situation.

"No, see," and I made the classic mistake of laughing as I spoke; "if he lives, he gets charged with attempted rape. Hah! And if he dies, Mallory might be in for it."

"If he dies, it's better for everyone in the long run, including Mallory." Margot rolled her eyes.

Our morbid conversation apparently disgusted the people at the table to our left, because they scooted out without finishing dessert.

"What about you?" Julie motioned toward me with her fork.

"Me?" I frowned, as I hate being the target of anyone's critique.

"Your knuckles," she insisted, and I stared down at my right hand, where the wounds from hitting Ibarra in the face had healed, leaving pale scars across the darker hue of my skin.

"Oh, I'm...doing good." I nodded.

"Doing good." Now it was Margot's turn to laugh.

"I have decided to absolve myself of any responsibility to that issue," I explained.

"Bullshit." Margot was still laughing at me.

I felt hurt, but I hid it. Even after we toned down the conversation, and had espresso, which usually cheers me up, I was stinging. I'm pretty fair about dishing out dirt, and under most circumstances, I can take it. Tonight, already thin-skinned from the pummeling of the past weeks, any jab ached.

All the way home, with my hands tight on the wheel, I felt the unease, and I realized that no matter how hard I tried to resist it, to thrust it away, I was doomed from the moment Jesse Ibarra walked into my closed fist in the smoky innards of JJ's.

* * * *

Two days later, and seated at the breakfast bar in my house, I was eating the last of Grandma Enida's birthday food, which thankfully hadn't gone bad. I'd been smart enough to stow the leftovers in a plastic container and shove it into the freezer. This kept me fed, as I'm averse to cooking, but I do know how to use a microwave oven to heat up someone else's culinary efforts.

The doorbell rang, and I considered ignoring it. Then came an irritating knock, and I tried my best to pretend it was an audio hallucination, but my curiosity got the better of me, and I went to the door. Peering through the spyhole, I recognized the detective from the evening of Uncle Bill's accident.

Chappell, I recalled, still staring through the spyhole. Reluctantly, I opened the door, but kept the chain across.

"Lieutenant," I said casually.

He was intuitive enough to stand one step below the landing.

"It's Ben," he corrected.

"Lieutenant Chappell," I said, and he sighed.

"Ms. Benités."

"What can I do for you, Lieutenant?"

"Actually...I'd like to talk with you, if you have a moment."

"Okay." I stood with the chain intact. "I'm listening."

"Would you be amenable to having a conversation inside of your house?"

I eyed him for a moment. After all, who uses words like that? But because he didn't behave with disrespect or impatience, I decided to let him in.

I headed straight for the kitchen, and Chappell, after closing the door, followed closely on habitually soft cat's feet, as though intent on keeping me in sight without my actual knowledge.

"I'll have you know that I'm not doing anything illegal," I assured, as he noted the contents of my plate closely. "I promise not to waste it."

"Wasting food's not against the law, Ms. Benités," he replied to my straight-faced teasing.

"Waste was a sin, when I was a child," I disputed. "Do you want coffee?"

"Sure."

"Sorry, all out of donuts."

"Thanks, I had my allotment for today," he said, in all seriousness, as I put together a pot of coffee. "You have any particular mistrust of law enforcement, Ms. Benités?"

"What mistrust?"

"Your apparent incapacity for seriousness, your continued cynicism."

I shrugged. "My brother-in-law's a Sheriff's deputy in Lassen County, and my sister is Highway Patrol."

"Whatever *that* means."

"You're right, it doesn't mean anything. Even though they're family, they're not automatically forgiven."

Pulling in a stool at the breakfast bar, he announced my current meal.

"Chocolate meat," he said, pointing to my last few bites, which were mixed in with rice.

"That's right." In defense of his knowledge, I cleared my plate, scraping the precious *dinaguan* into the trashcan, because it had congealed in shades of cooked blood and white fat.

"My ex-girlfriend was a Filipina," he supplied, to quantify his knowledge.

"Wow. How uncommon." The coffee maker burbled its appropriately obscene comments from the counter.

"Well." He seemed slightly embarrassed. "What can I say? Filipinas are God's most triumphant creation."

"My sisters and I used to try to find the mirror image, an Asian man with a white woman."

"Any luck?"

"Most of the time it's the white man with a bizarre hunger for Asian women."

"And you're the result of such a pairing?"

"No. Filipino father, mostly white Indigenous mother. I'm the new breed, Lieutenant. Watch out, we're taking over the world."

"Do you think of yourself as Filipino?" This felt more like an interview, than a discussion.

"How I define myself ethnically gets deeper than I'm willing to go."

I made certain my tone reflected sudden irritation, which stemmed from the practice of definition that had chased my entire childhood and adolescence, the habit people practiced in pigeonholing ethnicity. Not that I wasn't guilty of the same practice, it was just frustrating there was never quite a niche for me, as the white kids had me labeled inaccurately as Asian, and the full-blood Filipinos in the high school FilAm Association snubbed me for being a *mestiza*.

"What can I *really* do for you, Lieutenant?" I asked, hurrying the conversation toward its conclusion.

"I understand you were involved with an incident in San José recently."

"I haven't been involved in any incidents," I denied, and honestly, I couldn't think of anything; no tickets, no warnings; and then, I recalled JJ's. "I thought you worked for Santa Clara P.D."

"It's a small world, Ms. Benités. Word gets around." He rubbed his chin. "I heard you attacked a police officer."

"Oh, that! I punched a stranger in the nose."

"You admit to assaulting a peace officer."

"Well, he didn't identify himself as a cop before I punched him. Seems to me I wasn't arrested, so my take is that it didn't happen," I said, utilizing my father's *annulment* technique for a memory-wipe. "And if he *was* a peace officer, I don't know why he went out of his way to stir things up. Does that sound like peace to you?"

"I knew Officer Ibarra's father," he said, brushing my comments aside. "José Ibarra worked for San José P.D. for over thirty years."

I poured the coffee. "You people sure flock together."

He took a sip of his coffee, and set the mug carefully down onto the counter. That slight hint of pain indicated the coffee was too hot to drink.

"It's interesting how you might make that type of remark, and then as soon as you need assistance, you're the first to make the call."

"And why do you think police officers are paid? You get it all, benefits, retirement. Who the hell do you think pays for my social programs, Lieutenant?"

"What about you, who do you associate with?" he countered, as though building up to prove a point.

"Do you see anyone else here?" I challenged.

"Who are your associates, Ms. Benités?" he persisted.

"My family." And then I remembered Kevin Gerard, though he was more of an occasional drinking buddy, most of our socializing relating to our profession.

"You don't keep company with contractors?" he asked.

"I'll tell you, Lieutenant, contractors, we're worse than jealous housewives. We don't want anyone stealing our clients."

"Hmm. You're a loner." His eyes roved the kitchen briefly. "And you're single. Not even a cat or dog."

"Since you're making assessments of my personal life, I'm going to take a wild stab at yours. You're single, previously married but now divorced—contentiously, maybe? And you can't keep a steady relationship."

"That's pretty accurate. What gave it away/"

"You're a cop. How else do you people live?"

"Kind of like...contractors, eh?"

125

"I haven't alienated anyone yet."

"Can't alienate someone you don't have."

"Are you going to make a point, Lieutenant?"

"I don't have a point to make. I just wanted to follow up with you." He finished his coffee, which had subsided from scalding hot to consumable. "Where do you want me to put this?" he asked, of the emptied mug.

"Wow. So tempting," I joked, taking the mug from him, and placing it in the sink.

"You really should iron it out with Ibarra."

"Wait, *now* I know where I want you to put that coffee cup!"

"Too late, you had your chance, Ms. Benités," he said with a grin, and headed toward the front door.

"Don't let it hit your ass on the way out!" I called, as he shut the door solidly behind him.

I paused for a moment, and then went to the bedroom, where I'd placed Ibarra's rain-soaked business card beneath the wooden box of obsidian stones upon the mantel. Try as I might, searching high and low, it was nowhere to be found.

I pondered the hearth. I suppose I was talking myself into believing it had fallen into the flames, but the core of me knew better. As a contractor, I have to be on top of my tools and equipment, and because I'm self-employed, I keep strict record of each transaction, and account for every receipt. Ibarra's card was no exception, and therefore, its absence was a burning mystery.

The mute black glass glittered back at me. The box was too heavy to simply allow the card to catch on a sleeve or fall unheeded to the carpet or into the fire. The only rational explanation was that the card had been purposefully removed.

I've been getting telephone messages from Jesse Ibarra, Mallory had told me, when she came to visit me after my return from Susanville.

I'd been absorbed in my dark mood, so it didn't dawn on me then to ask Mallory how Ibarra had acquired her telephone number, or her name. I thought back to that day, and then reflexively lifted the wooden box just to be sure. There was nothing beneath it, save for a dustless rectangle.

I was forced into considering that Mallory had removed the card when I was in Susanville repairing the mobile home. With my eyes closed, I pictured the extra key stashed in its cache in the redwood planter box.

Who else would know about the key? Certainly not Mallory, and I'd never revealed the hiding place to a single soul.

Suddenly inspired, I grabbed up the key to my motorcycle, and headed out the back door.

* * * *

The beauty of two wheels is the speed you can attain outright without being killed, though the hazard is always in the back of my mind when I ride. There's nothing that beats 1600 ccs of street bike between one's thighs. I once expressed this to Miranda, who only pointed out the fact that she could do one better with a real live man.

Personally, I'd rather have the motorcycle.

In the afternoon chill, I drove straight from the flatlands and into the hills via highway surfaces, the marvel of modern civil engineering. The Nomad rode smooth and heavy, and was agile enough once I reached the curving roads of Woodside, purring through stands of fir and big-leaf maple that cast deep green shadows dappled with golden sunlight. Hairpin turns seemed to disappear into black pockets as the road wound toward a blue sky diffused with tendrils of fog.

Mallory's cottage stands back from the main road, accessed by a ribbon of asphalt fractured by roots of a row of redwood trees that guard the descending slope. Above, the wind catches in the grove of looming eucalyptus trees, diminishing the house's importance in their heft and girth. The shock of their smell was dog-urine musty, sweeping through the vents of my full-face helmet, the earthy spice of the redwoods, and oily tang of the eucalyptus trees.

You can't see the end of the driveway from the county road, until the final rise, and by then, I knew what I'd find inside. There was no mistaking the brown Suburban in the shade of the carport, guarded by Mallory's steel gray Infiniti.

Though the Kawasaki's exhaust pipes aren't as loud as a Harley's, I knew anyone inside the house could hear me as soon as I approached, trapped by their brazen truth. All it would take to reveal their subterfuge would be a knock upon Mallory's door.

But I couldn't bring myself to it, not right away. I just stood with my helmet in hand, staring at the house, at the reflection of trees and brush off window glass, at Virginia creeper clinging to the chimney bricks, fresh green leaves springing forth from the crumbled death of last season. I weighed the inscrutable nature of lust, how it persuades its victims to build their secrets in complex deception and hasty sidestepping.

I knew what I had to do, and I dragged myself into the doing. As soon as Mallory opened the door, draped in a silk robe, her hair disheveled, and our eyes met, what could I say?

She is my eldest sister, and as such, she has been granted respect by our Filipino culture. When we were young children, Mallory was our *manang,* the sub-hen to Mom; in fact, that was the title I first learned, *manang,* rather than *Mallory.* I only comprehended the gist of her given name when I was five, and skipping off to Kindergarten.

Therefore, I said, "*Manang*, I love you, you're my sister. Please tell me that I'm wrong."

"Maddie." She cleared the hair from her eyes. "What are you doing here?"

Her voice had an underlying tone of guilt, and her cheeks were flushed, both sure signs of eternal damnation. My worst fears were verified by Jesse Ibarra in the flesh, shuffling out of Mallory's bedroom, tied up in the red plaid robe that Mallory had used in college days.

I heaved the helmet onto the nearest surface, the foyer table, definitely not the heaviest weight dropped in that room.

"How long?" I asked Mallory, who stood to one side, clutching her crossed arms with the veined strength of her hands.

"Since you were in Susanville, fixing Mom and Dad's place," she admitted, though I'd already figured it out.

"You entered my house without permission. You took the card." To me, I sounded flat, but I could tell my *Killer Voice* was searching for weaknesses.

She dismissed me with a roll of her shoulders, and just about the ugliest expression across her face, which bears no describing.

"So?"

"How did you know where I keep my extra key?"

"I don't know. I just...looked around. You really should move it, or to just make it easier for a thief, put it under your mat."

"You could've asked. I would've given it to you."

"And then you would've known."

"But it doesn't matter, Mallory, I found out." I scratched my head where the tightest pad of the helmet had rested. "What's it like?" I asked, forcing the *Voice* down, swallowing a demon.

"What's *what* like?" Mallory sounded suspicious.

"Sleeping with your brother. What's it like, Mallory?"

She waved her hands in the air.

"You can't prove we're related!" she spat.

I wanted to ask, *is it like banging half of me, only with a penis?* But words thus expressed become tools of incitement. So, instead, I kept it clean.

"Do you love him?"

Her eyes filled with tears. My beautiful Amazon of a sister, with her sinister manner of psychologically cold cocking a man just to watch him fall, had been infected with a disease. That evil glee prevailed, wherein you crest the wave, only to be knocked flat with the worst regret hangover when the man has done with you.

"I swear, Mallory, you didn't wait, you didn't check him out, and now it's too late." I didn't need the volume of the *Voice* to convey its acrid bite.

"Fuck you, Madeline," she hissed, but she was too wounded to do me any harm, and there were those burning tears in her eyes.

"Why did you do it?" I could feel myself trembling, but I wisely kept my voice clean of vulnerability.

"You know." The flames of her indignation, created to excise personal guilt, were building.

"Why?" Persistent, eh?

"Because." She smirked. "He was there."

I don't remember breathing, so much as turning in slow motion, and grasping my helmet. Fleeing out the door, I crammed my head into its maw, and buckled in. On the fissured driveway, I manhandled the Nomad, until it faced downhill, and once it started, rolled it toward the grade.

In the rearview mirror I glimpsed Mallory. She'd stepped out on the porch, the flowered robe held tightly with what I supposed were bloodless hands. I would have carried my wrath home, but Jesse emerged, and put one arm around her shoulders. Not one word had passed his lips, not a glance, and yet there he was, guiding her back inside, and all my rage was crushed in that single compassionate gesture.

* * * *

If you drive into Livermore on the former Highway 84 connector, Vallecitos Road, past the wineries and the odds-out fruit stand, there's a concrete bridge across a creek. The bullet-dinked sign reads *Arroyo Del Valle*, plainly put, "Valley Stream," but I prefer the elegant Spanish translation. The streambed is choked with cane and willows, and the twisted bodies of living sycamores.

To the right, and just before the bridge, bared to all travelers journeying northeast, is a homemade sign nailed to posts. It reads *CARPE DIEM, Seize the Day,* in blood red paint upon plain, white-primed boards. The rustic monument is an awkward marquee, gauche in its simplicity, but its content mimics the housing subdivisions encrusting the rolling, grassy hills, and the vineyards' reach to where blacktailed deer browse, and wild turkeys forage.

Much later down the line, someone changed the sign, modified it to read, *CARPE DIEM, Pay It Forward,* though I much prefer the original message.

When we were living together as a family, this was our corridor to the Central Valley, and on to the Sierra Nevada or Cascade Mountains. I've logged countless road-trips alerted mentally for the sign, a constant reminder I must make merry now, for tomorrow I will be dust.

My father often pointed out the sign; in fact, we couldn't cross the stalwart bridge and its wilderness of bottomland flora without Dad quoting the wildly popular version, *seize the day,* although he was more likely to insert the word *fucking* right after *seize the,* especially when we'd hit puberty, as though to drive home the concept.

"There it is, kids, look Moira, it's the sign! Seize the fucking day! Repeat after me kids," but Mom, ever wise, would quash Dad's offering with a high-toned *Carpe Diem.*

"*Carpe Diem,* you'll never forget what it means," she'd say with the confidence of the blessed.

And we never did forget it. I note that we all *Carpe Diem*ed ourselves to death, with our careers and family axioms, with the relentless severity we apply to romantic relationships, when we manage to find a qualified partner. There are social and personal expectations Filipino family culture instills, and which evolved, over time, into the butt of jokes written into a snide oral tradition by my Caucasian counterparts when I was in high school.

But this premeditation by Mallory exceeded the bloody words, the hypothesis of grabbing up what pleasures we can collect now, because by the time the earth makes another full rotation, we will probably all be dead.

* * * *

From Woodside to Santa Clara, it's a mere twenty minutes mounted on the plush seat of my cruiser bike. The wind arcs over the top of my helmet, deflected by the windshield and its complement of insect carcasses. I can look through and around the insignificant splotches that mark their instantaneous deaths, but I cannot avoid the collision of Mallory's act. This, I never would have expected of a woman who enjoys the hunt, and the endless tease. Mallory is a heckler of men, she knows her physique is their addiction, and she uses it for punishment, which is her method of self-gratification.

If I had been in any shape to grieve, I would have paused at Stanford Hospital and said a prayer at the foot of the bed of Mallory's last victim, hoping to mumble loudly enough so God could decipher my voice from the chatter of artificial life support.

Instead, because I'd been raised to believe some higher power is always tuned to my silent thoughts, both pure and ignoble, I kept on, until I pulled into the driveway of my parents' house, and cut the engine.

Mom and Dad were both at home, seated hip to hip on the sofa watching the news. Rarely ever parted, they spend nearly every waking moment, and all their unconscious hours, deliberately avoiding the privation of physical separation. They are lovers, so crazy about one another that it made sense to have children as an expression of their utter, diabolical passion, but it's impossible to break into their coterie. They have some hoodoo spell on each other, a constant chant that derives from the heart. Inseparable, they are identical to the coupling of geese, mated for life, so that when one dies, the other will pine away in abject misery. We learned as children that we could never play one parent against the other because they were like a fused granite wall without any telltale fissures. Oftentimes it was difficult to know where one ended and the other began.

And it will be my good fortune to find any person so well fitted to me.

"Madeline, come in and sit," went my mother's invitation. And then, a tilt of her head, when she said, "Are you all right? Are you sick?"

I suppose my face was red, and my eyes were smoldering deep in their sockets, because there was energy that hummed in my head, egging me onward, while caution rattled the bars of the cage.

"No, thanks, Mom, I'm fine. Really fine."

Dad, no fool, gauged my face, body language and voice in an instant, and knew I was far off the mark of personal harmony. And in his predictable habit, he pried the edges of my unrest, as an alternative to changing the subject.

"Why're you sweating, then, Madeline?" Dad asked, but he doesn't know I have an Ace in my hand.

* * * *

How to describe my father, his dire need to embody the definition of "provocative" across the board?

A superb anecdote calls to mind my parents' favored morning activity (aside from the sex we all pretended not to hear; I'm sure they figured they were being extra quiet), which is reading the newspaper together during breakfast. Dad always reads a certain advice column aloud to my mother. She never leaps ahead and scans it. She waits until Dad's finished with the front page, and then she settles in for their daily discussion, a facet of their matrimonial intimacy.

Starting in the era when we were preteens, Dad included us in these discussions, if we by chance risked eating breakfast simultaneously.

One incident that stands out occurred when this particular advice columnist dedicated one month to *Random Acts of Kindness*. Readers were urged to respond to the deficiencies in their communities, with a verve of compassion, and crammed with enough energy to "start a prairie fire."

My father, with a trademark smirk upon his face, scoffed, "Yeah, a prairie fire. Huh! I'll tell you what, get a bull-horn, drive into east Oakland, and yell *nigger* on that thing, and you're sure to start a Goddamned prairie fire."

As a man of color, Dad always figured he had exclusive rights to ethnic jokes and controversial pronouncements, and the power to stun us into pained silence.

Occasionally he extended these platitudes to his children. A prime example would be the year Margot was readying for her Sacrament of Confirmation, and was requested by the catechist to choose a saint name for the rite. Margot chose *Cecile*, the patron saint of music, in honor of our father, an embedded musician, whose sword wielded on behalf of a higher power is a guitar.

"Cecil?" Dad repeated, deliberately twisting it into the male form, with the angle that he was aghast at Margot's choice. "I never heard of a Saint Cecil."

Evaluating my father's psyche (and calling to mind my brother-in-law Gilbert comparing me to Dad), evidently, he believes he's wickedly funny, aside from his compulsion to be our constant pedagogue of life's

132

lessons.

* * * *

"Because," I said now, on stage before my expectant parents, gaining control of my emotions in the dawning realization that I owned the eight ball. "Mallory's fallen in love with a man too young for her own good."

I made a serious face, as though caught in religious contemplation, before continuing.

"He's only twenty-five, the same age as I am. He told me that his mother's name is Clea Ibarra. He said I would know the name, Mrs. Clea Ibarra, but I just don't think I've ever heard of it. Maybe you know the name, Dad."

I raised my brows, innocent to the core, my vindication in pure thespian mode.

I have never witnessed that turnabout, the total withdrawal of Dad's countenance from the over-eager wisecracker, into the dupe.

"I'm not sure," Dad hedged, rubbing his nose, the sure sign of a falsehood. Mom saw it. She reads us all like a book, and because Dad's her intimate succubus, she knows him through and through.

"What did you say, Mitchell?" Mom asked, gaze intent to my father's face.

"Never heard it," he said, offering another lie to our ears. Or, maybe he exempted himself, because he hadn't cast *Clea* as *Mrs. Ibarra.* A lie is a lie, but somehow, Dad can ferret out all the loopholes.

"Well, then." I rose to my weary feet, and hiding it, made my way cheerfully to the door. "Got an early day tomorrow, so I'd better get home."

"What's tomorrow?" Dad asked warily.

"A construction gig in Pacifica, another kitchen renovation. I have to be there at seven o'clock with a crew."

"You're leaving town?" Dad asked. "Tonight?" Now I know just whom I'd inherited my staying power from.

"Well, no, but real early in the morning."

My father indicated desperation to continue our conversation, *any* conversation, because I was positive Mom would interrogate him as soon as my wheels hit the road.

"Gotta go," I repeated, and I hugged them, Mom first, feeling the muscles in her back, and then Dad, who was exuding the heat of the guilty. I might have laughed maniacally, as my Dad's face was fixed and indecipherable, yet bursting at the seams. Imagine trying to hold back the tide, and it ain't pretty, though Dad is the undisputed master of self-control.

"You'd better be on your way, then, Madeline," he said in that tone he'd use when we knew we were in trouble, but the yelling hadn't commenced, and we fervently wished for the wrecking ball to hoist so we could just get it over with. He was smiling biliously, and I felt a sudden ache for his self-made predicament.

Fine, I'm going, I remember thinking, and then, I walked out.

The drive is quick, only about a mile to my house. Though I was truly in no condition to drive my motorcycle, I mounted up and guided it home. Perhaps the act was the same as being intoxicated, because I really don't recall doing it. I could have plowed down a child running after a ball, and still kept going, those blood spots on the windshield as invisible as insect kills.

But the ride was unremarkable, and home was a blessing. And once I cleared the door, a shot of tequila and mental exhaustion guarded my sleep.

* * * *

The telephone woke me up, my cell, vibrating in the pocket of my jacket, which I still wore, bundled up on the sofa inside of a throw blanket. Somewhere in my dreamless sleep I'd twisted up so tightly in the throw, I had to roll onto the floor to unwind myself. I hit the carpet with a grunt, tussling with the cover, until I lay, spread-eagled, staring up at the ceiling.

By then, the phone had stopped ringing, but I dug it out of my pocket anyway. Squinting at the screen, I saw my father's cell number as a missed call.

I rolled onto my stomach, and punched in his number. At almost three a.m., he had it coming.

"Madeline," he answered to my first ring, calm, a rock. My father usually maintains control of his emotions, except when he's cleared the deck, and then there's no turning back.

"Hello, Dad."

"We need to talk."

I used the sofa to rise to my feet. The room was cold, and my head ached as though I'd tied one on, and then I saw the shot glass on the edge of the bar.

"I don't know what you could say to me that would mean anything, Dad." I found the switch, and grimaced painfully at the light, but managed to locate the fridge behind the bar, and surface with a bottle of cold water.

"Are you going to let me in, Madeline?" And so I knew, Mallory-like, he was waiting outside.

"Yes, Dad."

I opened the door, and he trudged in without a word, except to sit on my sofa with a sigh. Leaving him to wordless simmering, I went off with an excuse for tea. Closeted in the kitchen, I prepared the pot, waiting with the patience of a nun while the kettle came to a boil. I swear it *does* take a hell of a lot longer if you watch the damn thing.

We sat in the living room, and drank tea, tough without alcohol, but better to keep a clear head.

"You were out of line, Madeline," was the first thing he said. No *sorry,* or other forms of apology, he threw the blame my direction.

"Out of line about what?" I feigned innocence. "Ah, do you mean my mention of Clea Ibarra?"

"You and I both know what that was all about."

"Did you or did you not have an affair before I was born?" I asked, getting to the point.

"I had an affair. It was a one-night stand."

"Oh, *that* makes it all good."

"Don't patronize me. And don't assume your mother was clueless. I told her all about it."

"*When* did you tell her, Dad?"

He frowned at his tea. I could see a tremor in his fingers. Maybe he was weighing the aspects of truth.

"Two years later."

"Two years later, Mom was pregnant with Margot."

"That's right." He put down the cup and shifted, clearly uncomfortable. "I was careful, I took precautions. There was never supposed to have been a child."

"I got news for you, Dad, there's a man out there who thinks he's your son. Because his so-called father died, and his mother thought he could handle it."

"She never told me there was a child," he repeated. "I don't see how it could have happened."

This, from the man who had quoted to each of his four daughters, *don't have sex, unless you intend to get pregnant.* I passed this honorable cliché back to him now.

"You never said it was supposed to be recreational, Dad. Sex is for a reason, you don't do it unless you expect pregnancy as the end-product."

I imagined him in his eternal justification: *Recreation is the best reason of all.*

But for once, he was quiet, until, emboldened by his silence, I tried to make this an adult conversation.

"And you never told me you'd had an affair."

"What happens in our marriage is between your mother and me. It's none of your business, including this affair."

I stood and walked around the room, as though searching for the right words.

"If my husband cheated on me, that'd be it. I'd get rid of him," I concluded.

"This explains why you're single, Madeline. There isn't a man out there, not one man alive who can live up to that ideal."

"Cheating on a marriage isn't inevitable, Dad."

"I prefer to define it as dishonoring my vows," he amended in that maddening, pious tone he so often utilized when we were children.

"It doesn't matter what you call it, it's shoveling shit, Dad."

We were left in silence, Dad making sure he knew every inch of that teacup, and me, hovering over the bar convinced I could find solace in another shot.

"I'd like to do a paternity test," he offered.

"Fine, then I have something for you."

I left him for a moment, went to the second bedroom I use as an office, and found the DNA report on my desk. Carrying it back to my father like a loyal, well-trained gun dog, I dropped it on the coffee table, the paper whispering across his fingers, as he caught the fluttering page.

"Send in your own sample. You don't even have to approach the guy, just use the numbers and the password from the test to see if your DNA matches."

He read the report, outwardly amused, because his mouth was turned up in a smile, though his eyes were filled with what I can only define as fear. I don't know what transpired between my parents after I let loose the invisible cloud of angst into the air. A secret is only as good as its dubious nature. As long as my mother kept Dad's sexual flimflam confidential, its poison was contained. I'd revived all the toxic emotions Dad's brief liaison had inflicted upon the marriage over twenty years ago.

"Do you mind if I take this with me?" he asked, rising to his feet. I could hear his knees crack, the body-speak of mortal frailty.

"I don't care."

"Well, Madeline." He shook his head. "I'm sorry about all this. Though it seems you enjoy the intrigue."

"What makes you think I enjoy any of it?"

"This," he said, snapping at the paper with his fingers. "How you ever collected DNA from these two people. And one of them wasn't even me."

He looked at me directly, but his eyes were kind. My father is a man of deep curiosity, fascinated by human nature and the machinations of the cosmos, convinced that psychology couldn't be readily defined and labeled, just as the laws of physics aren't confined to a well-ordered universe. He ruminates outside of science's regimented box, with the philosophical idea that thinking springs a notion into actuality.

"I hope—" I started, and then I bit my lip. Whatever I hoped had no influence on my parents.

"I hope, too, Maddie," he agreed, gathering me into his arms. His embrace is endless, and comforting, though he might have been the one who needed consoling. "I love you," he said, the same as always, nothing changed in the heart of this man who just happened to be my father.

"I love you, too, Dad." And then, he went out into a new morning.

10. Lovesick

When I arrived at the job site in Pacifica, my work truck was loaded with a crew of day laborers hired off The Home Depot parking lot in Colma. I reflect on a town inhabited by more dead people than the living, as Colma is a reservoir of cemeteries, their peaceful acreage of clipped lawns and stately trees complemented by mausoleums and headstones. But there seemed to be plenty of people with a measurable heartbeat to hire.

In the parking lot, the animate gather to keep up with daily existence. If one is fortunate to be swept up into the cab of a general contractor, a wife and children in some natal village will be supported financially. I admire these men, their stoicism and humor, and hidden loneliness. It's rare that I am ever treated with disrespect.

When I pull up with a crew it's six forty-five a.m. I slide the truck into the driveway of the 1970s-built house whose kitchen is being rendered whole again. At the top, is the expectedly enormous dumpster, and I glimpse the green form of the rental toilet which has been stashed behind a cypress tree. As I exit the truck, there is the sea, a line of rumpled, misty blue beneath a gray, fog-laden horizon.

I can't help but think about my father once more, however intent I am to avoid it. I don't often visit the ocean, but when I do, the smell of it prompts certain memories, and not all of them pleasant. The most prevalent recall is laying prone on the bottom of Dad's fishing boat as it rides the crests and troughs of ocean swells, deck bloody with slithering mackerel, which precede my dry heaves. *Deep-sea fishing*, it was termed, in my parents' confident marathon style. This made us either wholly embrace the outdoors, or flee from its heady stench, our childhoods shattered by the dual torture of seasickness and exhaustion.

Working so close to the surf and tide, I felt always on the verge of queasiness, which I could suppress with attention to the remodel. But when that distraction passed, I figured it was better to face my adversary head-on.

At week's end, when we had cleaned and finished, I paid the work crew, returning them to their parking lot niche and refrigerated wind that snapped the American flag. Colma and Daly City are flumes for the wind and fog. But the true source is due west, and as I merged onto Highway 1, with the deep blue of the Pacific Ocean juxtaposing the green chill of the land, I actually felt faint.

Back in the town of Pacifica again, and lashed by the wind, I parked the truck near the municipal pier, and walked slowly toward the breakwater. Long gray rollers crested beneath the pier, slamming the supports, which seemed to me too spindly to hold back the surge. The tide was in, and waves seething with foam washed as high as the seawall, inundating the narrow beach.

I walked along the concrete pier, where scattered groups of people, mostly men and some women, hung their hopeful lines far down into the water. Sometimes a lucky fisherman would pull up enough perch, smelt or white croaker to fry up for supper. Maybe a luckier bastard would hook a striped bass, and there would be hell to pay, as the attempt was made to bring the catch to its favored conclusion.

All the way to the end, and I was forced to stop, gazing at the horizon with my eyes slitted against the awful strength of the wind.

I noticed a man nearby, leaning on the top of the wall, gingerly though, because of bird guano and bait scraps. A dog sat at his feet, a motley canine cross of indeterminate breeds. The dog looked over its thick shoulder at me, and thumped its tail reflexively on the concrete, turning its lips up in a satiric doggy grin. Distracted, the man turned around, and gazed at me, and in the mood of his companion, he smiled.

Sorry to intrude, I thought, thinking to move away, but the dog had a better idea, trotting over to me with leash dragging, and pushing against my hand with its wet, cold nose.

"Rat!" the man remonstrated, and the dog threw him an expression of apology, walking back reluctantly with a sideways grin. "You're a naughty boy, Rat," he told the dog in beaming praise, while Rat lay down with a whine and grunt at the man's feet.

"I don't mind at all. Your dog seems friendly."

"I'm sorry about that," he apologized, and smiled again. "Sometimes people just don't like Rat's approach."

"Well, I do," I promised.

We stood together at the edge, and talked about the sea, how the colors change constantly with the tide and the seasons and the height of the sun. We tried to identify the various specks of anchovy gut and pile-worm mouth part, and he told me the Latin names of the different gulls vying for airspace above our small section of pier.

I finally got around to asking him why he'd named his dog *Rat*.

"He's ugly, don't you think?" he asked, straight-faced.

Studying Rat's countenance, I might have been repulsed, if not for the sweetness in the dog's eyes.

"Yes, he's ugly. Absolutely. Well, I agree with his physical self, though he's not exactly horrendous, just...different. But he has a heart of gold, and that seems to make everything else about his appearance kind of nominal."

Now the man was grinning at me. I felt as though I'd passed some kind of a test.

"You're the first person to agree with me," he laughed. "Everyone always *oohs* and *aahs* my poor dog, insisting that he's fucking handsome. But you're the only one who said that about his heart."

I felt embarrassed. The anomalous meeting on the pier, the very fact I was even on this pier to begin with, was troubling in itself. But I had failed to mention that the strange man with the equally peculiar dog was beautiful.

And I'd never have said it, not in a hundred years, nor for a million bucks. Imagining myself, Madeline Benités, still dirty and sweaty from the construction job, holding a conversation with a man who reflects the kindness of his pet, it was incredible. More so because I could sense a light shining off the man, too, it was blinding.

I could feel my face burning. I hadn't felt that for...ah, hell, for a long, *long* time. All those hours toiling, I made my living and paid my dues, and capped it with tequila or a beer or a glass of wine, a sure-fire pathway to sleep. Sex, though, physical intimacy, I wasn't inclined to search for it, and because I dressed to deflect, it had rarely bothered to find me.

"I...I have to go now," I said regretfully.

The man seemed concerned by my announcement too.

"Do you *really* have to?"

"Yes, yes, I do, I have a long drive."

I could feel my nose beginning to run, which suggested another point of embarrassment. I was a construction dude with a woman's body and a schoolgirl's clumsiness. The closest I'd ever get to *Mr. Light* would be to touch myself in my own bed, before passing out from what might promise to be a full glass of Port, or some equally potent alcoholic beverage.

140

"I was kind of hoping we could talk some more," he said wistfully. "Maybe get a bite to eat."

I was now backing away slowly. I realized that this probably made the man think I was suspicious of him, but then, no dog that nice would hang with a monster.

I hope he knows that, I was thinking.

"I'm sorry, but I do have to go. Thanks for the talk," I said, picking up the pace. "Good-bye."

I turned and headed for my truck. I'm literally making a dash for it. Looking back once, the man was still there, watching me. Rat sat on his haunches, one of the man's hands resting on the dog's head.

* * * *

I tried to telephone Mallory once I arrived home, but she wasn't having any of it. Either she was 1. screening her phone calls; 2. she was in bed with Ibarra; or possibly 3. down in Los Banos, what she'd termed *his turf* to me, in some parallel universe of the recent past.

Frustrated, I stripped off all my clothes, and took a long shower, then loaded the empty belly of the washing machine with my sodden, everyday attire. By the time I'd put on my pajamas and wandered through the bar, full wine glass in-hand, I was more than ready for sleep.

I turned on the TV, and flipped through the channels. While I was surfing along, I could hear my cell phone ringing in the bowels of the jacket I'd worn on the pier. For a moment, I had a wild thought it could be that man, but then, I'd never given him my name.

When I found the phone, it had stopped ringing. There was Margot's number, so I phoned her back.

"What took you so long?" she asked. "You're usually such a phone jumper."

"I've been drinking," I pretended, taking my first sip. "That's why I'm not so quick on the draw."

"You shouldn't drink alone," she warned. "Everything okay with you?"

"Well, since you asked." And I summarized what had transpired after our meal in Saratoga, where Julie had made light of family tribulation.

"Really?" she asked, at the end of my long-winded diatribe. "I'm impressed. You have balls, Maddie."

"Yeah, that's the problem." I forced a tag ending with a short skit about the man on the pier.

"Maddie, if you don't mind my asking, when's the last time you got laid?"

"It's not in my recent memory."

I wouldn't count the event, two years ago, when I picked up a drunken reveler at Julie's company Christmas party, and made *Happy Holidays* with him at the Super 8 Motel right off Highway 101. The room was cheap, and the lay sleazy, but its effects, including the private shame in my stupidity, could last a lifetime. The worst part of it was when my partner, known only as "Doug," threw off the efficacy of his imbibing, and it suddenly registered to him that he was in bed with a less than hottie. Even my retreat from the pier hadn't matched the speed in which dear old Doug flew from that motel room. To soothe my ego, I tactfully concluded to myself he'd been a married man.

"Say, the reason I called, is that Julie wants me to go to this party with her."

"I know, I know, you need a babysitter," I teased, since they had no children, nor dogs. Margot is a feline aficionado. She has two sleek black cats she christened *Devil* and *May Care*, and is smart enough to keep them inside the house at all times. As felines, they're self-maintaining.

"No, you dumb-ass, we're inviting you, too."

"What do I wear? Would they allow me in with my *Maddie* shirt?"

"They'd probably have you be the valet, dear Maddie. I have an idea, let's go shopping."

I groaned, because shopping with Margot meant going into a Macy's Women's and finding something clingy and inappropriate. Heels are torture devices, and a purse is a joke, but you'd never see my petite lesbian little sister in anything less formal than five-inch heeled pumps and silk. With flowers, mind you.

"Margot, is it one of those black-and-white affairs?" I asked, trying to take the reins away from her.

"Well, no," she admitted. "It's a barbecue. Up in the Santa Cruz Mountains, a week from tomorrow. Some author Julie knows, it's his birthday, and I guess his girlfriend is throwing him a party."

"Is it a milestone? Because no one ever just throws a big party unless it's a milestone year."

"Forty?" she said uncertainly.

"Look, I'll compromise. I'll wear chick jeans and let my hair down. I'll even shave my armpits. Would that satisfy you?"

I could practically hear her smiling on the other end.

"That'll work just fine, Madeline." She paused. "What was it you said, about the man on the pier?"

"Huh? Oh, light. He glowed. I don't know, I think I'm tired, that's all, but he was kind. Even his ugly dog was beautiful."

"What was he?"

I hesitated. After all, it's common practice, when you are the product of an interracial marriage you are inherently fascinated with the ethnic backgrounds of others from your figurative clan. We have terminologies for the inter-race and multi-ethnic, for which we can brandish many flags. In this case, I was searching for the term to characterize the man at the Pacifica pier.

"Blasian," I described. *Black* and *Asian*.

"Really? Lovely combination. I'll see *you* next Saturday, ten a.m."

When we were finished, I sat in a dim room with the wash of the television, and thought about the brief encounter. The feeling was magical, and in the spirit of all conjuring, sadly ethereal, and could never be repeated. Not in any combination of time whatsoever would I be able to regain the moment again, the gentle Rat and his human companion with the brilliant, friendly eyes.

I swallowed the wine, and, ready for sleep, pulled on a throw blanket and lay down alone. I wasn't even in my own bed, but on the empty sofa with theatrics of the nightly newscast shadowing across the floor.

* * * *

I had a couple of minor jobs that week, a shower stall installation in Newark, and a granite countertop in Los Altos. Up in the hills for the latter job, I smelled the sun-warm earth and the grass, and perversely remembered the sea, this time, without the malaise attributed to my stomach.

Kevin hired me to assist him framing and hanging a high-end entry door in Menlo Park, and quickly noted my distraction.

"What's his name, Maddie?" he asked intuitively, as we shimmed the door.

"I don't know, Kev," I said seriously. "But I surely wish I did."

On Friday, rather half-heartedly, I wandered through a low-budget department store, and bought a new pair of jeans.

Standing in the fitting room, I stared at my reflection, the image of a feminine stranger from the waist down. I don't wear women's clothes often, my wardrobe consisting of sturdy men's clothing appropriate for my profession. Pants like these flimsy Janes wouldn't last a moment while tiling a floor or hanging drywall. I do, however, have a muscular feminine body, and while my work clothes blur my gender, the dime store jeans accentuated every curve and shapely, round protrusion.

Just to complete the ensemble and the myth that I was, in fact, a female, I bought an earthy peasant blouse to go along with the jeans.

True to my word, on Saturday morning, I took a shower, and shaved my legs and armpits. I had even purchased a bottle of pink nail polish with the girls' jeans and blousy thing, and painted my toenails. I'd decided to wear a pair of sandal flats. The strappy shoes had been in my closet for years, and worn with a pantsuit to my grandaunt's funeral. Stored in their carton, they were virtually unused. In no way would I paint my fingernails, but at least, and barring the faint scars from Ibarra's face across the knuckles of my right hand, they were clean.

"My, *my*," said Margot, when she and Julie pulled up in Julie's Camry, and I emerged from the house, dressed like a woman for the first time in a decade. "You sure don't look like Maddie," she claimed. "You must be Madeline."

"Watch it, buster," I warned, but I smiled to remove any edge.

The drive seemed hellishly long to attend a party. We passed through Saratoga, up the twisty Highway 9 grade—avoiding the morning bicyclists—leapt across Skyline, and down the next series of hills and more winding asphalt of the Highway 9 continuation, to reach Ben Lomond.

But Julie is an excellent driver, and after the hardship of riding in my father's offshore boat as a child, I'm seldom afflicted with motion sickness in a car. Close enough to the allotted hour, we were at the access road to the birthday boy's property, marked by a right-leaning mailbox tethered with a shock of colored helium-filled balloons.

"Oh, please," said Margot, in jest. She enjoys childish touches as much as the next person, despite her sophistication.

"What is this place?" I asked, craning my head around as we ascended the road, and emerged in a wonderful clearing ringed by dense woods. In the green-filtered light, was an assemblage of marvelous old buildings—a house, barn, three-car garage, various small out buildings, and what appeared to be an artists' studio.

"It used to be a hunt club, a rich man's retreat," Julie explained, finding a parking place near the garage, along with the other cars of partygoers who'd beat us to the punch. "Built by a wealthy San Francisco copper magnate in the mid-1920s, so I hear, and you know what happened when the stock market tanked in '29."

"What?" I asked seriously.

"You really have to read more about history," Julie said, clucking her tongue.

I carried a bottle of wine under one arm, my contribution, because I didn't know the honoree, didn't expect to know anyone beyond Margot and Julie. The wine was a decent choice, a bottle of *Reserve Red* from Clay Creek Winery near Lodi, and I figured I couldn't go wrong.

"You'll love this place, Madeline," Margot was telling me. "Jake had it renovated about ten years ago, you know, modernized without losing its ambience."

I opened my mouth to speak, when I saw a dog approaching us, wagging its tail.

"Dear Lord, that's a *really* ugly dog," Julie said, pointing, but I was on Cloud Nine.

I dropped to my haunches, the wine leaning against my calf, and held out both hands, wiggling my fingers.

"Rat!" I cried, "Rat!"

Julie regarded me as though I'd lost a screw.

"Stop calling it that," she was urging. "You might offend somebody."

But Rat remembered me. He headed right to me, and lay down on the ground, belly-up.

"He seems to know you," Margot said, deliberating our familiarity.

"Of course!" I was a little too excited. "This is the dog I told you about, the hideously ugly dog on the Pacifica pier with the really gorgeous pet man."

"Let's go find the guy, then." Margot helped me to my feet. "He must know Jake Keene."

"Who?"

"You know, the person for whom this get-together is being held?" Julie put forth her wicked sarcasm.

"I'm ready!" I declared, with the enthusiasm of a prepubescent girl.

Following the sounds of revelry, and with Rat in our wake, we found the party on the expansive back deck of the house. The area was occupied by at least forty people, who were grouped around a couple, comprised of a very attractive thirty-something white woman, and the man who was the prettier half of Rat.

"There he is," I elbowed Margot, and pointed.

"Is she *serious*?" Julie asked.

"Do you mean Jake Keene?" Margot shook me.

"I don't know, but *that's* the man!"

"Madeline." Julie put one hand on my shoulder. Both she and my sister regarded me with pity. "That's Jake Keene, and the woman is his girlfriend, Sophie Whipple."

"Oops." I felt like a complete idiot. Of course, it made sense, and why *would* such a good-looking man *not* be attached to an equally fine woman?

Rat, however, nudged my hand, as though to say, *what do you have to lose?*

I went forth with that ugly dog, and Julie introduced Margot and me to Jake Keene and Sophie Whipple. I mumbled a birthday sentiment, and handed over the bottle of wine, while Jake nodded and smiled his gratitude. When Jake shook my hand, I think he faintly recognized me, because he kept glancing back at me with a pondering expression. Sophie scanned us all over once, and probably decided we were no competition, two declared lesbians, and a plain hippie chick.

I told myself it didn't matter, my personal disappointment buffered by the festivities.

Aside from the company hired to cater the barbecue, there was a small jazz quartet playing beneath a canvas gazebo. Helping myself to a paper plate of food, I sat to one side, and listened to the band, shades of my childhood, and the rich musical culture our father exposed us to.

While absorbed in the ensemble's rendition of *Polkadots & Moonbeams*, Jake Keene snuck up, and took a seat beside me on the hard wooden bench. Being this was a truly professional group, they were expressive, yet not too loud, so I could hear his voice clearly.

"Madeline, did you say?"

I nearly upset my plate.

He leaned close to study my face. "Have we met?"

I gathered my loose hair, holding it in a ponytail, and pointed to a feigned shirt pocket, saying "Maddie," as though reading from my work-shirt's nametag.

He slapped his thigh, laughing. "I *knew* we'd already met!"

146

"Yes, at the pier," I agreed. I let go of my hair, the strands thankfully hiding the sudden heat rising to my cheeks.

"I know, that was an off-chance, wasn't it?"

He was smiling at me. I've never had anyone except maybe my own father seem so transfixed by me. His hypnotized concentration was interrupted by an outcry from Sophie.

"Jake, oh, get it out of here, gross!" Sophie, seated across the porch, and talking to several guests, looked down at Rat's face stuck deep into her plate of barbecue. The plotting dog didn't think he was revolting, though Sophie obviously held a difference of opinion.

"C'mon, Rat!" he called, and Rat came running, potato salad smudged across his nose.

With Sophie looking pissed, it seemed only logical Jake wanted to clear out for a while.

"Want a tour?" he asked me, and, done with my meal, I replied that I sure did.

"My sister tells me you're an author," I said, to make conversation, as we headed away from the core of the party, Rat galloping around the trees. The sounds of the band and layered conversation faded into nuances of wind and bird sounds.

"Yes, that's right. Do you read very much, Maddie?"

"Ah, yes, I used to read a lot of fiction when I was a kid, but then I discovered power tools. Now *how-to* books are my line. I don't suppose you write *how-to* books, do you?"

"No, I'm a novelist. I write, what some might refer to, as *bullshit*. My latest release is *New Fall Blood,* it's about a demon-hunter in post-Colonial Massachusetts."

"Hmm, sounds scary."

"What's scary is the copy of *Gates & Fences* Sophie bought me," he claimed. "She's thinking of a picket fence, though I can't fathom it in the middle of the woods. Really, Maddie, the book terrifies me, and all because I can't do anything with a hammer or a saw. I still don't understand why she's trying to change me into a fixit-man."

"What about Sophie? Maybe she can handle tools."

"Attorneys don't do manual labor either, they're as bad as novelists," he said, and rolled his eyes.

We arrived at a place where the woods, a mixture of oak and bay, parted to reveal a small creek in a deep ravine. The air smelled of the overpowering bay trees, and the damp from the flowing water. I picked up a random stone, and tossed it down the ravine, listening to it bouncing off the earthen walls until it hit the water with a faint splash.

"So, what kind of dog is this Rat of yours?" I asked.

"He's a mix of Shar-pei and Chinese Crested, and personally, neither breed is very attractive."

"But a great combination of ugly," I joked.

"His litter mates weren't as bad. Rat was the last pup that no one wanted. Fortunately, I appreciate a good canine personality."

"Rat must've had nice parents to be so sweet. What about you? What's your ancestry?"

I inquired with complete innocence, and yet, had a compulsion to know.

"My father was Thai, and my mother was African-American and Japanese."

I nodded, because it all fit so perfectly, expressing this man's exotic physical character.

"You said *was*, are your parents still alive?"

He sighed. "They died thirty years ago in an auto pileup in the Central Valley. Tulé fog and a big-rig."

"I'm sorry I asked," I apologized, but he waved his hand.

"It's fine. I had my therapy, and I moved forward." He looked at me intently. "What about you? What's your ethnic background?"

I quoted that familiar dirge, which made him laugh impulsively.

"And your folks, are they still alive?"

I found another rock, and sent it after its cousin.

"Yeah, alive and kicking. They live about a mile from me, but believe me, there's no umbilicus."

"Well, you seem mature, anyway, for your age."

"I'm twenty-five," I defended. "*And* I'm self-employed. How many twenty-somethings do you know who own their own companies?"

"Not too many, I'm afraid, not being affiliated with your immediate generation."

"How old *are* you? If you don't mind me asking. I mean, depending upon how many candles'll be on your cake, we might need to have Cal Fire standing by."

He laughed again. He seemed to find me particularly humorous.

"I'm forty."

I shrugged. "You're a healthy-looking forty," I gauged, as though complimentary, but he snorted at me.

"Forty's not decrepit, Maddie."

"The concept of forty is, if you're twenty-five."

I headed for another rock to throw, but he grasped my hand before I could bend down. Rat, seated in the leaf litter, watched us curiously, one ear upright, and the other flicking at a fly.

"Maddie," he said, and then paused, as though the dam had burst, and he was about to gush out words that would obliterate the town below. He thought better of it, and released my hand. "I'm really glad you came to my party." There was a melancholy undertone to his voice.

"Don't sweat it. It's a nice gesture, I wish I had someone who thought enough of me to put together a party on my behalf."

He glanced back to our point of origin; the merrymaking hidden by the bulk of the house.

"She wants me to get rid of my dog," he admitted, the source of his disconsolate aura.

I hesitated to enter that argument. Lots of people consider a partner's pet as interfering in the human union. Still, watching Rat snap at the fly that had been pestering him, I couldn't imagine this particular dog serving as a barrier to any serious relationship.

"I remember when my father wanted to buy an Athena," I began, a story to circumvent Jake's problem, while demonstrating that I understood.

"What's an Athena?"

"It's a very sweet-sounding archtop guitar, built by a luthier, Ted Megas. Dad already had an L5 CES and a couple of Gibson ES-175s, but he'd wanted an Athena for years, a *true jazz musician's piece*, he called it."

"What did he do?"

"Well, I could see my mother felt it was superfluous, even to his profession. The joke being, a guitar player needs just one more guitar. He's a professional musician, teacher, that stuff. I mean, he already has several really nice jazz boxes he never uses. They just sit around waiting to be played. But this guitar was going to cost more than just a few thousand dollars."

"Then what happened?"

"She let him buy it."

"And?"

"It was a move that saved their marriage. He wanted it, and she was practical, but she made room for another archtop guitar."

"Soooo...." He frowned. "How does this relate to Rat?"

"I guess what I'm trying to say is that a person should always make concessions for their significant other's passions, without expecting a return on emotional investment. If it's a beloved pet, then a compromise should be made to include the pet. I imagine it happens with single parents all the time, trying to integrate children into a new relationship."

"You're wise, Maddie, for being such a spring chicken."

"Thanks."

I found another rock, and sailed it down the ravine. A mourning dove, which had been perched upon a protruding branch in the ravine wall, startled and flew toward the canopy, its wings whistling as it rose skyward. A blur swept in from behind us, a sharp-shinned hawk, that took the dove out in midair with an explosion of feathers. The kill happened so fast we stood there stunned as the hawk winged away to eat its prey in privacy. Small feathers from the dove spiraled down into the earthen wound.

"Wow," said Jake. "That was fantastic."

I nodded, but it seemed to be an omen, more than anything else. The shade of the trees became pointedly cold.

"You know what I do for a living," he turned toward the house again, oblivious of my momentary pause. "What's this business you say you own?"

"I'm a licensed general contractor," I explained, while Rat walked at my heel, his nose nudging the palm of my hand. "You know, I'm sorry, but this is a really nice dog."

"Rat likes you, Maddie." He didn't bother to add that Rat probably didn't like Sophie as much.

"Animals always like me. I think it's because they sense I won't hurt them."

"Just wait until you meet a man who owns a dog *before* your relationship. Try and work that one out."

"I don't see it's an issue, unless the dog's a killer." I described my Uncle Mark's former hunting pack of pit bulls.

We reached the front of the house, and he walked me through, revealing the little touches the renovation had wrought, such as the refinished oak floors, old-growth Douglas fir beams, the beautiful stones of the fireplace, and its hand-carved mantel with a peculiar burl pattern in the redwood.

"Wow," I sighed. "This is a museum piece to me."

"I knew you'd really appreciate it, when you mentioned you're a contractor."

Now we could see the porch from the great room, which faced out toward the back of the house. Strains of *Jordu* filtered through the screens.

"Maddie," he spoke in that dam-buster voice once more.

Rat had followed us in, a polite, eager child, and it wasn't lost on Jake that his dog really took to me.

He shook his head vehemently.

"If the circumstances were different," he said cryptically.

"C'mon, it can't be that bad reaching forty," I said, deliberately misinterpreting his statement.

Sophie entered the house from the back door, and though she saw us together talking, she wasn't obviously threatened by me. She did note that Rat lay placidly on the floor by my feet.

"Oh, good," Sophie broke the moment. "Looks like you found someone to take your dog."

Jake turned toward her with the most vicious expression on his face, but Sophie, engrossed in sticking forty candles into the huge birthday sheet cake, missed the daggers entirely.

"I'm *not* giving Rat away," he spoke in a resonant voice.

"Now, Jacob, we'll talk about it later," she said, shoving him off. "Right now, you have to come out and let everyone sing *Happy Birthday* to you."

The candles blazed, having been lit by Sophie from the flame of a butane torch. She walked out the sheet cake backwards, cued to the first few bars of the song.

But Jake just stood there, glowering. When his eyes met mine, the smoldering fled, and he shrugged.

"I'm not giving Rat away," he repeated.

"Do you...maybe you want to go outside?" I asked, motioning to the screen door. I could hear the symphony of mismatched voices, some in tune, others wandering in a chromatic rush, but at least in sync to the lyrics, *Happy Birthday, dear Jacob...* "It *is* a public-domain song, after all."

"I owe her that," he assented through clenched teeth, and after taking a deep breath, headed out the door.

Rat wasn't having any of it. He simply lay on the floorboards, while I stroked his tufted head, and he gazed up at me with soft brown eyes that

151

said it all.

* * * *

For the remainder of the afternoon, Jake remained in proximity of the porch, and of the guests, and I had no other chance to speak candidly with him. That wasn't important, I told myself, because he had a very complex dynamic with Sophie, and I didn't want any part of it. I keep my life simple, and straightforward.

But in the car on the way home, Julie and Margot talked to me with a hint of sympathy in their voices.

"I know, I *know*," I grumbled. The gnarled limbs and dead snags on either side of the road seemed to be closing in on me. "Can't you just chalk it up to a bad mistake?"

"How long has Jake been with Sophie, Jules?" Margot asked.

"I don't know. Couple of years at the most." She sighed, because we were out of the hills, and headed down the straightaway toward Highway 85. Now the evening sky beckoned me from my funk.

"They're not married yet, Madeline," said Margot sagely. "I don't even think they're engaged."

"Oh, Margot," Julie scolded, "don't tell her that! A bond's a bond."

"She doesn't like his dog." I put it out there. "She wants him to get rid of Rat."

"I don't blame her," Julie wrinkled her nose. "That's a phenomenally hideous dog."

She glanced at me through her rear-view mirror, so I knew the comment was meant to measure my outrage, but I subsided into silence, and just brooded all the way home.

Once she rolled me to the curb in front of my house, Julie opened her window.

"You're no fun anymore, Maddie," she accused, winking. "Lighten up, will you?"

Margot got out, and hugged me close, then tweaked my nose. That's her way, ever since she was a toddler, always picking on me affectionately.

"He isn't married yet," she reiterated, whispering in my ear, but I only smiled bravely, and found my way back into the lonely cottage, as that is my home and my life.

11. Pulling the Wool

Just before a last-minute construction job in San Benito County, I happened to read about Mallory's case in the daily newspaper.

At six a.m., razing a maple old-fashioned and washing it down with coffee at an early opened donut house in Morgan Hill, I was reading the *San José Mercury News,* and it leaped out at me. The title was onerous: *Peninsula Woman Charged with Attempted Murder.* The article mentioned Mallory's full name, her profession, the San Mateo County Sheriff's version of the event, and the explicit reason for Mallory's near lethal act of self-defense.

And it also identified my sister's attacker—now her victim—a real-estate broker by the name of Jeffrey Clarence Donegan, and the position of his mother regarding what Mallory had accomplished.

"She attacked my son, and left him in a coma," Mr. Donegan's mother, Virginia Donegan, of Boyes Hot Springs, contends. *"Why didn't she call the police if she says Jeff was trying to rape her? That's not true, she just wanted to kill my son!"*

Mrs. Donegan went on to state that her son is no rapist, but rather, the victim of a "man-hating money-grubber."

"The police said they were familiar," Mrs. Donegan continued. *"Why would she try to kill him? I'll tell you why! It was all over a property they bought together!"*

I slammed the paper down, eliciting the shocked stare of the counter clerk.

"Sorry," I apologized. "I was...just trying to wake myself up," I lied, and then, I scratched the side of my nose.

Annoyed now, I hurriedly cleaned up the table, tucked the section of the paper with the article into my jacket (e.g., stole it), and left to drive out to the job site. With the printed quotes of Mrs. Donegan in my head, and the greasy aftertaste of the doughnut coating my throat, I knew I'd have a hell of a hangover tomorrow, as I intended to liquor-up once I arrived home that evening.

* * * *

The job was at a winery in San Martin, Tanner Valley Vineyards, quick changing their public toilets from decrepit half century-old water suckers, to low flow champions. According to the foreman who telephoned me, a woman by the name of Charlotte Burgess, the toilets, all eight of them, had already been delivered to the facility a week ago, and were simply awaiting my arrival with tools, plumber's tape, 1/2" water connectors, and wax rings.

"If you don't mind my asking, Ms. Burgess," I started.

"Call me Charlotte," she enjoined. "Both *Ms. Burgess* and *ma'am* make me feel oodles old."

"Charlotte, then," I amended. "How did you find out about me?"

"Oh, through an acquaintance of mine. Jacob Keene, he said you're a friend of his?"

"Aha, yes, Jake Keene!"

Oh, shit, I thought.

"He assures me you do excellent work, and that you have great taste in wine." I heard the shuffling of papers. "He mentioned that I should tell you the code word is *Rat*."

I laughed as a consolation, got the job, and headed out early in the morning to satisfy the faxed contract.

The winery was located at the end of a two-lane road, past farm fields greening with an unidentifiable crop, and backed up to a rise of tree-clad hills. The winery looked orderly, with an immense main house, undoubtedly used for weddings and other events, and surrounded by endless rows of emerald vineyards. The tops of trellises were mounted with strips of Mylar tape meant to chase off marauding birds, each streamer sparkling in the breeze. In the trembling morning light, it seemed contrived, almost a landscape in freeze-frame.

But Charlotte Burgess was definitely real. She met me at an access road blocked by a chained gate, which led the way to the rear of the facility. She was a tall, mannish woman with a sun-lined face and laughing eyes, seemingly on the verge of a joke or story, and confident in my purported abilities.

"Jake spoke highly of you," she repeated the yarn. "And how about this *Rat*?"

"His dog," I revealed, as I inspected the crated toilets. "Rat's the ugliest pooch you'll ever see, but his heart's in the right place."

Her own dog was a blue merle Australian Shepherd that sat in the cab of the winery truck, a magnificent specimen with flowing hair and alert posture.

"Well. He said you gave him a bottle of wine, and it was de-lish."

"I'm not an expert, I just know what I like."

"Pshaw! You're too modest." She patted the dog's head, stuck through the half-opened passenger window. "Come and see me in the office whenever you're done, sweetie."

Sweetie. I shook my head. If that had come from the lips of a man, I might have cringed, but in Charlotte's winsome voice, it sounded benign.

I finished in a couple of hours, and only because I had to locate the main water shutoff for the bathrooms. Once that'd been put down, the toilets were an easy change out. I cleaned up the job, heaping the old johns and hardware in the bed of my truck, destined for the dump, and headed out to find Charlotte.

The office was partitioned off inside the foyer of the main winery building, a structure of grand proportion. Built in 1958, the architect seemed to have blended Mission California with southern France, and still managed to come out of the mix looking classy.

At my step upon the tiled floor, Charlotte smiled up from her desk.

"I see you've finished."

There were neat stacks of papers in her work area, and a full bookshelf completely covering one wall. Since the office occupied a corner, two tall windows brought in the light and lushness of the vineyard-covered valley, with the occasional sharp flash of Mylar in the wind.

"Do you want to inspect it?" I asked, but she shook her head.

"So long as they flush effectively and don't leak, I'll take your word."

"Out of all due respect, that's...kind of contrary to my business practice, Charlotte."

"Dear, if you want me to sign off the job, I'm more than happy to. I'll worry about the rest."

I scuffled with my sensibilities, and then, let it go.

"You'll let me know if you encounter any problems, won't you?" I insisted.

"Of course." She slid the check over to me, and I wrote her out a receipt.

"There's something else," she said, and she rummaged in her desk, surfacing with a bottle of wine. "Complements of your friend." She handed me what appeared to be an elderly and very expensive bottle of 1979 Tanner Valley *Symmetry*, their version of a reserve red.

"From my friend?" I must have seemed baffled, so she gently reminded me.

"Jacob Keene."

"Ah. Well, thank you."

I drove home pretty unwound by the entire day. Not only was my sister being charged with attempted murder, following what seemed to be a hurried Grand Jury indictment, Charlotte Burgess didn't inspect my work, however flawless I knew it to be.

And now this bottle of wine...it was almost the same as that right punch I gave to Jesse Ibarra, and I still was at loose ends.

* * * *

When I reached home, following a dump run of the demolished toilets, more of the truth revealed itself to me, because there in front of my house sat Jacob Keene in a midnight-blue Eclipse, accompanied by Rat's ridiculous visage.

Without so much as glancing their way, I poked the automatic garage door button on my visor, and slid the work truck into its cubbyhole. Through my rear-view mirror, I could see Jake and Rat had emerged from the car, so I jabbed the button again, closing the door to all comers.

Once inside the house, I might have considered pretending they'd been a shady figment of my imagination, but Jake was determined to knock continuously on the front door until I chose to answer. Out of sheer curiosity, I relented, and opened it.

"Hi," I said cautiously, without forcing cheer, though I was discreet enough to refrain from pessimism.

"Hello." He pointed to the dog, waiting on the step politely. "Rat missed you."

"Did he tell you that?"

"Yes, indeed, Maddie, he's been sending me telepathic messages."

I laughed convulsively, my low-key gloom nearly defeated.

"You can both come in," I invited. "Want a drink? A glass of, gee, I don't know, some Tanner wine maybe?"

He slapped his leg. "So, you got the job, *and* the wine!"

"Sure did." I patted Rat, who lifted his lips in a grin, and then settled onto the edge of the rug, head on his paws. "I guess I'm supposed to thank you for both," I added with sincerity. "I have to tell you, though, I'm kind of not with it tonight."

His smile faded. "Why? What happened? Was the winery foreman difficult?"

"Oh, no, nothing like that, Charlotte was, well, to be frank, an easy lay."

He snorted at my descriptive.

"I have something for you to read, and then hopefully you'll understand. I'll be right back."

I left briefly for the truck, where I found the newspaper in my stowed jacket pocket, and carried it back to him. By that time, he'd already located a bottle of red wine in the bar (not the Tanner; I was saving that), and decanted it. Two glasses stood at the ready.

I opened the paper, and indicated the article.

He took the paper, and read carefully, while I poured out the wine. Taking a glass for myself, I settled into a chair, conscious that I was wearing my mucky work clothes, and hadn't yet showered, but at least the wine was a plus.

"Maddie," he said when he was through reading. He seemed to like to say my name.

"Yes?"

"This person, Mallory Benités. She's your sister, is that right?"

"Yes, the eldest. I picked her up from the Sheriff's department the night she assaulted that man, Donegan." I rubbed my hand across my eyes wearily. "Anyway, I've been thinking about it all day." I described finding the newspaper in Lombardo's, and how elements of the story had disturbed me.

He nodded thoughtfully. "And no one from law enforcement has spoken with you?"

"Oh, sure, I've talked with a couple of cops since that night, but not related at all to Mallory's problem." I went on to explain meeting Jesse Ibarra in JJ's, and Lt. Chappell's unannounced visit after Uncle Bill's train accident.

"Your life's been fairly busy in the last couple of months," he observed.

"That's why I was out on the pier that evening. I'd been working a remodel in Pacifica, dropped my crew back in Colma, and then found the pier on the bottom of Sharp Park." I shook my head. "My parents used to take us fishing near Pacifica in my dad's big-ass offshore boat. We'd launch at Pillar Point in Half Moon Bay, and head north. I swear, I'll never forget the smell of the harbor at low tide. I think there's a picture of me and my sisters in the dictionary, redefining *seasick*."

"Too bad. There's something appealing about the ocean."

"The ocean's fine, as long as my feet are on land."

"I never would've thought, Maddie, when you showed up on the pier, and agreed so candidly about my dog, that all that history was part of you."

"That's like everyone, you walk down the street, pass strangers, and they all have a history you'd never suspect."

"I suppose," he said, and frowned.

"What *were* you doing there that day, if you don't mind my asking?"

"Clearing my head," he said mysteriously. "I had a lot to think about." He smiled, his eyes gentle. "I'm happy you were out there, working off your nausea, or else we'd never have met."

"We *did* meet again, at your birthday party," I supplied.

"Yes, but the pier was special," he insisted.

"So." I'd finished the wine, and set down my glass. "How did you find me?"

"Did you know you're the only Maddie listed as a general contractor in Santa Clara County?"

"I don't believe you."

"Actually, I called Julie Fife, and asked for your name."

"And she *told* you? Can't trust the in-laws these days."

"No, Julie put your sister on the phone, and *she* told me where I could find you, she gave me your address and phone number."

I shook my head. "Margot's too crafty for her own good."

"That's what Margot said about you."

"Hah." I glanced at Rat, who'd fallen asleep on the floor, one of his ears twitching in a dream. "By the way, did you ever resolve the Rat issue with your girlfriend?"

He waved his hand. "No, it's still a sticking point with her."

I sighed, and hauled myself from the chair, carrying the empty wine glass to the kitchen.

Jake followed, and watched me in silence as I elaborately cleaned the glass, and set it into the dish rack.

"Did you have dinner yet?" he placed the snare.

"Jake." I tugged at my ponytail, aching for a shower, which meant I would have to turn this man out of my house. He'd already used Sophie in the present tense, and invariably, cheating-ass doesn't have much potential at everlasting.

"Rat doesn't mind waiting in the car." Maybe he thought he'd use the *love-me-love-my-dog* persuasion.

"I wouldn't do that to Rat. I wouldn't do that to Sophie, either."

He nodded slowly. "I see."

"Don't get me wrong, I appreciate the referral, I know I'll enjoy the wine, and it's good to see your dog...well, and you too, I admit, but I don't know you. I don't enjoy hidden agendas."

He raised his brows.

"I like you, Maddie," he told me softly. "If that means just being friends, I guess I can handle that."

"Well, I *can't*," I said quickly.

"Like you said, you don't know me."

"And you don't know me," I countered.

"What better way to get to know someone, than by simply taking the step?"

I then remembered something my father had said many years ago, about his relationship with my mother.

With you, Moira, I get to have my cake and eat it too.

I didn't know what he meant at the time, but I was wise enough to use Dad's comment as a tool for the moment.

"Look, you either have your cake or you eat it, but you can't have it both ways."

"I get your metaphor," he said. "Would you want to go out and just get a bite? As friends? I'm not implying anything else, Maddie."

I studied his face for a moment trying to decipher his intent, but I was too damn blinded by the light.

Not trying to keep your options open? I thought.

I squinted. "Just give me fifteen minutes."

* * * *

And that is how I embarked on an initially platonic, and intellectually passionate relationship with Jacob Keene.

Following a late dinner, we came back to my place and split the bottle of Tanner wine. As I suspected, it was pretty good, although I'm not a *sommelier*, more of a blue-collar wine drinker, I can generally discriminate between fruity crap and a sincere dry red, and this one was age-refined.

We must have talked until three a.m., and then Jake fell asleep on my foldout sofa bed.

My rare, mean-spirited side lulled me to sleep, assuming how he'd feel in the morning, quieted by the fact that he'd ache for the next twenty-four hours, a penance applied toward the man's redemption. This was destined to become a familiar emotional dance for me, a love/hate thing for Jake, pitying Sophie, and then despising her for the lung-clenching grasp she had on the man. But blame myself? That stewed for a long time, before I took responsibility for any of it.

* * * *

I could forecast Jake Keene's appearance on my doorstep with more thorough science than a meteorologist's satellite. On a steady basis, usually three times each week, I'd arrive home from a job or the store to find the Eclipse parked on the street containing the man and dog. Eventually that graduated to Jake parking along one side of my narrow driveway, as though he were so privileged; and if the weather were good, seated in the yard with Rat sniffing about.

He even developed a place in the house to put his keys, inside of a drink glass on the bar counter. I suppose this makes for a quick getaway, when you know where your keys are at all times.

We spoke about many subjects. I can't even keep track, though we avoided mention of Sophie. For all practical purposes, I knew he went back to her when he left me, and I think that's what lent us the aversion to sleeping together. I know it was a huge deal for me.

The closest we ever came was one evening when we'd gone bowling.

I never bowl, but there we were, rolling those scarred, hired bowling balls down the shining maple lanes in our rental shoes, drinking Blue Moon, and laughing it up in a brilliant portrayal of your everyday couple. Somehow, I managed to beat him, outscoring him three-to-one, though he was really trying, or at least, gave the impression that he cared about winning.

When we arrived at my place, I must've said something witty, as he grabbed me up in his arms, hugging me close. For a moment, we stared at each other, maybe three inches between his lips and mine. I was the first to back off, laughing about it. But though it was the first time, it wasn't the only time. Every time he arrived, it was more and more difficult not to give in.

Don't get me wrong. I wanted to go a lot further. If it weren't for

Sophie in Ben Lomond, and my own malicious sense of humor, I would have. I *would* have.

But I was content with what we had. Sometimes we sat around the house, comfortable, but with the unspoken sexual question lurking. He would work on his laptop while I finished paperwork, and sent out bids. His body reckoned to the sofa bed, the way muscles find familiarity to a certain workout, they adapt. I had nothing to quiet my urge for revenge, and all he had was plain honesty.

* * * *

While I was playing with fire, Mallory was sitting in it, straight out of the frying pan, because Jeffrey Clarence Donegan, relegated to the definition of *brain dead,* was allowed to pass on.

Two weeks after Mallory had been arraigned on attempted murder charges, Donegan's mother authorized doctors to remove her son from life support. As the *Merc* stated, once Donegan died, two events were set into motion—his organs saved five dying people, and my sister, Mallory Marie Benités, was charged with murder.

Marie is the French version of the Blessed Mother, but Mallory's saint name is a misnomer, having never lived by the rules of the Church. I have come to believe that my eldest sister has a buried side, ruthless and premeditated, even self-serving. Her occasional dedication to community service, as in her donated self-defense training of battered women in San Mateo County, complies with an agenda to forward her career.

I visited Mallory, the first time since I confronted her about Jesse Ibarra, as he stood there, naked beneath the plaid college robe. Set loose on a twenty-five-thousand-dollar bond (the amount of which Virginia Donegan hotly protested to the San Mateo County D.A.'s office), Mallory was home, her work schedule thinned by the attrition her so-called crime weighed upon her clientele.

She was happy to see me, hugging me tightly, but when I studied her face, there was stress etched as fine lines and dark circles. No hope for peace, or reconciliation to the future, now that Donegan was officially deceased.

The first thing I asked was if she'd retained a lawyer.

"Jesse found me an attorney who handles cases for cops," she said.

"Is that good?" I peered into her face, and she waved me away impatiently.

"I trust Jesse. And I have to trust the lawyer."

"Cops are almost always exonerated simply because they're cops," I said, recalling Dad's smart-alecky tone, and parroting it. "You're just an everyday person, Mallory, the law treats you differently, worse even."

My sister, the perennial drama queen, rose out of her chair, and walked in a circle around the living room.

"God, Maddie, stop being such a prick!" she protested, hands pressed to her temples.

"I'm being realistic. If that means I'm a prick, just wait for the prosecution to make its case."

She paused, and then settled into her chair again.

"What's this about buying property with Donegan?" I asked, referring to the news article.

"I didn't buy any property with that man," she shook her head. "I never even knew about him until he showed up at the gym, and started stalking me."

"Well, his mother seems to think you tried to kill him because you wanted the property put in your own name."

"Maddie, I didn't fucking know him!" she cried.

"Yeah, just try *that* with a jury."

"Maddie," she said reproachfully.

"Have you even looked at your loan papers?" I persisted.

"I went through every page on the day I signed them at the title company. And my lawyer's been over them, too. He told me he's subpoenaed the title company's records."

I believed her. Mallory has always been a stickler for details.

I unrolled the article, now in a plastic sheet protector, because it had become dog-eared.

"Did you see this in the paper?" I asked, handing it to her, but though she held it in her hand, she barely glanced at it. "Maybe you'd want to give it to your attorney," I suggested.

"I will."

"And have him *really* research the property title, Mallory, I think there may be something wrong with the transaction." I scratched my head. "You *sure* you didn't know this man?"

"Madeline." She grabbed my wrist so tightly that on the following day, there was a bruise where her fingers met her thumb. "I didn't know the man, we never socialized, we never dated, and we never bought property together!"

"Then why," I continued, extricating myself from her grip, "why was Donegan even there?"

She hesitated. That second of indecision forged my doubt for my sister, no matter her candor. Prevaricating corners the criminal, and I figured, *Wow, she's guilty, she's really guilty.*

And when my face reflected my skepticism, she asked me to leave, using her middle finger to send it home.

"Don't forget to tell your lawyer what I mentioned," I was rambling, as she assisted me across the threshold with one good shove, closing the door firmly in my face.

* * * *

I was halfway home, when I remembered the photographs I'd taken of Mallory's bruises the night of the assault, when she slept in my bed, and I writhed on my foldout sofa. By the time I reached the house (complete with the Eclipse, canine and dog's best friend), I figured to look at the photos, before I burned them onto a CD and mailed it off to Mallory anyway.

But Jake's presence caught me off guard.

"There you go, that serious look again," he accused, so unnaturally, I buried my issues with Mallory for the evening. No sense putting forth my worst side with personal problems.

I beamed. "Is this better?"

"Great!"

He sniffed the air as soon as he entered the house. He always did this, I think as an unconscious reflex, but I was constantly afraid the house would reek of shit or garbage. My vapid fears dissolved, as he would announce what he could smell.

"Mmm, sun-dried firewood and clean laundry."

"You say the same thing every time. Don't you ever smell anything else?"

"Well, if you'd been cooking...."

"Good luck to that," I dismissed with a snort, as I rarely ever cook, and then I might make a sandwich, which involved no activity whatsoever with the stove.

I then made a stupid mistake.

"How does it smell in Ben Lomond?" I asked.

I'd found a diet cola in the bar fridge, and was seated on the sofa with my feet propped rudely on the coffee table. But hell, it's *my* coffee table.

"Hmm," he said, and I could tell he was waffling. Rat seemed to sense a rise in tension, and sought out the kitchen floor a good twenty feet west of our conversation.

"Go on," I urged, taking a swig on the cola, as though downing liquor to gird my strength.

"It always smells like something delicious to eat," he said, in the tone one uses while reflecting upon a cherished memory. "Perhaps...I don't know, apple pie, or roast. Sometimes I can name the herbs she uses on the chicken."

"Who, your housekeeper?" I inquired boldly, asshole that I am.

"Why, no, Sophie," he replied. "She's an outstanding chef."

"Huh. And here I thought she was just a lawyer."

He eyed me, perhaps in a vain attempt to seem nonjudgmental, but since I was deliberately trying to be uncouth, I incorrectly supposed he was having a difficult time not feeling irked toward me.

Therefore, the next utterance completely threw me.

"Make love to me, Maddie," he coaxed softly. "I've been wanting you for such a long time."

Either I was hallucinating, or his dark eyes really were soft and filled with desire. He even placed himself on the sofa next to me, so I could get a feel of his erection against my hip.

Now, I don't generally think a man would be so bold, but I'm sure I'd given him plenty of reason to believe I wanted to sleep with him in the last few weeks, though I didn't see how he could misunderstand my signals of the moment. I surely had no reason to want to sleep with him, with the specter of *Sophie* whirling about the room, complete with a cast iron skillet designed to take down a choice rib-eye steak, and subdue it into a work of culinary ecstasy.

His face was buried in my neck, and I was sorely tempted. God bless Sophie and her will to endure what this man was dishing out.

I pushed him away from me, grunting as I hefted him back. With a twist of my body, I leaped off the sofa, and rubbed off the sensation of whatever he'd left behind from my neck.

"Jesus Christ!" I swore, and using that as an expletive is no casual feat. "Jesus Christ, Jake!" once more, only this time, adding his name for effect.

"I need you, Maddie," he said, standing up to possible defeat.

"Why, Jake?" I held up my hands, to demonstrate how this perplexed me. "Why?"

A fatal error, perhaps.

"Because, I'm in love with you," he claimed, knowing that would be the last thing to say if you expect cooperative, recreational ass. That phrase subjugates the other person, especially if they've been secretly clamoring for it. "You're different from any other woman I've ever known," he stupidly elaborated. Yes, all cliché but designed to bag the prize.

"Jake." I sighed, and hung my head. "You and I are not meant to be...doing what you're implying."

"Oh, I didn't imply, Maddie, I said it, I goddamn *said* it!" he declared in a flash of passion.

I held up one hand. "I didn't think that was part of our deal."

He grasped my upheld hand to remove the barrier, and his arms drew me close.

"Maddie," he said my name tenderly. "I don't know what I'd do without you."

I was thinking I knew *who* he'd do without me, but I resisted the urge, and in my clumsy, erudite style, I gave in. Word by whispered word I was transformed from this unrefined woman with a tendency to secretly brood, into an articulate, graceful *inamorata,* my wicked edge momentarily sheathed.

* * * *

I'll tell you how lame my family is, and how our awkward humor is a genetically inherited tendency. We are self-amused. We believe we're witty, but we'd fall far painfully short of being able to hold our own in stand-up comedy. Grandpa Feliz, Hawaiian-born, enjoys giving everyone his standard greeting of *Hawaii-ya!*, while my mother's favored literary source is *The Complete Works of Laura Ingalls Wilder.*

As children, we historically bypassed opportunities to vacation at Disneyland, in exchange for enthralling daytrips to the California Academy of Sciences, Exploratorium, or the Tech Museum of Silicon Valley.

The telling point in our family history is highlighted by an event from Margot's *Sweet Sixteen* birthday party.

Of our immediate family, Margot is singularly sophisticated, an inveterate socializer (not to be confused with *party girl,* Mallory's deadly trait), who owns the stamina for whirlwind carousing. In her adult life, it's the strength that keeps Margot's clientele infatuated with her, while she punishes them with highly opinionated leftist political intrigue. In summary, she can persuade an inhibited wallflower to dance fanatically all night.

At first, the premise of Margot's birthday bash contained potential. An enormous gymnasium-sized hall was rented at the Sunnyvale Community Center. Three hundred of Margot's school friends and acquaintances were invited, with most inclined to attend.

Dad, being a professional musician marked by a penchant to hoard professional-level equipment, brought in a sound system that included subwoofers in near-unmanageable cabinets that stood taller than Margot's diminutive height of four-foot-eleven. An A-frame mounted with stage lights was borrowed from one of Dad's musician allies. Miranda was enlisted as the emcee and disc jockey, supplied with CDs representative of the latest and greatest in the techno-dance genre. Great platters of food were ordered and delivered.

And then, disaster, as Miranda, predisposed to a law-enforcement mentality at age twenty, utilized such words in her emcee vocabulary as *latent* and *superfluous*. Although Margot's endless friends weren't exactly uneducated, Miranda's selective idiom put a damper on what would normally be an upward spiral of dance energy and party fever.

But nothing could be worse than Mom and Dad, who interrupted the feverish libations of revelers with their interpretation of *Pearly Shells*.

Imagine the unlikely pairing of Mitchell and Moira Benités, offering two-part harmony, Dad on a ukulele, and Mom's rhythmic Powwow-step, her unconscious manner of counting out the meter as she sings. They wore rayon Hawaiian shirts to really drive home the performance, misty-eyed as Margot, forced to sit before them in a community center chair, set her face into stoic lines, while within, she fumed.

My sister's frustration was made all the more impotent by the reasoning that our parents were singing as their sentimental gift to Margot, who, as a three-year-old, once stood on a similar stage at a family function, and sashayed to that very song.

The last straw was Miranda's gushing praise, once the performance had been agonizingly fulfilled. Did she use words like *amazing* or *sensational*? Rather, Miranda, clapping energetically, said that our parents' presentation had been *prodigious*.

How fucking socially inept we all are. And yet, I wouldn't change anything. We are family-oriented to a fault, busybodies in one another's lives, elated by triumph, and soothing lament.

Which makes my transgression all the more incredible, that I could wean myself from the moral teachings of our matriarchy, a family where women tend the flame, handle the family finances, and watch out for one another's back. What was I winning by losing myself, by trading in right for wrong?

* * * *

And there I lay in my lover's arms, content, until I awoke and began to stir. Only then, did the outside world intrude, the reality of *Mallory* and *Sophie*, as though I'd neglected the inner strength at my command. I was as steadfast as a field of mustard in full bloom, sprung up from tiny seeds, yet plucked dry, flowers and sprigs, by the elders who consume the leaves, and pass this cultural food along to their descendants. Leave behind the hunt, and there remains the will to gather.

I have eaten the bitter greens, embracing their flavor, their bright hue captured at the moment of boiling, suspended in time, as if to say that life extends past death, defying its reality. But the truth is, though Uncle Mark killed the lion, I dug the grave, shovelful by shovelful, hiding the corpse beneath winter's grass, subdued with lime, and sealed by the fear of discovery. My guilt by association is just as unshakable as my faith portends.

* * * *

My father paid a visit, and thankfully, it was one of Jake Keene's off nights, when I was alone with Grandpa Feliz's antique phonograph, and an old vinyl recording of Joe Pass and Ella Fitzgerald I'd been gifted by Dad.

"You have good taste in music, Maddie," was my father's first comment, after kissing me. Then, "You have a brother."

I made us both drinks to stave off the shock. Bourbon and cola over ice, evil companions that suggest a medicinal quality, as they combine into a malevolent toxin that slowly seeps through your veins. But it did shield the blow, as side-by-side, we read the lab's DNA results: *99.9% paternal probability.*

"So, there it is," I said.

"Yup," Dad agreed.

We acted so casually, a fatalistic mood, as though we'd already known, and it'd been only a matter of official decree.

"There'll be hell to pay, you know, Dad," I noted. "Mallory's in love with him." But I wouldn't say Jesse Ibarra's name.

"The way I see it, Madeline, no matter what the test indicates, he's not my son. He was raised by his real father, a man with a different set of rules and someone else's culture. I have four daughters, and that's all that matters."

We drank our ill-tasting concoctions, and then we talked lightly about immaterial subject matter, *minutiae,* my father calls it. That was the buffer to save our wretched souls.

I didn't ask about Mom. They were not commonly parted, but I didn't want details. All I wanted to believe was that the moment my father left this house, he would be back beside his wife, and the world would go on turning.

* * * *

Kevin Gerard telephoned to hire me for another entry door installation. This one included leaded-glass sidelights and a fanlight, and was built out of expensive stain-grade mahogany.

"Who the heck buys these things?" I marveled.

"Los Altos Hills," he elaborated, which explained it all.

I arrived at the job site at nine-twenty on a Friday morning, ten minutes ahead of schedule. At the top of a very long, asphalt driveway, Kevin had assembled his sawhorses, and was laying out tools, when he saw my rig.

I've never witnessed a man, any man, jump up so fast and run to me, even Jake Keene. But there it was, Kevin limping up to my truck with a huge grin and waving one gloveless hand.

I opened the passenger window, and regarded him dubiously.

"What's got you all juiced-up this morning?" I asked.

"Yo, Maddie, I'm in a good mood, so you'd better be, too."

He leaned on the sill of the opened window, and smiled at me for a good count of ten, and then, slapping the door, took off to resume his layout.

Nearly two hours were required to fit the door and its accouterments, and then we were merely waiting for the stucco patch to set, and admiring the entryway that almost qualified as an art piece. I helped Kevin clean up the work area, and then there was nothing left to do, except wait for my pay.

I sat in my truck, while Kevin settled with the homeowner. When he returned, that big grin still on his face, at least he had a check to comfort me with.

He stood, this time, on the driver's side, and passed me the check in an envelope.

"Aren't you even going to look, Maddie?" he asked, squinting behind his sunglasses.

"When I get home," I assured, tucking the envelope into my jacket. "Why, did you rip me off or something?"

"No," he said, and grinned. "I'm not that stupid."

"That's debatable," I joked, winking.

"Let's go eat," he said, without waiting for me to agree. That's been our way, our friendship, so I followed his truck down the driveway, and toward flatlands.

He took me to lunch at a Mexican restaurant in Los Altos, where even in our rough clothes, we were graciously served. Over a basket of chips and salsa, Kevin gave me the news, which I supposed could be construed as good or bad, depending which side you're on.

"I'm moving to Astoria," he said, and gave me that dazzling grin.

"Where's Astoria?" I asked, working on a Corona.

"In Oregon, right on the mouth of the Columbia River, just across the shore from Washington State."

"What made you decide to move up there, Kev?"

"There's a lady."

From his chest pocket, he withdrew an envelope of photographs, and set them on the table like a deck of cards.

One by one, I studied the photos, eye candy to a contractor. This was proof of work in progress on a tri-colored Victorian house tiptoed in a row of other similar antique homes, yet glowing with the work Kevin had already committed.

"How often...when did you start?" I set the photo stack before him.

"Six months ago, and I've put in every free moment I could get," he admitted.

"Is this the *lady* you mentioned?"

"Right on," he said dreamily. "She's a beautiful old girl, built around 1900. I got her on the cheap, Maddie." His insistence in referring to the house as a female entity amused me.

"What are you going to do, sell it?"

"Eh, not sure yet. I'm gonna live in her for a while and see what happens."

I was amazed this man had fallen in love, and *hard*, for a mere house, but was acting contrary about his feelings. Scooping up the photos once more, I had to agree the house was a beautiful thing, elegant and elaborate. I imagined Kev working his way skyward on scaffolds to detail the exterior, or replace the windows. Although I'm not necessarily acrophobic, the uphill angle of street side photos made me flinch thinking of climbing spider-like up the face of that house.

A thought struck me.

"What about your roommate?" once more passing him back the photos.

"Who, Jeanine?"

"Yeah, your lawyer-girlfriend."

"She's getting married in June," he said evenly, so I guess that didn't bother him.

"But she still lives with you?"

"She did until two months ago. Go figure. But once she found the guy, we stopped sleeping together."

"I'm sure that's a comfort to her fiancée," I said sarcastically. "So, when are you leaving?"

"In three weeks. I already sold my house in San José. It's in escrow, and now it's just a matter of packing up and shipping out. And I got my Oregon general contracting license."

"Well, I might come up and visit you, if you have a spare bedroom."

When we were done and parted ways, and I was on the freeway heading south, I pondered Kevin's unrealized ardor for the Victorian, which readily eclipsed Duke Snead's River Street prize. Measured abreast, Kevin's elegant devotion made Duke's hick gusto seem like a cheap fling. Even my own Santa Clara bungalow hadn't elicited enough passion to anthropomorphize its character. In my line of work, I'd stood witness to countless clients who expressed candid affection for their homes, whose eyes lit up like a sex-junkie once the makeover was complete.

I know it's a strange emotion, but I felt at that moment sort of envious of Kevin, compounded in degrees exponentially greater than I ever experienced toward Sophie Whipple. I wanted that intensity, to be fired-up and soaring high, falling into the arms of the greatness of the inanimate which will never let you down, and never disappoint.

12. Whatever it Takes

I'm not often prone to visitors, lacking certain gregarious tendencies. I'm not lacking a place to entertain, it's just that, aside from myself, I perceive this house I own reaches out to no one else, and in that unshakable belief, I have one solid thing that keeps the faith.

My house, circa 1916, a cheerless epoch for America, was built in the Agnew neighborhood served by the little turn of the century train depot, which is still located on a strip of stony earth along Bassett Street, and fronted by the pitiful ornamental pears. Inside of the depot's walls, which have settled to fit the shape of the ground where it stands, is the California Central Model Railroad Club, members who built a stupendous layout complete with folded dog-bone rail line. This was one of those forays that stood in lieu of Disneyland, and that's why I know it's locked in there.

The streets in my neighborhood are wide, remnants of a horse-and-buggy era. Sidewalks didn't exist until the 1980s, when the city swallowed the edge of each property with a network of concrete walkways over patches of earth worn smooth by shoes and tires. But, like everything else about this charming community, sidewalks were long before my earthly time.

Up and down the asphalt stretch of my particular block, children ride bicycles and play along the tracks, laying out coins for the freight trains to stamp into lustrous ovals. We did this in our day, accompanied by our father, who, with one hand, would indicate a train churning southbound from the Alviso curve, its headlamp burning unmistakably in broad daylight. With care not to slip on the rails or catch a foot between ties, Dad set out a penny for each of his girls along the humming rail, while we crouched beside him. We then lit out for the sound wall, which had been raised as symbolic demarcation between our humble blue-collar neighborhood, and the towering upscale townhouses crane-necking on the opposite side. When the freight had thundered past, we would find our prizes, rendered smooth, and holding brief heat from such tremendous friction. To this day, the deep reverberation of passing trains brings to mind these burnished treasures.

When at age 19, I moved out of my parents' house and installed myself in my first (and last) apartment in south San José I discovered among my things a ceramic box of distorted coins, a testament to hoarding the memories of a sharply defined childhood.

The house was a beaten shack when I bought it. The previous owner neglected it out of financial necessity, and had lived and died within its walls. His name was Gus Wenstad. A widower and former maintenance worker at National Semiconductor, Gus had been retired for twenty years, and afflicted with insulin-dependent type 2 diabetes. Apparently by the end, Gus was fed up with his insulin, because he simply stopped injecting, and died of a glucose overload.

His granddaughter, a schoolmate of mine from Wilcox High, who had gone on a Sunday to visit her Gramps, discovered Gus. As Amy Wenstad related, it appeared that Gus, exhausted due to starvation at the cellular level, had simply crawled into bed to sleep, and never awakened.

The family had wanted to put the house on the market, but it was twice a pariah - so ramshackle that it would take a bulldog of a contractor to fix it, and marred by cradling Gus Wenstad's passing inside its walls. Amy, knowing I was neither lazy nor squeamish, contacted me first to gauge my interest. After a walk-through with the family, I made an offer I figured was fair, two hundred thousand. I landed a loan, and the house became mine.

Much effort was required to right its wrongs, but it was work I was more than willing to embrace as the house's caretaker. There were serious problems. The foundation needed reinforcing, the plumbing and wiring were outdated, and for months, I continued to find used syringes. I'd rip out a carpet, and there'd be a syringe, stuck alongside the tack strip. When I gutted the kitchen, there were syringes lying in the rear of cabinets, and even inside the pan storage drawer of the Wedgwood gas stove. No wonder Gus got sick of injecting, the damned syringes were just about popping out of the woodwork, and a real hassle to dispose of.

Amy's comment, when I shared with her the finished restoration of the house, was "It's a show piece, Maddie." And then, "You could sell it for three times what you bought it for." Kind of wistfully, as though she wished she'd been in on the deal.

I vowed to Amy that I'd never sell. The house with its offbeat history, and Gus Wenstad's windbag of a ghost, has grown on me. There are moments when I drag my ass home, completely burned out from a job, and there it is, the resurrected, peculiar bungalow with a fitted front porch, and planter boxes that in good weather, are filled with *vinca,* droopy and colorful. The cold winter nights are soothed with real wood fire, and in the blistering heat of summer, when the neighbor kids are shooting each other with water cannons, central air conditioning (or *AirCon,* if you're a true Filipino) is my repose.

If Kevin is in the honeymoon stage with his Astoria beauty, then me and this bungalow are old married folk. I withstood *giddy,* and went straight to *geek,* complete with wooden shutters, butter-yellow walls, eight-hundred thread-count sheets, and a ceramic cache of train-stamped pennies, imprinted with a child's tribute to her father.

* * * *

Grandma Enida and Grandpa Feliz had been to my place only once. This was in the early days, when I needed help plotting the yard, and my grandparents equated that with farming. They carried seedling *sili,* which are sweet peppers, and tomato plants, in the trunk of their chugging 1973 Mercedes. There was a basket of spiny *sayote* fruit, over-wintered in the cool of their garage, and now split with the promise of a living sprout. Those dragon eggs grew into vast mats of foliage that draped across my fence, adorned with more of the prickly meat-stew fruit than I could ever hope to enjoy.

I had set down pavers, and the only viable soil bordered the fence, and this is where they planted. Shamefully, I'm not a willing cook, because those were the best tomatoes I've ever tasted. Sometimes I would just stand there in the yard, eating them sun-warmed and directly off the vine after rubbing the dust specks on my shirt. Most of the produce went to my neighbors, a Mexican couple with four children, who delighted in the peppers and tomatoes. Perplexed by the *sayote*, I found a Filipino woman in my parents' neighborhood who welcomed the bristled fruit.

This, then, would mark the second time my grandparents paid me a visit.

Let me state you do not wait for your elders to come to you; you go to them first. Countless times I have been at the home where my father was raised (though having moved thrice before settling in their chosen Sunnyvale neighborhood, due to Grandma Enida's call to better her family, and wisely ignoring Grandpa Feliz's predictable *money grumble*). Here is the unconscious honor the younger generation bestows upon parents and grandparents, mobility to their doorstep as a sign of respect. You do it, because you see your parents doing it for their parents, and we expect to teach this to our children.

Therefore, when my grandparents rolled up, I knew there must be a significant reason.

On a Sunday, I was idling on the porch, reading the morning paper, and drinking coffee. I do not begin my day without coffee. The fragrance is designed for dependency, though it's an addiction I wholeheartedly embrace. An entire American sub-culture has been created around the redolence of the brew, corporations reaping billions and employing a multitude of blissful coffee stoners who cheerfully foster succeeding generations of caffeine-addled druggies.

They had driven their older car, the vehicle not stolen by Uncle Miles. That contraband had been a flashier, more streamlined late-model Mercedes, one the elders refer to as *Class-A Number-1*. They pile into luxury sedans, and zip off to Reno, or in these civilized times, a California Indian casino.

Grandpa Feliz, to spite the sport version he shined each morning before my grandparents departed for McDonald's, made a point to hang onto the 1973 coupe, with a carburetor and seldom-used air conditioning. The coupe reminds me of a miniature version of an American classic, but German-engineered, whitewalls fresh against the tire-blacked rubber.

"Grandma, Grandpa," I greeted them. I met them at the bottom of the porch steps once the initial shock of actually seeing them had released me.

My grandmother handed me a container cradled in a plastic grocery bag, hanging heavily like dangling *sayote*.

"I brought you *giné-ta-an*," said Grandma, "made just today."

"Oooh." I smiled in anticipation, which pleased Grandma. I could feel the faint heat through the plastic bag of the stove-warm dessert, made with a base of sweet rice and coconut milk. I anticipated the sweet-rice dumplings Grandma included in her standard version.

"Did you eat yet? Can I get you some coffee?" I asked, leading them up the steps.

Grandma laughingly mentioned they'd had their breakfast visit to McDonald's, but Grandpa said he'd take his coffee inside the house, so I hustled the newspaper indoors, to prevent the wind from picking it up and dragging it down the street.

I placed the *giné-ta-an* on the kitchen counter, and brought my grandfather a cup of hot coffee.

Grandma got right down to business, after first making herself comfortable in a chair.

"We are here to give you the car, Madeline."

From the purse she clutched tightly, she withdrew the title paper to the '73 Mercedes, and I received it gratefully, though I knew I'd probably be clobbered with a huge fix-it bill. The symbolism was as ripe as those thorny fruit that kept hitting me in the head during the height of the growing season.

"Thank you, Grandma; thank you, Grandpa." I kissed them, careful not to spill Grandpa's cup. "But don't you need the car?"

"No more!" Grandpa Feliz complained. "Your Grandma made me buy another car."

"With the insurance money," Grandma Enida interjected, so that I would know the whole story. My grandfather, monetarily frugal as a byproduct of the War, could outright win the lottery, and still haggle over a few pennies for the price of a pound of fruit at the local farmer's market.

"You bought another car?" I asked, after securing the pink slip to a magnetic clip on the refrigerator. This, so I would not overlook transferring the title.

"Your Daddy bought the car," said Grandma, sending my mind reeling in another direction completely.

I paused. Did she mean to say *your Grandpa,* because I could swear she just mentioned my father.

"My Dad bought a car for you?" I asked carefully.

"Sure," Grandma smiled brightly. "He drove me and your Grandpa to the Mercedes dealer, and she bought the car from him, he paid the balance after the insurance money. And then she drove us home, and I told him we can no longer keep two cars, and that she should take the old Mercedes. But your Daddy said to give it to Madeline, because she said that you like old things."

Forsaking my grandmother's loosely utilized pronouns, it was a marvelous story.

I nearly laughed out loud. "Old things." I felt the words in my mouth, and then, thinking the phrase. It *was* true. I did like "old things," this house as the prime example. And my truck, it was by no means new, having been manufactured in the year before my birth. I suppose it could be defined as "old." And look at Grandpa's ancient record player, faithfully turning vintage vinyl discs for the pleasure of my ears. Then, there was this affair with Jacob Keene, he was forty, so would he be considered "old" in ratio to my "youth?"

As I ruminated, I must have been making a weird facial expression, because Grandpa nudged me.

"Madeline is having a stroke," he teased.

"I'm okay, Grandpa," I assured, "I'll save the stroke for when I get the estimate to fix the car," I added, and everybody laughed at that.

"Just don't get a stroke when you drive us home, Madeline," Grandma said solemnly.

* * * *

I had decided to pressure wash and repaint my fence. Dusty spider webs clung in the joints, and a layer of silt had built up at the top of the kick board.

Wearing a pair of earplugs and eye protection, I meticulously removed dirt, webbing and old paint, until the fence was prepped for a fresh coat of paint stain, that earthy green I preferred, a shade lighter to compliment the dirt-green of the house. I leaned over to shut off the compressor, when I spied Mallory out of the corner of my eye seated on the porch swing—which I'd repainted a week ago, the same preferred color—and watching me intently for any gaps in my shield.

"Mallory!" I squeaked, nearly dropping the nozzle onto the pavers. Instead, I popped out the earplugs, pushed back the goggles, and joined her on the seat.

"Maddie." She opened her arms, holding me close. "I missed you."

We rocked to-and-fro, the chains jingling, chime of a more familiar time, when our father had installed a jumbo hammock between two trees on the back lot of the Susanville property. That was in theory an excellent place to laze away the drowsy hours of hot summer afternoons. The wind would nudge the hammock back and forth while the hardware clinked, and we girls lay four-to-a-row, motionless. We didn't care if we sweated, we just watched clouds sail across an azure sky between gaps in the pines, languid and companionable, until we noticed the first of a horde of carpenter ants and assorted spiders that made their way across our unassuming bodies.

Only then I saw Jesse Ibarra standing near the alley, as though poised for a quick getaway. I made a point to smile and wave, a peace gesture, but he only nodded once with his chin.

I turned to my sister, who seemed gaunt behind the bug-eye

sunglasses.

"Do you want some coffee?" I asked, pushing off of the swing and standing.

"Sure, all right." She smiled wanly.

"Come inside," I invited, and Mallory followed through the back door, but Jesse lingered in the yard, walking the squared lengths of the fence, and exaggerating his interest in its water-blasted appearance.

"How are things?" I asked, now alone with Mallory in the kitchen, as I put together the makings of a pot of coffee.

"Pretty good," she said, nodding. "Jesse got an email from the testing lab," she went straight to the issue.

"Yeah, I heard about that. But I don't think it matters too much to Dad."

"He said that."

"You talked to Dad?"

"He came up to the house with Mom. They brought a whole watermelon, and Mom baked a cake." She smiled. "You know how Dad likes Mom's cakes."

With you Moira, I get to have my cake and eat it too.

"It's a metaphor," I broke, suddenly understanding the cryptic statement.

"The cake's a metaphor?" Mallory was puzzled.

"For greater things," I reasoned aloud. "For love." I shrugged.

"Well, anyway, Mom's cake was good. It always is."

"I know," I agreed, but I wasn't speaking of the cake Mom had baked and left for Mallory. I had a revelation about the condition of my parents. To Dad, our mother is sustenance, the air he breathes, the beating of his heart. That his life is complete due to loving one woman creates an island of uniqueness to the man.

I shook my head to refocus.

"Tell me, how are things going?" I asked.

"Not too good," she conceded. "They could be better. The D.A. is pushing my lawyer for a plea deal."

"That's because the D.A. can't win this case," I said defiantly. "Don't make a deal with them, Mallory."

"I was considering it."

"Absolutely not!" I grasped her hand; she squeezed back. "That's how cops and finks work. It's just business to them."

I paused, because our biological half-brother had taken a seat on the swing chair, and I'd defined Jesse as one of the untouchables.

"My lawyer won't plead me out without my cooperation. But he says he's having a difficult time proving it was self-defense."

"Of course it was!" This was starting to rile me up. "I saw your bruises, the scrapes on your face, that cut on your lip. Nobody gets those from just standing there."

"Oh, *that*," she said in an apologetic tone. "I staged those, Maddie."

The coldest wave pierced me.

"What do you mean? How could you stage them?"

"With a rock and a stick. I placed them in his hands afterward to get his prints on them, before I called the cops."

"Mallory!"

"I *had* to, Maddie, he was going to kill me. He had...*intent*."

"Does Jesse know about any of this?"

"No, he's never been in on any of my meetings with the attorney."

I staggered to my feet, and poured out the coffee, but an awful feeling of unease had descended on me.

"Mallory," I whispered, and I took my seat. "How did you manage to get anyone to even believe that it was Donegan's idea to attack you in your carport? That he wasn't coerced by you?"

"I don't know!"

She impatiently stood, and paced around in front of me, a caged tiger. I decided her body language already determined her guilt, at least for me, the sudden release of energy, the same gesture as scratching the side of her nose.

"All those notes you told me that he'd left you. All the stalking behavior. Was any of it true?"

"It was *all* true! He wanted money. He said I owed him money on the house. But I *never* bought that property with him. It was a scam, my lawyer's been able to prove that at least, some fraud he was in on with a woman in the title company, plus another man, an outside broker." She stopped pacing, and took a breath. "I'm not the only one they cheated, Maddie. The D.A. has their hands full of these real estate swindlers. And maybe Donegan's lucky he's dead, because the others are going to prison."

"That still doesn't make it right."

She stared right at me through the shaded lenses, having neglected to remove her sunglasses once inside the house, though I could still see her eyes. Her gaze was troubled, eyes wide in perpetual fear, waiting for the moment she was no longer free, and prepared to take flight, even if it meant she'd hit a wall. There was a crazed vibe to her, a hopelessness that I found terrifying; not for myself, but for Mallory.

"Yes, it does, it justifies everything," she insisted.

"And what about Donegan? What *did* you do, Mallory, to hit a man just one time, and hard enough to kill him?"

"The block," she spoke in a voice far removed from her physical self, distant, as though she were reliving the moment in her mind. "I only meant to hit him once, but then his forehead, it caved in, all of the skin fell forward, with his nose, too, and then it was all hanging down from his brow, peeled right off. His skull was exposed, I could see the bone underneath and his eye sockets, and blood, nothing but blood; the blood was everywhere."

She looked around herself, as though to hang onto reality, take stock in her surroundings, and that's when Jesse entered the house from the yard, in time to put his arm around our sister's shoulders.

"What about the two of you?"

I was strangely untroubled by their dynamic, though horrified by Mallory's recount of her attack upon Donegan. I could create the impassive face, an inscrutable force, a plane of least resistance.

"We've talked about getting married," Jesse said for the first time.

"Dad won't contest it," I assured, and I could swear I saw in Mallory's face a stark reluctance.

"I know," he agreed. "He told me that."

"Not like you're...well, you *are* related, but...you weren't raised together." I shivered involuntarily. "No, it's not right, but you can make it right, if it means anything to you."

"I can't have children anyway, Maddie," she said, resigned.

"What?"

"Well, you know, remember that time while I was in high school, and I stayed in the hospital for about a week?"

I thought back, recalling a time frame when I might have had the bedroom all to myself.

"I vaguely remember," I said slowly, noncommittal.

"You were twelve, Maddie. Building bird-houses in Mom and Dad's backyard."

"Well, I remember *that* clearly. But I'm not sure about the hospital."

179

"I have MRKH, it's a prenatal condition. I was born without a uterus. I had vaginal reconstructive surgery when I was sixteen, just so I could have normal sex with a normal man."

"I guess that settles things between the two of you," I voiced the mean-spirited thought. "You won't have to worry about that tricky moment when your children ask you how you met."

"That's uncalled for, Maddie," Jesse defended our sister. At least I knew where he stood, but Mallory had an aura of retreat about her.

"I'm sorry, you're right." I raised my eyebrows. "I never knew about the surgery, Mallory, no one ever talked about it."

"And here you thought our family was so open and close," she said bitingly.

"I guess I did. I guess I thought you and I were pretty close, too."

When she and Jesse were gone, I went back out to the yard, and sat on the porch swing, deliberating, trying to summon pity for Mallory. The emotion sparked, but never fully bloomed.

My sister is a reckoning force. She manages her life without deviation from personal goals of any sort, primed and at the ready. I had thought her flaw, the declaration of her failing, lay in love. But there is an undertone to Mallory that impedes love, something impervious that resists the strongest force known to humanity.

Enough of idling, I thought, and gathered myself for the next task, which probably should have superseded painting the fence, and that was changing out the front door lock. This required less than five minutes of my time, because I'd become such an expert at fixing the doors—and problems—of others, that I'd neglected my own issues.

Standing back, I studied the fresh brass deadbolt, pleased at the outcome, however influenced by Mallory's casual breaking-and-entering. This time there'd be no dependence upon a key stash; and now my bargain-basement home, my better half, was secure.

* * * *

Reclining in the wind-torn haze on the perimeter of the southeastern San Francisco Bay, is the mostly forgotten settlement of Drawbridge. On a day of clarity, when the wind rips across Mission Peak and scours the air of particulates, you can almost count the tops of its squat, abandoned buildings poking up from Station Island, in the midst of pickleweed and salt grass.

My parents used to day-trip Margot and me to Drawbridge on our bicycles when we were in our teens. Closer to Fremont than to Santa Clara, the site with its posted signs warning of unequivocal closure fit perfectly into their marathon mentality. They would hustle us up the levees from Santa Clara, through sleepy Alviso, and across the flattened landscape. Dad rode at point and Mom on drag, with the two of us strung between, laboring against a stiff northwest wind. Coming home was a cinch, gorged on mumbled profanities, and the wind now at our backs. I often wondered at the parental logic in following most of the laws, with the exception of trespass and the carrying of a loaded firearm, which Dad kept in his rump-pack as an obscure safety measure.

The trains pass Drawbridge regularly on the same line that continues past my Bassett Street house. At one time, they used to pause at Drawbridge, which, after 1979, faded to a ghost town slowly subsiding into wet soil. All that echoes in the vacant dwellings between trains is the moaning of the wind through the blank windows and doors.

I rode my mountain bike out there on a day that started with fog, parting to a brisk wind that bent the wings of ravens patrolling levees for carrion and food scraps. Fat ground squirrels sped across the trail, perfect targets for a hawk, though brawny contenders against any bright-eyed raven, which are too smart to squander hard-won energy chasing anything their equal in size.

I had a purpose for this ride of fifteen miles or so, which served as an attempt to rid myself of Mallory's admissions of the previous day. I could bury myself in the open terrain that smelled of circulating tides and salt marsh, richly alive with birds and brine flies. The levee trails coursed around obscure fragments of sloughs with unpretentious, forgotten names such as *Grey Goose* and *Mud Creek*, pathways encrusted with forbs, wheel tracks and shoe prints worn into dried mud. I encountered pairs of Canada geese that would amble off, highly inconvenienced by my approach. And all around, tidal ponds teemed with herons and egrets, formations of feeding white pelicans, and diving brown pelicans; squalling gulls, and rafts of waterfowl that fed and dabbled in complete ignorance of commercial aircraft flying overhead.

The lengthy ride and my illegal crossing onto the Island were uneventful, the best kind of medicine. Luck was with me that day, as there were no trains approaching the south bridge to the Island. I really scrambled to make the crossing safely, first hiding my bike in the brush, and then running along the bridge pretending hell was at my heels. The tide was heading in, and I counted three small boats in Coyote Creek slough fishing for sturgeon, bows pointed seaward on their anchor ropes as the Bay waters surged inland, fighting successfully with the lazy downstream current.

From the height of the rail line, there lay the duff buildings of Drawbridge, probably painted at one time, but faded by the general tone of sky and water. Engrossed in my adventure, I startled a harrier hawk out of a building, and it winged off in a huff across the distant flats, screaming at me as it disappeared into the marsh.

I walked through a few of the buildings, though most were surrounded by moats of water that percolated to the surface. My feet echoed across creaky wood floors, accentuating dire emptiness. I thought about Drawbridge in its heyday, back when the lawless crowded to the Island, and trains paused ten times each day, five northbound and five from the south. This must have been a perfect place to hide out and gamble, or buy the time of a prostitute, or acquire bootleg liquor during Prohibition. And it had all started with a single cabin built for the lonely operator of the two drawbridges, which were long since demolished. The town faded away, and the only rumblings arise from the trains that use the corridor.

A southbound freight train with its day-breaking headlamp gained the north slough bridge, and I put a nickel on the track, before ducking into the closest structure, and hiding my body as well as I could. The engineer was no halfwit; he'd seen me at the rail, and made a point to lean on that horn and nearly scare me out of the resonating shack. The floor felt like a rippling sponge while the train roared past, and once it cleared the Island, I ran up to find my prize.

A few moments I searched, and there it was, pulled into the familiar shape, and warm to the touch. Like a child, I laughed as I slid it into my pocket. The coin heated its own space, reminding me as I followed the train, really running hard to cross the slough southbound, that being a child never truly ends.

* * * *

Jake arrived in the Eclipse, with Rat in tow, my usual pair of fools— Jake, due to his indecision, and Rat, simply because he knew we could all do a lot better.

There was luggage in the trunk of the Eclipse, and an airline ticket hanging out of Jake's overcoat, which he wore, though the weather was mild. I could see the unmistakable folder, the crisp flop of the Southwest

Airlines logo catching my eye.

"I came to tell you good-bye," he said, and kissed me, a mistake, as you never bait the lion, and then foolishly stick your head inside its opened mouth.

"Wait. What?"

"Don't worry, it's not *farewell*, Maddie. I'll be back." He held me by the shoulders, and kissed me again, apparently blind to the presence of my bared teeth. "I have a bunch of book signings in the Seattle area. I'll be out of town for about a week." As an afterthought, he found a brandy snifter beneath the bar, and set out his keys for display in their customary place.

"I didn't know you had plans," I said, wishing I could let it go.

In ignorance of my feelings, he pressed against me, and we briefly scuffled on the sofa. I have no guilt, you see. By the time we were done wrestling, the overcoat lay beneath a pile of our clothing, my contrariness had been corralled by sex, and the clock was ticking away.

But with Jake's arm tucked beneath my neck, I was in no hurry to release him to his departure.

"I could do this. Anytime," I professed, which is a fact, as we'd been doing "it" a minimum of three times each week since he'd declared his love for me.

He ran one hand along the contours of my body, the taut muscles formed by carrying sheets of wallboard, and piloting the occasional rented jackhammer.

"You're lovely," he breathed in my ear, "and beautiful. Inside and out." His eyes, when they met mine, held regret, but I wasn't sure to whom or what it was directed. As if to cover his blunder, he told me that he loved me, and I, uncharacteristically, had nothing to say.

Because, you see, there had been two pieces of luggage in the trunk, one red, and one blue.

Grabbing up my clothes to separate *mine* from *his*, I admired Mallory's ability to objectify most of her life's ills, though ultimately wrecked by love, evil choking vines sprung from an incorrupt seed. Does it seem impossible to reconcile the two in equal measure? Somewhere down the line, you either climb upward or take the ultimate nosedive. Just ask my parents if you don't believe me, as they're still on their ascent.

He glanced at his watch, the only item covering flesh, as I had already covered him.

"Flight's in four hours," he mentioned, insensitive. "Maybe I should get in a shower before I go."

I frowned down at Rat, who, following the lovemaking, had decided to reenter the room, wagging his tail, and smiling up at my apparently nasty mood. The fact had just dawned on me that Rat wasn't likely to buy a seat on the airplane.

"And so what, you're taking Rat with you?"

"Well, no," he said sheepishly. "I was...kind of hoping you could watch him for me."

"What, Sophie can't handle him?"

"Sophie doesn't like Rat. Rat doesn't like Sophie."

"And Maddie has a fucking life, Jake." I felt the surge of my *Killer Voice.* "You could, at the very least, have asked me before you dropped in at the last minute."

"My, Maddie, so recalcitrant."

"So what, I'm headstrong." I used my cussing tone, translating his writer's terminology, this self-willed woman who was no idiot. A sucker for love, maybe, but not an idiot.

The overcoat was beckoning, the ticket sleeve blindingly bright in the colorless room. I reached out and yanked it from the coat, before he could stop me, or protest, and out it tumbled.

There were two tickets. And there were two names.

Jacob Keene. Sophie Whipple.

"I know why Sophie can't handle him." My voice was so soft he had to lean forward to discern my words. "Because. Sophie is going to Seattle with you."

For a moment, our eyes met, and I knew he was wondering, but I handed over the tickets in their sword-sheath.

"Madeline," he cajoled, "listen to me," but I'd been dealt enough for one day.

I picked up the pile containing *his* clothes only, including the overcoat, and, with a purpose, carried them to the laundry room, jammed them into the washing machine, turned the dials violently, and started water gushing, a super load. Fortunately for Jake, I had pulled his wallet out of the slacks, and flung it against the backrest of the sofa, where it bounced into the catchment of his bare crotch. As for the clothes, he would either have to wait until they were finished with the entire cycle, and wear them wet, or wait longer for the dryer's effect, thus pushing his envelope for clearing airport security, or—

"Madeline, for God's sake, you have to listen to me, please!"

I slammed the lid down, and stood there, hands on my hips, both of us naked and burning.

"Please, Madeline, it isn't what you think!"

"You don't even know what I think!"

By God, he didn't.

Grasping the throw blanket from the ridge of the sofa, he wrapped it around his naked, sex-tainted body. Like an expert, he hooked the keys with one finger from the snifter, and walked out to the Eclipse. I observed, fascinated, and from behind the locked front door, as he heaved open the trunk, extricating one of the pieces of luggage (the red piece—so I'd been wrong about whose luggage, defined by color), and humped it up the steps.

But now it was problematic, because I wouldn't unlock the door. I finally did open it, talking beneath the security chain.

"Have a lovely trip, Jake. Good luck on those signings. And, I've decided to watch your dog for you."

He had to sit on the passenger seat of the claustrophobic Eclipse in full view of my neighbors, feverishly pulling on clothing before someone thought to call the police.

And, unless he managed to shed himself of my scent at some random bathroom sink, he was destined to smell like a woman other than Sophie all the way to Seattle, notwithstanding the glaring fact of the alien throw blanket in his car, which he might have to explain. But Jake writes fiction, so I'm sure he'll think of some yarn to solve his situation.

In the shower, I knew in my heart this would be the last time I'd be able to cast off the engine of my self-loathing. Why I had been so willing to consume someone else's bitter dregs, I'll never know.

And when I emerged, energized, there was Rat, sweet clueless Rat, politely waiting for me in his usual curl by the wood stove.

13. Fruit

I drove my grandparents' former Mercedes to an authorized mechanic, an older gentleman who had served as this car's grease monkey for twenty years. His name was Pat Mazar, and he knew my grandparents by first name.

"Nice people, Enida and Feliz," he assured, with an ambiguously European accent.

I tried to pay him for a once-over of the car, to list all the repairs it would need, but he looked at me funny, and then produced a work order, which proved who engendered the culture of generosity in the Benités family. There, at the bottom of a sheet of lengthy, expensive repairs, totaling a hair under five-grand, was Grandpa Feliz's signature, and a date back about a week before they delivered the car to my doorstep.

"You must be Madeline." Mr. Mazar held out his hands, palms-up, as though introducing me to someone else in the room that was invisible.

"Yes, I'm Madeline Benités."

"*Das ist gut,*" he said, which I presume was German. I started suspecting that knowing German was a prerequisite to fixing Mercedes and Bimmers, even if your clientele ain't getting it.

"*Es ist Ihr Guburtstag,*" he added.

"I'm sorry?" painfully not understanding.

He proceeded to sing, *Happy Birthday,* shades of Jacob Keene's fortieth birthday in the not too-distant past.

"Oh," I smiled uncomfortably. "It's really not my birthday."

"They say, 'it's for Madeline's birthday,'" he told me. "Your *Großmutter,* she's so kind."

"My Gross-farter signed it," I said, apparently botching what I assumed to be the German form of grandfather, extrapolating from his term.

He laughed at me, very loudly. Grabbing up the copy of the repair order, I left the office, embarrassed, but not before Rat, who'd been tied outside near the door, lifted his leg and peed on the corner of the building.

"Good old Rat," I praised, as we rolled away.

Now I understood why the car ran so well, why there weren't any oil spots in my garage. The car was sound enough for a road trip, and when I arrived home, setting Rat loose in the yard to urinate or defecate or whatever the hell dogs do while out of doors, I checked my calendar. I could reschedule at least a week and a half of booking dates, maybe more, which made me think of Astoria.

I telephoned Kevin at the phone number he'd emailed to me, the new one up in Oregon, but though the phone rang through to the correct voice mail, I never actually got to talk to Kev. I left a message anyway, and when I'd hung up the phone, I was starting to feel a bit of verve. Maybe a road trip was just what I needed.

At around three o'clock, Rat scuffed around to the side alley, and began to bark in earnest. Thinking it could be a skunk or a raccoon, two prime carriers of rabies, I went out back to investigate. All I found was Rat with nose to the gate, growling.

While I stood there gawking, the doorbell rang. The sound was faint at first, almost as though I imagined it, but after it kept *ringing-ringing-ringing*, like something possessed, I took it upon myself to check out who might be standing on my step.

Eight months ago, it had been some scruffy white kids trying to drum up money by painting my address on the curb. When I politely refused, pointing out that they needed a city permit, they pretended to leave, and then, when I wasn't looking, they sprayed a swastika instead of the address. Last I'd heard, they were arrested for the hate crime, though the cops made me wait a week until they acquired all their evidence, which finally allowed me to obliterate the foul message by covering it up with my actual street address.

As a precaution, I left Rat in the yard, though he grumbled about it.

But this time, instead of soliciting scumbags, it was a very tall, older white woman, with a familiarity to her face and carriage.

I hauled open the door.

"Charlotte?" I said, puzzled. "Charlotte Burgess?"

"Well!" she snapped, though I could see amusement in her eyes. "It's about time!"

"Is there something wrong with your toilets?" I asked stupidly, because I couldn't fathom why this woman, who I'd only met on that one contracting job, would drag herself all the way from the San Martin winery, to my rail line bungalow.

"The toilets, dear, are quite functional," she insisted.

"Then...I don't know why..." I stamped my foot reflexively, which made Charlotte startle. "Forgive me for asking, but just why the hell *are* you here, Charlotte?"

"Do you mind if I come in?"

"Well...yes, I *do* mind, but I'll let you in anyway."

I ushered her in, and she sat on the selfsame sofa that served as Jacob Keene's thrice-per-week bed.

"Would you like some coffee?" I offered, still dumbfounded.

"I would *love* some coffee, Madeline," she confirmed, so I went off to put it together, a pot and sugar and cream, the usual, including a cellophane package of cookies I'd picked up at the store on the last grocery run.

This was uncanny, serving her coffee, which she accepted in the gracious tone she'd used at the winery, our only other encounter.

I pinched a store-bought sugar cookie from the plate I'd set out, and asked the inevitable: *how is it that you know Jake?* And then I was dealt the final blow.

"He's my son."

"Oh."

I felt very small and cold inside, a dread, not unlike the anticipation of discipline meted out in our home when we were children. The punishment—usually standing in the corner, being grounded, or, as consequence for the worst offenses, a solid spanking—was never as agonizing as the terrible suspense involved in wondering just when the hell the hammer was going to fall.

"You...you don't look African-American," I mentioned, in a well-mannered, tinny voice. "Or Japanese, for that matter." And then I remembered that Jake's parents had died in a horrible accident when he was only ten.

Charlotte laughed. She was a woman of great humor, this was the only trait I'd seen in my original narrow view, but now I could predict what she concluded of my part in Jake's wayward activities.

"I'm not his birth mother, Madeline, I'm his *adoptive* mother."

"I see."

I reflected on a comment I'd made to Jake once, characterizing Charlotte as an *easy lay* in a business sense. Swallowing the memory, I politely supplied a brief account of my own mother's escapades of youth, being raised by Grandmother Beth in the stuffy enclave of Burlingame Hills.

"Well, Jacob had the winery," Charlotte nodded, understanding. "Did you think I was merely the foreman?"

"I thought so." I cleared my throat. "Not that I'm kissing ass, but even a mere foreman is very important."

"A foreman would have to answer to the winery owner, and not simply take at face value what a contractor is dishing up."

"But you believed me."

"Of course, Madeline." She studied me intently, as though she expected great things from me. "Jacob spoke very highly of you. He continues to speak very highly of you." She winced. "I'm sorry that I cannot say the same about Sophie."

I wisely abstained from asking if that meant what Jake said about Sophie, or Sophie's opinion of me.

"And you want him to marry Sophie." I was getting her drift.

"I believe that Jacob should marry his own kind. Otherwise, he will regret what bed he makes."

"How is Sophie in any way Jake's *kind?*"

She sighed, as though I was either too thickheaded, or perhaps brilliantly astute in the realm of a lawyer, requiring that she spell it out so that all loopholes—and potential misunderstanding—be negated.

"Sophie Whipple's family hails from Pebble Beach." Charlotte hit the target, drawing blood. "They're rich, they're sophisticates, they are socialites, and they are good business for Jacob, and for Tanner Valley Winery. With Sophie, he can waste his entire life writing, and it won't matter if he makes a trillion dollars or a paltry cent, because she will ensure he will never want for anything."

"Yes, he will," I protested. "He'll *want*, as you put it."

"For what?" Charlotte exhaled a sigh of impatience.

"For love," I insisted.

"Ah, Madeline, *dear* Madeline." Charlotte used a pitying tone, but maybe it was heartfelt, rather than condescending. "Love doesn't mean anything, don't you get it? Love doesn't pay the bills or raise the children. It doesn't pave the road to an Ivy League University. It doesn't even have the power," she leaned forward, pressing my hand, "to keep two people faithful."

She removed her hand, and waved it in the air as though the concept of love was meaningless. I knew she believed this, and I also knew she was dead wrong.

I paused, thinking about my own parents, how they share two minds and a single heart. Not a day passes without my father telling my mother that he loves her, and vice-versa. They are spawn of the far left, their libations of affection keeping them fit and intoxicated in the same breath. They are dedicated to their love affair to a fault, and yet they are impeccable in the burden of their love that they accept with open minds. My father's ancient transgression might have killed a fragile love, but theirs withstood and forgave. I knew, without any doubt, the greatness in their template, and I suddenly felt very sorry for Charlotte Burgess.

"You're wrong, Charlotte," I spoke with conviction. "I've seen it, and I know it's true, love means *everything*." I smiled. "But you're worried about something, aren't you?"

"Not in the least," she said quickly, and then, she rubbed the side of her nose.

"It's not all roses in Ben Lomond, is it, Charlotte?"

I had a sudden insight about Jake, how he'd tried so hard to get me to listen to him, before he wrapped himself in the throw blanket, and risked arrest for indecent exposure by dressing out in the car.

"I'll admit," she looked chagrined, "that my son flew to Seattle without taking Sophie with him."

"What?"

"That's right, dear, Sophie met him at the airport, but he tore her ticket up, and gave her back her valise, then told her they were done, and to remove herself from Ben Lomond. She was devastated, she telephoned me right away, and I vowed I'd fix things."

"Charlotte." I shook my head. "Some things, they're not fixable, even if you wish it with all your heart." I pondered her directly, my eyes sharp. "Except for love, *that's* fixable."

"Well," she scoffed, and rose to her feet; and I knew I'd driven home a shard of truth that she could only deflect by leaving. "You think anything your silly mind wishes. Thank you for the coffee, and have an abundant life, Madeline. You are a decent person, and I'm sure some roofer or dock worker will see your value in good stead."

From the porch, I watched her climb into her pristine BMW, her statuesque height minimized by the stately car. I waved to her, and she raised one hand in reply, but there was dark sorrow in her eyes that I, in my lucid state, could easily discern.

I let Rat in the house, after that, and he sniffed around, muttering at the remnants of Charlotte's spoor. I imagined the two women in cahoots, Charlotte and Sophie, leveraging Jake to rid himself of his dog, the simple joy in a boy's life.

And Jake, leaving Rat with me, apparently the only person he trusted in the event that post-breakup, Sophie decided to dump Rat by the side of the road or at the city pound. I felt that I'd misjudged him, and all the while, underestimated myself.

The telephone rang, and I jumped.

"Maddie!" Kevin, calling from northwest Oregon, and it sounded as though his proverbial tail was wagging. "You're coming up?" His voice crackled with excitement.

"I have some time off," I said, and then, I advised I'd be bringing Rat with me.

"Bring the little bugger," he said. "If he likes you, he's all right with me."

We then parted. I hung up the phone, and packed my bags. I settled my business, left messages, emailed people, talked to a few. When that was handled, I printed out a map, the route from Santa Clara to Astoria. Twelve hours and twelve minutes, a winning combination in cryptic numbers.

* * * *

I had gassed up the Mercedes, and then stopped at a pet store to buy food for Rat, when my sister, Mallory, called me. Sitting in the parking slip with the novelty glow of the trip still alive, I studied the number on the caller ID, and resigned to answering it.

"Can you meet me for coffee?" she nearly pleaded.

I was reluctant. After all, Mallory was partly the reason to blame for my sudden flight. But her voice... I gave in.

"All right," I said with a sigh, and agreed to meet her at a Starbuck's near her house.

She was already in the lot when I arrived, and I don't doubt she was probably as anxious to see me, as I was to skip town. That steel-colored Infiniti, a lethal bullet carrying my sister, knowing she was partially operative, and slightly deranged; yet I pulled in and greeted her anyway. If it meant I had to suffer one last conversation before I was out of the Bay Area, I'd gladly do it.

"Thank you for seeing me," she obliged, frowning as Rat exited the car, sticking close to my heels, the leash slack. "What the hell is that?" she asked, standing back to prove to Rat she wouldn't accept any attempts at a physical introduction. Rat, ever the gentleman, sat on his butt, and merely grinned.

"This is...er, a dog owned by a friend of mine," which was the truth. I didn't need to elaborate on any of my private life. Unlike me, Mallory seemed to catalogue the secrets of others, and form resentment afterward.

"Well, he's so damned ugly!" She seemed to find Rat laughable. "Why do you have him?"

"The owner went out of town, so I promised to sit the dog."

She nodded at the Mercedes. "I heard you got the car. How's it running?"

"Great. Apparently Grandma and Grandpa fixed it before they gave it to me." I hesitated. "I'm going out of town, Mallory. Kevin asked me to visit him in Oregon, so I'm taking him up on the invitation. I'll be gone for a couple of weeks."

"Okay. Do you need anyone to watch your house?"

"Thanks, but no," I replied evenly. "It's got a shiny new lock, and no key outside."

She smirked at that statement, and I smiled back.

I found an umbrella-screened table out of doors, while Mallory bought us coffee. Rat curled up by my feet, panting a little in the semi-shade, as it was a beautifully warm sunny day in Redwood City, the usual fog beaten back by a high-pressure system. That made me wonder about Astoria, as in Kevin's photographs I'd glimpsed a fog-wet sky, coastal northwest Oregon weather. Then my mind rambled on to Jake, up in Seattle without Sophie, so I was pretty much occupied by the time Mallory returned with the coffee.

"So," she began, passing me my allotted cup. "The D.A. dropped all the charges against me."

"That's just great. Is it because they believed your scenario?"

I could say that word, without making it worse by referring to Mallory's side of it as a *tale* or *fable*. It would have been counterproductive to our sisterhood.

"Yes, that, and the real estate scam." She laughed nervously. "Though there *was* this assistant D.A. who was just so sure I'd set up Donegan, and murdered him."

"Good thing he didn't know all the facts, then," I took a stab at *tale*.

And then she poured gasoline and flicked the match.

"I broke up with Jesse."

I nearly choked on my coffee. "*What*? Why, Mallory? The last time I saw you, he was leaning toward marriage."

"Yeah, but no," she shivered. "I told him I wasn't ready."

I looked closely at my sister's face, because I knew there was more to it. I'd seen the mental and emotional exodus the day I mentioned our father wouldn't contest her relationship with Jesse Ibarra, as though she had thrived on the possibility of conflict, her physical attraction to Jesse embodied in the potential for deeply wounding Dad.

At that moment I remembered, as though it weren't so long ago, shortly before Mallory turned eighteen, and she had arranged to go out on a date with a young man a few years older, whom she'd met at a party. He was perhaps twenty-three, and he materialized at our parents' house to pick up Mallory on a motorcycle, dressed in a leather jacket like a 1950s rumbler punk, smelling of cigarette smoke and pot.

My father, who'd not been privy to the "date" Mallory agreed to, protested strenuously. After all, Dad knew this character, having taught the young man in a music class a decade earlier at one of the district middle schools.

"He's a Goddamned deadbeat," Dad told Mallory, the words spewing from his mouth.

This guy, Tony something-or-other, had been standing right there, but Dad utilized the third-party directive, communicating to one person by talking to another, thus delivering a blow that becomes indirectly confrontational, and which nobody could fault you for.

But Mallory faulted Dad.

She argued up and down, right and left, while our father stuck to his principles.

"Look at him now, some people just *never* change," said Dad. His voice, always resonant in that big head of his, had stepped up the volume quite a bit.

"I'm almost eighteen, I'm going anyway," Mallory threatened. In retrospect, I guess she wanted to start using that new vagina of hers.

"Go ahead," Dad warned.

"I *will,* just *watch* me!" she asserted insolently.

And then, he proceeded to remove her personal effects from our shared bedroom. One by one, they flew out the window, clothes on hangers, single dresser drawers filled with more clothes, the empty dresser, a mattress, and then the bed frame. He didn't stop, until just about everything she owned lay in a mangled heap on our front lawn. Neighbors witnessed this; people driving down the street turned their heads to get a glimpse of the crazy fucking father making dead sure his stupid, impulsive daughter got the message.

Mallory sobbed. Tony what's-his-name wisely departed when the first few items began to fling out of the window. The pile lay on the lawn all night long, subject to dew and more scrutiny by the neighbors. But strangely, nobody called the police, either too afraid of Mitchell Benités' temper, or privately admiring of his archaic manner in handling his daughter's rebellious hell raising. I'd like to think it was the latter, but I'm betting it had more to do with Dad's infamous will, his loud voice, and the utter reluctance everyone possessed in crossing him.

My sister slept on my bed that night, while I, compassionate yet wary, took a blanket on the carpeted floor. She cried most of the night, and by morning, she was pithed. Afterward, Dad and Mallory worked together to bring her things back into the house, but things were never the same between them. She hated him. I knew it, because she repeated that mantra to herself in unbroken chant all night long, while the snails crawled over her best dresses, leaving slime tracks that glimmered in the morning sun.

Right now, seated in the shade on Woodside Road, with cars whizzing past, and my sister nearly thirty years old, I could see she still hated him. Oh, I know, Mallory loves our father, she always will, but she hates him, too, unforgiving, and unrepentant. I'm positive our father regretted his act of imposed will, but if handed the same circumstances, I know he would also repeat the same act. He is who he is, and a lesser father would have buried a daughter such as Mallory by now, a victim of her own recklessness.

"You did it to get back at Dad," I said.

I had nothing to lose. I love my sister, but she seethes with self-destructive tendencies that require reining-in.

"Yes," she said, nodding, knowing exactly what I was getting at. "But it backfired."

I opened my mouth to say more, blessedly saved by my cell phone ringing in my back pocket; that slow rise into a soft-core porn theme. As I pressed the button, I made a mental note to change the ringtone, as it's embarrassing to have perfect strangers in your vicinity lift their heads to stare.

"Hello?"

"Maddie," said my father. Speak of the devil.

"Dad."

Mallory's face drew into lines of caution.

"Madeline, your Grandmother Beth had a heart-attack this morning," he informed in that rock-solid voice of his.

"She did? Is she dead?" So inappropriate, I know.

"She's not well, but she's alive. I'm up here at Sequoia Hospital right now with your mom, so if you want to come, it might be a good idea. The doctors don't think your grandmother has a lot of time. Her heart took a really big hit."

I explained how Mallory and I were in Redwood City, so close, less than ten minutes away, and that we'd be right over. He promised to call Miranda and Margot, and when I hung up, I realized that he'd phoned me first. The realization was humbling, but also an accolade, to know he trusted me that much.

* * * *

I stashed the Mercedes in the shade of the hospital parking structure, leaving Rat safe with the windows mostly wide open to the breeze. Mallory, who'd followed in her gun-barrel car, walked with me arm-in-arm to where our father had promised to be.

Grandmother Beth was bedded in the ICU. When we arrived, Dad and Mom were in the room, as they'd only allow two visitors in at a time. I remember waiting in the doorway as Dad stood to greet us, and how Grandmother Beth was gazing at Mom with bleary, loving eyes.

And I heard the words, too, unexpected praise from Grandmother's lips to an adopted daughter who for so long had unjustly been a grave disappointment to an adoptive mother.

"Moira, you're a blessing," Grandmother said, and my mother's eyes spilled with tears.

I had once thought to tell Grandmother Beth's corpse that vengeful phrase, *who's shriveled now*, but I'd been disarmed by Mom transforming from a *curse* into a *blessing*. Instead, because I have learned how to forgive—though I am still in my spiritual infancy—I kissed Grandmother Beth, and told her how much I loved her.

When I came out of the room, I saw my father seated on a bench with Mallory. One of his arms was around her, and her head lay upon his shoulder the way she'd done, how we'd all done, when we were children.

* * * *

Last year, when she'd been cleaning up one of the bedrooms in her Sunnyvale home, my Grandma Enida came across a photograph she had thought she'd lost. Because our family is afflicted with *Pack Ratterism,* we keep everything and forsake nothing, so the photograph, buried but not forgotten, had a high likelihood of turning up somewhere down the line.

Grandma Enida, a very enterprising person, had managed to supplement Grandpa Feliz's income by working the Libby's cannery, and later standing swing shift at Fairchild Semiconductor, and then Teledyne, working on the assembly line. Grandma inevitably chose the swing shift, so there would always be an adult home with the boys.

On the side, she made extra cash by selling the likes of Avon, Tupperware and Sarah Coventry jewelry. This particular bedroom, utilized for storage, was cluttered with the byproduct of her lengthy association with door-to-door sales, forty-five years in all.

Over time, she ignored Grandpa Feliz's rant about wasting money, and made quite sure that her family was raised in a safe neighborhood, and they all had what they needed, a college education or a new car, or down payment on a house.

This life in the United States was made possible, because Grandma Enida brought my father and three of his four siblings to California in 1959, traveling by ship to meet up with Grandpa Feliz, who at that time had lived in the States for almost two years, estranged from his wife and children. My father, who'd been born in Narvacan six months after Grandpa departed for the States, was the only one who didn't know his own father; even the next eldest, Miles, had vague memories of Grandpa Feliz, and accepted him readily once the family was reunited and moved in together. Mitchell, however, fought by using the stubborn rule, to prevent Grandpa Feliz from administering love or discipline, and it took, as I observe it, a good fifty years to disprove their alienation.

Grandma was distressed that she'd lost the picture, so when she rediscovered the photo she was so ecstatic, she asked my father to copy it, and give a printed photo to every one of our family members. Dad scanned the little 3x5 inch photo, and produced stunning 8x10s of the revealing scene, taken by Grandpa inside of their first abode, which was a converted garage on the property of a Japanese-American-owned flower nursery in Mountain View, where Grandpa worked. The date inscribed at the time the photo was developed, and included in the scan by Dad, shows *June 1959*, though Dad said the picture had been taken in April, less than a week after their arrival at the Port of San Francisco.

The photo is a bit grainy, but clearly shows an old chrome and Formica dining table, and the open room of the garage, with a kitchen counter block and a bare water heater, and frying pans hanging from the wall. Grandma is seated at the head of the table, with two children on either side. On the far left is Marianne, the eldest, then Michael, my Grandma, my father, and Miles. Grandma is drinking from a cup, and most eyes are fixed upon Grandpa and the camera, except for Miles, who is in a trance and for my father, who is reaching toward a carton of milk with one hand, as though thirsting for more. There aren't enough chairs, just four, so Uncle Michael is pulled up on a tricycle, and you can see the front wheel under the table.

This photograph symbolizes a lot of things to me; it records, obviously, a moment in time that is probably very similar to many immigrant families, both then and now.

There's more: Grandma Enida's great courage in bringing her children to America, her patience and strength in caring for four children on board a ship, three of them very boisterous males, where the passage lasted in excess of three weeks.

And I am reminded of their deprivation, however temporary, that Enida and Feliz were apart for nearly two years while my grandfather established a job and a home in California, sending for the family when all was settled. My Uncle Mark was conceived in May of 1959, even in that densely populated garage, a one-room arrangement, and a study in family socialism. That my grandparents were making love while their restless children slept is a testament to endurance.

But the fact that my Grandma took all risks by embracing a faith in God to better the lives of her children is the exemplification of love. There is nothing else but love.

And I have been so equally blessed. I am the by-product of their tree, the traditions and habits and quirks of the Benités family, connected by our hearts. My grandparents, my parents, they've all gifted me the strength and honesty to make the most of my life, on my own and in due season, because I have been given the tools of culture. The elders sowed the seeds, so that I could reap the sweet harvest of their blood fruit.

About the Author

A California native, Karen Kennedy Samoranos has a deep and abiding love for the Golden State, reflected in the settings of her books. She believes in love at first sight, undying passion, and the rare balance of two souls in sync. As an author, all of these elements are a constant theme of her work. In her off hours, she hikes, is an avid fisherman, and motorcyclist (both dirt and street), and is an advocate for regular exercise, red wine and whole foods. By day, she and her husband are committed to a music education business that forwards the cause of live jazz stage performance for children, ages 4 through 18. Family is the ultimate fulfillment—the author has four adult children, and six young grandchildren.